TWISTED GLASS

TWISTED INTENTIONS

SAVANNAH RYLAN

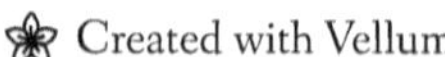 Created with Vellum

1

———

BRIELLE

Thinking about my kids was the only way to keep the pain away. But my fucking God, they did their best to break through.

"Miss Lancaster! Look!"

I turned at the sound of my name. "Way to go, Johnny! Just be careful up there, all right?"

He gave me a thumbs up. "I will!"

I cupped my hands over my mouth. "Both hands on the jungle gym!"

"Miss Lancaster?" someone asked as they tugged at my dress.

I peeked down and found little Miss Lindsey standing next to me. So, I crouched down to her eye level.

"Hey there, pretty girl," I said with a soft smile, "what's up?"

She tugged at one of the curls that I had painstakingly placed in my hair and giggled as it bounced. "Sproingy."

I touched her nose softly with my finger. "I curled my hair just for you today, cutiepie."

I had to admit, curling my hair wasn't something that I did often. My pin straight bangs matched the pin straight demeanor of the rest of my jet-black hair, and sometimes the temporary *curls weren't worth the pain I went through in order to place them. But oh, the curiosity of the kids in my classroom at work made it worth the effort. A pang of pain rushed through my side, and I hissed as I snapped back up. "Johnny?"*

"Yeah, Miss Lancaster!?"

"You be careful up in that tree now. I don't want you getting hurt!"

"Again."

My body grew weak as I sank to the ground, feeling the grass cushion my knees.

"Miss Lancaster!?" Johnny exclaimed.

I held my hand up as I struggled to catch my breath. "I'm okay. I'm good. Just... a bit hot."

"Again."

"Are you sure?"

"Did I fucking stutter? Again."

My eyelids grew heavy, as if they were being weighed down with lead as yet another pang of agony shot through my ribcage. I had to hold on. I had to hold onto my kids. Hold onto their smiles, laughter, and joy.

It was the only way I knew I'd stay alive.

"Hey, kids?" I called out as I shook my head.

I wanted to hold onto my little ones for as long as I could.

"Miss Lancaster, look!"

"Get the spotlight."

"Miss Lancaster! Watch!"

"Are you sure this is her?"

"Miss Ell!? Can you hear me!?"

"Miss Lancaster?"

"I love your curls!"

I swallowed hard. "And I love you."

"What the fuck did she just say?"

"Right there. Yep. Point it right at her."

"Miss Ell?"

"She has to be disassociating. No one's that good at ignoring pain."

That brought my head up from its dangling position. "Challenge accepted."

The stinging sensation rushing through my side was met only with the buzzing of the harsh light that dropped down onto my face. I winced as the bright light burned a hole into my forehead. My shoulders tensed as my mouth drew in short bouts of air. I felt it coming. Felt it brewing as something dragged its way across the floor in front of me. The hairs on the nape of my neck stood on end. My arms shivered from a cold my body didn't feel. The rough carpet beneath my feet taunted me as whatever was being dragged got closer. Then, something thudded in front of me before my seat lurched with a resounding thud.

I wanted to be back with my kids. Back at the school, where I knew that it was safe.

"Aaaa-cho!"

I sneezed all over my lap before a brutal voice hit my ears.

"Don't get snot on my fucking floors."

Panic gripped my throat. I tugged at my wrists, but they didn't come free. I outstretched my legs, or at least tried, before I realized I wasn't sleeping. The pain coursing through my body reminded me I was alive.

No. It had been a dream. It couldn't be real. There was no way that—

Oh, God. I'm really not at home.

"Where am I?" I croaked out.

A shadow cloaked me, giving my aching face a rest from its harsh light. I peeked up with one eye, managing to pry it open from the sealant of fluids and crust that had painted it shut. My ankles throbbed. My wrists ached. And for some reason, it felt like I was about to vomit.

"Who are you?" I managed to choke out.

I heard what sounded like shuffling around before the shadow abated, leaving me exposed to the harsh buzzing light.

It took my eye a second to adjust, but I found the devil himself sitting across from me when it did. The spindly chair he sat on did nothing to confine his humongous stature. He spread his legs wide as a grin slithered across his face. He looked positively murderous.

"Who are you?" I asked, trying to thread some strength into my voice.

But the man sitting in front of me with shoulders as big as the canyons simply stared. Sitting there, unwavering in his stature, while that glaring light blasted from behind him. It cloaked him in a weird sort of ambiance that would have relaxed me had it not been for the bloodlust in his eyes.

If he wasn't going to kill me, he wanted to.

And that was enough for me.

"Look," I said, shaking my pounding head, "whoever you think I am, I'm not. I'm just a schoolteacher. I work with students who need extra evaluation and care. I put together their IEPs, I get them set up with intervention tactics. I work with them on—"

"Does the name Luca ring any bells?"

I blinked. Was he serious? "Really, you've got the wrong girl. I'm just a—AH! NO!"

The thundering footsteps made me cry out before something pulsed against my lips. The chair creaked beneath a weight that shifted the arms of the chair beneath my arms. I felt his presence, even though my stare struggled to focus through the tears. His shadow loomed over me. Even though I couldn't see him—even though my eyes ached from a pain that ricocheted all the way down my spine—I felt him hovering. And when my gaze finally managed to focus on him, the disgust that curled his lips down stopped my heart in my chest.

Before he leaned me back, tipping the front two chair legs backward until I did nothing but dangle from his grasp.

"No! Stop! Please!"

My feet, moving around in the air.

"Oh, my God," I choked out as tears flooded my cheeks.

My body, suspended.

"Don't kill me, please. If I can't help, I will, I swear. What-ever it is. Just please, don't kill me."

Completely under his control.

"Please," I whispered as tears brewed in my eyes, "my parents are waiting for me. I know they must be worried. I won't say anything. I-I-If you let me go, I—"

His stare stayed still, as if torturing a woman did nothing for him. "Does the name Luca ring any bells?"

I scoffed. "I dated a Luca in college for, like, three days. Do you mean him?"

The chair's legs slammed back down before a resounding crack filled the room. It wasn't until after I'd caught my breath, however, that the searing pain ricocheted through my cheekbone.

Before something trickled down my jawline to my neck.

"Ouch," I whimpered.

"I won't ask you again," the man snarled, gripping my hair and pulled my head back.

"Ah! Please! Stop!"

His disgusting breath fanned against the shell of my ear. "Tell me the truth, you slimy little cunt, or you'll stay down here until your stomach eats away at your muscles."

I had no idea what he wanted. I had no idea what the hell

he wanted me to say. But if I was going to die, I sure as hell wasn't going to die a liar.

So, I swallowed hard. "I don't know who you think I am, but you've got the wrong woman."

At first, nothing happened. Even though I braced for the pain. Even though my entire body locked up, preparing itself for the man's fists, nothing came. One by one, my muscles relaxed. One by one, the hairs along my arms and legs finally settled back down against my skin.

Until I found myself suddenly staring at the ceiling and gasping for air.

"Oh—huuuh—no."

"Do you believe her?"

I didn't recognize the voice as I laid there with heated pain rushing through the marrow of my bones. What day was it? How long had I been there? What the hell did that man want from me? I gasped to try and catch my breath. My skin tingled. My ass burned. Tears flooded the sides of my face as my lungs felt as if they were collapsing, air sac by air sac. Why couldn't I catch my breath? I forced my stomach to press out as I tried breathing through my nose. But it was no use.

My body seemed to be protesting the fact that I was still alive.

"Help," I sputtered.

From the corner of my eye, a movement caught my attention long enough to flood my body with adrenaline. My lungs set themselves on fire. It felt like my entire body was burning from the inside out. But as that shadow appeared above me, I knew I was in trouble.

I wasn't in there with one person.

I had been in there with two.

"Help—me," I managed to choke out.

"You sure we got the right one?" the voice I didn't recognize asked.

"Shut up," the brutal voice hissed.

"She doesn't match my profile. I told you this the second we—"

"If you can't handle a bit of work, then go the fuck upstairs."

Work? What the hell kind of work was this?

"She's gonna pass out if we don't sit her up," the unfamiliar voice said. "You want to do the CPR this time or are you gonna keep outsourcing that gig to—"

The room moved swiftly as my head sat upright on my body once more. The room spun around me as I leaned forward, gagging and heaving while trying to gasp for air. My body didn't know what to do. I couldn't blame it, either. It felt like I had slipped into a nightmare and didn't have a way back to reality.

For all I knew, I was already dead.

How long have I been here?

"They'll be looking for me," I murmured.

The men stopped arguing before a hand fisted my hair and yanked my head back.

"Ouch!" I yelped.

"What did you say?" the brutal man growled.

If I was going to die, he'd have to look me in the eye to do it. "My family. They'll be looking for me. And they won't stop until they've found me."

That crooked grin spread across his scarred face before a chuckle fell from his twisted mouth. He released my head, shoving it off to the side. He snorted and snarled. I heard him coughing and hocking, making my stomach turn as my mouth filled with saliva.

And when that fucking ball of snot slapped against my shin, I leaned over the edge of my chair and puked.

"Jesus, someone get her some water," yet another voice said.

Shock ran through my system as something snapped. The pitter patter of feet moved away from me, and I managed to stop throwing up onto the floor long enough to look up. Three. There were three distinct shadows moving in tandem with one another. And as their footfalls rushed up the steps, I froze.

There had been three men in that room with me.

Where the fuck am I?

2

————

AXTON

Dante barely got the door closed before he spat out exactly what I was thinking.

"I never profiled a family, you know that," he said as he whipped around and pinned me with a look.

Well, attempted to, anyway. Nobody pinned me for nothing. "I know. So, shut the fuck up while I think."

Maverick chewed his gun with those damned aviators of his sliding down his fucking nose. "Looks a hell of a lot like her, though, don't it?"

I ran my hands through my hair. "Exactly like her, actually. I need to think."

I started for the kitchen and set my sights on a beer. I needed a fucking drink. After all of the time we had spent planning shit and setting up exactly how her abduction would go, I couldn't shake the feeling that we had the wrong person. No, a woman's petty pleas didn't get to me. Nothing got to me. Nothing got beneath my skin. That was why my men had named me President, because they knew that I was good at picking up the fucking slack when shit mattered.

This mattered, though.

And for some fucking reason, I couldn't shake the fact that we had royally fucked up.

"Penny for your thoughts?" Dante asked, leaning his six-foot-five stature against the kitchen wall.

I ripped the fridge open and grabbed a beer. "Gonna need more than a penny to get shit out of me right now."

Mav blew a bubble with his gum before popping it with his mouth. "All right, what if I give you a twenty?"

I snickered, cracking the beer open and closed the fridge door with my feet. Dee stood against the kitchen wall; his hands slid into his pockets like the unassuming motherfucker people knew him to be. That was what made him so good at his stealth work. That was why I had named him our Enforcer after our President had been slaughtered. And when Dante sighed, that damn noise held all of the stress that had been on our shoulders ever since Luca's brutal death.

Fucking hell, I had been sure it was her. It looked exactly like her. I mean, down to the little button nose.

"Damn, Dante," Maverick said with a smile.

"What?" he asked.

"I'm surprised you can get your hands in there with how tightly those pants of yours are painted on."

I took a pull from my drink. "You asked for it, Mav."

Dante snickered. "I know you've already taken to her, Mav. You're ready to get your cock wet, aren't you? Probably reminds you of your mother a bit?"

Mav paused the chewing of his gum. "Shut up, Dee."

Dee pushed off the wall and walked toward him. "Soothing, and innocent?"

"I said, shut the fuck up."

"With those cute little doe eyes of hers?"

Mav straightened his back. "What the fuck did I say about that shit, huh? Quit profiling me."

Dee shrugged. "Funny that you think it's a chore when it comes to you."

"You stupid mother—"

"Enough," I said curtly before taking another long pull from my relaxing drink.

The two of them turned to me, with Mav's red face daring me to laugh straight in it. The guy was about as sensitive as they came, he had to know how easy the cheap shots were to get in with him. He was a great goddamn Vice President, though. Despite the fact that he was a bit of a pussy, he knew how to make calculated decisions without shelving his emotions. It was a trait not all of us possessed, and it was fucking useful in sticky situations.

Kind of like the one we had found ourselves in.

I drew in a deep breath before downing the rest of my beer and tossing the empty can into the trashcan. "Dante, give me your profile again."

He shook his head. "You already know what it—"

I charged him, wrapping my hand around his throat and pulling him close. "Again, Dee."

He slapped my hand away and cleared his throat. "The woman we are looking for is a recluse. Mid-twenties to mid-thir-ties in age. She much prefers watching her prey fall victim to her traps, so she's liable to stick around and watch the death occur. She grew up without a family or a home, so she was likely in the foster system when she was younger, or even on the streets. She's uneducated, nocturnal, and prizes her health above all else due to the nature of her mercenary ways. Because of her involvement with The Heretics, she's no newcomer to the scene, so she's probably been part of it most of her adult life, if not all of it. She works alone, with no ties to family or friends so that she's not vulnerable should people attempt to pursue her."

"I've heard enough," I murmured.

Maverick sighed heavily. "We've had her in that basement for two days."

I pinched the bridge of my nose. "I know."

"We've had her for two fucking days. We took her off the street. Injected her with drugs to keep her docile because we knew she'd fight back, and hard."

"I know!" I bellowed.

And yet, Mav still had the balls. "So, when are you going to admit that the profile doesn't match who we've got in that basement?"

"This is why we're bounty hunters," Dante said plainly.

I snapped as I whipped toward him and wrapped my hand around his fucking throat. "She killed our former President. She killed Luca. So, I don't give a flying mother fuck what bounties pass us by. Luca deserves vengeance. This entire crew does, after what those stupid fucks took from us."

Mav peeled my hand away from Dante's throat. "We know, Axe."

Dante's eyes locked with my face. "And that's why I keep reminding you of the profile. That is what's going to keep us focused while we step out of our comfort zone. The guys are depending on this. We put all monetary efforts on hold the second she popped back up onto our radar, so we need to do this right and get paid."

I cracked my neck. "We're still bounty hunters, and we're still getting paid for her capture. Everyone wants a slice of this bitch. It's a bounty higher than the likes of anything we've ever chased."

Dante came up and stood in my face. "Then, we owe it to our crew and to Luca to do this right. And you know that's not the woman we're looking for in the basement."

Mav spoke the obvious, of course. "Which means she isn't gonna have any information for us, whatsoever."

I swallowed back a growl because I knew they spoke nothing but truth. "All right, so, what walks like a duck, quacks like a duck, but isn't the goddamn motherfucking duck we need?"

Dante shrugged. "Maybe she's wearing a disguise of some sort? You know, in the footage we have? Changed her appearance, shit like that."

Mav pointed at him. "She's been off the radar for a little while now. She could have had some plastic surgery. Dyed her hair."

"What else?" I asked, folding my arms across my chest.

Mav cleared his throat. "She's a good actress?"

"No one's that good," I muttered, pinching my nose.

"Amnesia? Maybe it's her, but she's lost her memory somehow?" Dante asked.

I drew in a deep breath. "I mean, I suppose it's possible. But—."

Then, Mav actually had a decent idea for once. "What if it's the duck's twin?"

For a split second, I wondered if he meant it as a joke. But his insinuation gave me pause. "Dante? Is that possible?"

He leaned his body against the wall and jammed his hands back into those pockets of his. "I mean, the girl downstairs is adopted."

I slowly turned my attention to him. "So, it's possible that she had a sibling she got separated from?"

"Yes. Especially considering the photo we have of her. If they're not twins, they're at least sisters."

I pointed at him. "Use your connections to get her medical information. Any information on her adoption. We need to make absolutely certain that she's the woman we're after."

"You know she's not," Dee said plainly.

I snarled. "That's why we're double fucking checking, asshole. Now, go."

I flicked my wrist at Dante, and he shoved himself off the wall. He peered over his shoulder at me, his gaze searching my face as I drew in a deep breath. I knew the guys were pissed that we weren't chasing a new bounty every week. I knew they had grown tired of sitting around instead of riding off into the sunset to bag yet another suspect on the run from the law. But this was personal. This bitch had killed one of our own, and she had yet to pay for her transgressions.

I wouldn't stop until I had all of the answers I needed. Until that woman was tied up in our basement and begging for her fucking life. Until Luca's death was avenged, Road Raiders style.

We just had to find the right one first.

"What?" I spat.

"You're going to hate yourself once I come back with this information," Dee said.

I knew he was right. "Just go get it done already."

"What can I do in the meantime?" Mav asked.

I watched Dante disappear down the hallway toward the front door before I turned to the man I entrusted as my Vice President. My stomach curdled with sickness. Bile crept up the back of my throat. Dear fucking God, we'd beat on that woman downstairs for damn near forty-eight hours to get information out of her. If she wasn't who we were looking for, I wasn't sure what I'd do with myself.

"Bring her food," I said as Dee headed out the front door with a thud.

Mav tilted his head. "You must be faltering if that's the case."

"What are you, Dante? Shut up and do as you're told."

"Axton."

I cleared my throat. "I can't deny what's in front of me, and it's our fault for not considering it."

He shook his head. "You couldn't have possibly—"

I turned away from him and rolled my shoulders back. "Take her some food and make sure she eats. We need to start covering our asses, just in case."

And as I headed for the stairs, venturing up to my bedroom, I kept a lid on it just long enough. Long enough to get into my room. Long enough to rush into the bathroom. Long enough to get the water running to cover up the sound of my gagging and heaving before I unleashed the contents of my stomach into the bathroom sink. Because if I was beating on an innocent woman for information she didn't have, I wasn't sure I'd ever forgive myself.

I wasn't sure I'd ever be deserving of it.

3

___

DANTE

The roar of my bike's engine vibrated between my legs as I raced down the highway. Every turn I made was met with the sound of that lusciously thick dossier I had on our woman. The papers flopped against the inner walls of my bike's back compartment. ***Thwip, thwip. Thwip, thwip.*** It reminded me of all the research we had done. The pictures I had taken. The information I had pulled and teased from our colleagues and connections in town, as well as in the surrounding areas. With every flop of that folder as I crested corners and roared over peaks and valleys, I was haunted by our mistake. Even with all the stakeouts I had completed to line all of this up, and even with all of the payouts for information, and even with all of the dancing around we had to do at the hospital to get birth records...

Only for us to snag the wrong fucking girl.

"Come on, go faster," I grumbled as I soared through a yellow light.

So many facts raced through my mind. Her birth date. The layout of the hospital where she had been born. Her love of ranged rifles and her backup knives on her hips, just in case. For fuck's sake, we had a picture of the woman, decked out in an all-black, skin-tight suit with heels as high as God himself. Even down to that crooked-ass smile that made her face seem lopsided like a goddamn melted cake! It was all right there, from her doe eyes that tracked her victims from the darkness all the way down to those thick-thighed legs of hers that stalked her prey for fun. A lonely, solitary woman, with no one to leverage over her head because she cared about no one and nothing.

We had tracked a psychopath.

And yet, the woman we had in our basement was anything but.

"Hey, hey!" Roger said as I pulled my bike into the parking space next to his rust bucket of a truck. "Everything okay? You need something for one of your guys? Because I'm just on my lunch break and—"

I quickly killed the engine. "Just the male nurse I was looking for."

His smile quickly faded. "Is something really wrong?"

I leaned back and slid my hands into my pockets, fiddling with the small, foldable knives I kept inside of them. How did I want to approach this? Did I want to slit his throat and leave him choking in his own blood? Or did I want to give out one of those rare second chances I wasn't very good at giving?

But Roger backed up. "Oh, no."

I moved fluidly, sliding off the back of my bike and slipping my hands out of my pockets. "We really need to talk, Roger."

He shook his head, raising his hands in mock surrender. "I gave you everything you needed. I swear. Everything we had on that girl is in the files that I gave you."

I put my kickstand down before sliding my hands out of my pockets. "I just want to walk."

He watched me crack my knuckles. "I just got off a double shift. I'm exhausted, Dante. And, for what it's worth, you and your guys never look like you come in peace. Just tell me what you want so I can go home and sleep."

"This won't take long," I said as I stood mere inches away from his body. "Just got a few questions."

He sighed, tilting his head back to keep me in view, like most people around me had to. "You and I both know it's never just a few questions."

I tilted my head. "And the longer you fight, the longer we'll be here."

He groaned, slamming his car door closed. "What do you want now?"

I pushed off my bike and walked toward his car. "The girl. Was she a twin?"

Roger looked around before he rushed around his car and got in my face. "You risked me losing my fucking job for a dumbass question like that? The police are crawling around here today. You could get us both—"

I lowered my voice. "Was. She. A twin?"

"A—a twin? The documents would have—"

"If the documents had my answer, I wouldn't be here. I told you to get me everything, Roger. You gave your word that you'd give me everything. So, why do I feel like you haven't done exactly that even though I paid you to do a thorough job? Or do you not remember that little bonus we worked out?"

"Of course, I remember," he glowered.

I grinned. "How is she, anyway? Your... bonus?"

His voice fell to a hushed whisper. "Just tell me what you want. I'm exhausted, all right?"

"I already told you: I want to know if she was a twin."

His voice lowered into a hushed whisper. "How the hell am I supposed to know that?"

My hand bolted out and wrapped around his throat. "Get in your car."

He gagged for air. "Dante, please. You're—you're hur—"

I reached down and tugged at the locked car door. "Open it, Roger."

He fumbled with his keys. "I can't—you're hurt—I can't breathe. Dante, I can't—."

I yanked the keys from his hand and pressed the singular button that unlocked the door. I tossed him inside and looked around at the empty parking lot before shoving my head inside the small compartment alongside him. I whipped the knife off my hip and flipped open the blade. It twinkled beneath the rays of sun that continuously peeked out from beyond the clouds above our heads. Clouds that hung heavy and low with the impending doom of a thunderstorm. Clouds that would rain down the way I'd spill his fucking blood if he didn't give me the truth.

I traced it along his cheek as he shivered beneath me. His body, warning him of the danger hovering above him. His eyes, wider than the sun as they threatened to pop out of his head. I loved their fear. I smelled it two miles away and cherished the feeling every single time. I wanted him afraid. I wanted him crying. I wanted him to be a little pussy-whipped asshole in the palm of my hand. After all, it had taken me a great deal of time and effort to arrange a date between him and the woman he wouldn't stop gushing over.

Then again, most people would do anything for money.

Even compromise their moral code.

"You've got one last chance, Roger," I said, holding the sharpened blade to his jugular. "Go get me every fucking shred of information you've got on this girl and her medical records, including who the fuck was in that room with her the day she was born, or so help me fucking *God* this E.R. won't be able to help you once they find your mangled body in this pathetic excuse for a car you've got."

"Fine, fine, fine," he practically wheezed, "just get off me. Get off!"

I removed the knife. "You have until dinner time to get me what I need."

"What!?" he squealed. "But—but that's in less than one—"

I rose up and out of his car before I tucked my blade away. "Now, get. Time's a'tickin'."

I'd never seen anyone move so quickly in all my life. He practically scrambled out of that car, not bothering to close the door behind him. He tripped over his own two feet as he scrambled back toward the emergency room doors, and I put on my best smile. An elderly couple walked by me, their prying gazes slamming my heart against my chest. I hated Nosey Nancys, and it seemed as if this town was fucking full of them.

"Hello, there," I said as I nodded and waved.

I watched them like a fucking hawk while the woman stared me down. The man managed to lift his hand and wave, but if he didn't keep that wife of his on a leash, they'd be in trouble. As they flounced by, I thought about how I'd spill their blood. Maybe I'd string the old man up by his legs before asking his wife what she thought she was doing staring me down like that. Maybe I'd let her have a taste of me, the man she couldn't stop gawking at, while her husband watched upside down.

"Lovely day, isn't it?" I called out to them.

Much to my relief, though, the woman finally managed to smile and wave. "Looks like rain, though!"

I shrugged, holding out my arms. "Good thing I love the rain!"

"Hey, you and me both! We used to dance in it all the time," the man said, waggling his finger between himself and his wife.

His old lady swatted at him. "You know being in the rain gives me fevers now."

I pointed at her. "Try taking a warm shower right as you

come in. Helps to warm your body up before it compromises your immune system."

"See?" the man said as he and his wife walked away from me. "Even the doctor told us that."

The woman clicked her lips. "I swear, Elbert, you'll take the advice of a stranger before you take the advice of your wife."

"Perfect," I murmured, a grin spreading across my face.

What they had was lovely, and I enjoyed the fact that I didn't have to snuff it out. I would have, of course. Sometimes, that was simply par for the course. And with how long we had been working on tracking this psycho bitch down, I wasn't about to let some old ass couple get in the way of that. They kept chittering along, walking toward a group of cars off to the left-hand side of the emergency room building. The man dug his keys out of his pocket before pointing them at a surprisingly nice BMW, and I had to allow myself a moment to smile.

Because sometimes, people were simply a surprise. "Way to go, Elbert."

After I watched that man help his wife into the passenger's seat of their vehicle, I turned back to my bike. Long gone were the days that I yearned for a life like that. Gone were the useless dreams that had taken up years of my life while I wished for a good woman at my side. Good women didn't debase themselves for men like me. Men whose hands were coated in the blood of others. Men who smiled while they gutted their enemies like fish. Good, strong, valiant women like the ones I enjoyed riding my cock weren't stupid enough to attach themselves to someone like me.

So, I filled my time with other things.

Like following that stupid bitch around for as long as I had.

I perched against my bike as thunder rolled in the distance. I opened the lock on the back compartment, then pulled out that tattered manilla folder. The front cover was coated in pencil and highlighter markings. Things had been jotted down and erased over time as we brainstormed where she'd head next, or where we'd be able to intercept her without the radar of the entire community going wild in the process. We had missed something, surely. Not me, of course; I read people like open books for fun. But there had to have been something we overlooked, something in that file that changed the way we looked at everything.

Because if not, we were back at square one.

I pulled out that black and white surveillance photo. It was the only picture we had of that woman serving as proof that she had done it. That she had slaughtered our President before Axton had been thrust into a position that everyone knew he wasn't ready for at the time. Whoever that bitch in the picture was, she had taken out the head of our crew. The man who had helped found The Road Raiders. The man who had recruited me, who had taught me that my stealth work and people skills were of value to a brutish crew of motorcycle men who protected what was theirs while taking what was owed to them.

As I looked at that picture, studying the soft slope of her nose and the quick blossom of her hips, lightning streaked across the sky. She'd pay the price for what she had done to us. For what she had taken from us. But the longer I studied that picture of her standing over Luca's dead body with his blood spilled everywhere beneath him, I focused on that bloodied knife in her hand. The knife that had ended my friend's life.

"We're coming for you," I murmured as my fingers clenched so hard that they crumpled the edge of the picture, "and we won't stop until we find you."

I lost myself within the nooks and crannies of that file folder. I skimmed over everything. I devoured my own profile, making sure I could track down the lineage of information that drove me to that point. I fished out a green highlighter from the back compartment of my bike, highlighting any and all information that helped me come to certain conclusions and facts we had deemed true. I highlighted and numbered. I triple-checked my work in order to make absolutely certain there hadn't been another train of thought to take.

Until something slapped against my chest.

"There," Roger said.

I looked down at the plastic grocery bag of files. "Well, then."

"That's it. That's everything, though I'm pretty sure I just lost my job doing it."

I peeked inside. "You'll find a better one."

"Why? Because you're going to place some calls? Trust me, I don't need it."

I looked up and plastered on my best smile. "Wouldn't dream of it."

He folded his arms across his chest. "If I ever see you back around this hospital, I'm calling the police. You got it?"

Aw. How cute. "Good luck with that."

"Good luck with what?"

I slid our dossier into the plastic bag before I shoved it into the compartment. "With convincing the police that the receipt I have for our transacted services is fake."

"Goddamn it, Dante. Just leave me the fuck alone. What the hell did I ever do to you?"

I slung my leg over my bike and shoved the key into the ignition. "I'll let you know if I need anything else."

"No. I'm serious, Dante. If you come back around here, I'll—"

I cranked the engine. "Sorry, what was that? Can't really hear you!"

His voice got louder. "I said, I'll call the police if you come back around here!"

I revved the engine. "One more time for me! I still can't hear you!"

And when he narrowed his eyes, I reached out and patted his cheek. "Your job is just fine; I'll make sure of that. And in the meantime, keep an eye out. I may need you again soon."

I kicked up my kickstand and pushed off toward the exit. As people came through the gate, they nodded at me, and I waved at them simply because I enjoyed putting on a show. No one ever suspected the nice, kind man who waved at them every time they saw one another. After all, half of what I did was make sure we kept a decent reputation around town. We couldn't utilize the town's help without their trust. But that trust went both ways.

And for some reason, my gut told me to burn my contact with Roger.

I need the warehouse.

I knew the guys were expecting me back at the house, but I needed to think. If I was going to be walking back in there with answers, then I wanted all of them. I wanted every answer to every question, including why the fuck Roger hadn't gotten me this shit the first time we danced haphazardly around one another.

Goddamn it, how badly had we fucked up?

With the wind in my hair, wrapping around my waist, I merged onto the highway. The closer I got, the more the darkness called to me. Santaleah and its rolling desert hills dotted with cacti fell into the background, giving way to the warehouse district that had been all but abandoned out there in the dust and clay-rotted sand. The cracked ground reminded me of home. The chilly temperature reminded me that I was alive and breathing, prepared to take on another battle for our survival.

I also remembered when the place used to be alive.

Stores littered the facades of warehouses that sat directly on the street while shops and apartment complexes lined the inner roads. There were block parties in the streets and dance battles in the alleyways. People from all walks of life that usually ended up in the underbelly of society in the sewers came to seek refuge within those metal-stained walls. And oh, the solace I took in being around those like me. It used to be a safe haven for all of those outcasted by humanity.

Then, the over-policing started.

I eased down the abandoned roads, taking in the cracked concrete and broken glass and used condoms that littered the bowing sidewalks. I thought about all of the times I had challenged drug-addled gangsters packing heat to dance battles as a fucking ten-year-old, like I was all big and bad or some shit. The memories tugged a smile across my face. I loved this place, the warehouse district. For many, it was the stuff of nightmares. But when the sun started to set and those shadows were cast, it felt like coming home.

I eased myself right up to a door I used to trudge in and out of all the time as a young boy. A comic bookstore, of all things. I grabbed the files and headed inside. The rusted door took a bit of work to open, but it caved after slamming my shoulder into it. I breathed in the deep, musty scent of old books and dye-stained papers that had rotted away over time. I shoved the door closed behind me and pulled out my cellphone, using its flashlight to illuminate my way. I bellied up to a dilapidated table in the corner and flopped down into the cushioned chair I had left here the last time I had taken up residence to look this information over.

And as I sat back, I dumped the contents of the plastic bag out in front of me.

"All right," I said, cracking my knuckles, "time to get to work."

The sun casted rays of light through the shattered windows

as night fell all around me. I found all of the stereotypical information one would find within those birthing documents: birth weight, time, length, bilirubin levels, time under a heat lamp. And while all of it was important, none of it pointed me toward what we had been looking for.

Until a simple section entitled "birth order" popped out at me.

"Second," I murmured.

I paused. No, I didn't pause—I froze. Birth order. Did that mean what I thought it meant? I couldn't get to my fucking internet quickly enough. My fingers typed away as I chewed on my lower lip, my entire body shivering in that chair. And when the internet confirmed for me what the hell I was looking at, I knew we were sunk.

She was the second-born child.

So, who in the fuck had been the first?

4

BRIELLE

The silence bothered me. I didn't hear anyone stomping around upstairs. I didn't hear any harsh voices filtering through the ceiling. I didn't even hear yelling, which I had heard over the course of my time there. I still hadn't figured out how long I had been here, by the way. Judging by the ache of my body, it had to have been at least a day.

Maybe two.

A light turned on and I cowered away. "Ah, shit."

"Whoops," a playful voice said.

The violence of the light faded away until it was nothing more than a soft dim. With my body turned away from its source, I peered over my shoulder and out into the darkness. There were all sorts of sounds I couldn't place. Clinking, and tinkering. Soft footfalls as opposed to the valiant stomps of the man that had damn near killed me.

Then, that same playful voice sounded to my right. "I brought food. Hungry?"

I tried to scoot further away, even going so far as to dance my bare toes along the harsh carpeted floor. Jesus, I hadn't even realized I'd been missing my shoes. Was I missing anything else on my body? It caused me to look down, and relief washed through me when I found myself still clothed.

"Seriously," the voice said as a shadow emerged in front of me, "you haven't eaten since you got here. You really should eat."

"And how long have I been here?" I asked.

"Two days. Almost three."

I scoffed. "No, thanks."

"Are you sure? I hear that stomach of yours growling."

It betrayed me with another groan that made me sick in my head. "I said no."

Something scooted along the floor before a pair of boyish hazel eyes came into view. In fact, the man looked nothing like I expected him to look. His blond hair twinkled with the dim light that shone behind him and his shapeshifting grin spread into a smile that exposed his pearly white teeth. He was clean-shaven with a crooked nose, most likely from whoever the hell had cold clocked him for being a dickhead.

Then again, he wasn't coming off as a dickhead.

Just that... other one.

"Hope you don't mind," he said, placing a tray on his lap, "but I dimmed the lights. I figured they'd be harsh on your eyes with all this darkness around you."

I looked down at his hand movements. "What are you doing?"

I watched him hold a piece of meat stuck onto the end of a fork up to my lips. "Feeding you. Here. It's my specialty."

I leaned back. "For all I know, it's poisoned."

He chuckled. "Poisoning is Dante's thing. Not mine. And he can't cook worth shit."

There was something warm about him. "You take the first bite."

He shrugged. "Suit yourself."

I watched him pluck the meat off the end of the fork and he chewed. He chewed, and he moaned, and he gave me a thumbs up before he swallowed. Then, he jammed the fork down into what smelled like potatoes before he shoved one of those into his mouth as well.

"Man, I can fucking cook," he murmured.

"It does smell great," I said as I peeked over.

He chuckled again before he held up another piece of what looked like chicken to my mouth. "Ready to give it a go?"

When my stomach growled out, it damn near made me dizzy, and I knew I couldn't hold off any longer. So, I parted my lips and slid the chicken off the fork. The warm, juicy goodness flooded my mouth. I moaned as I flopped back against the chair, savoring every moment my teeth collapsed into that tender meat. I hemmed and hawed, allowing my eyes to fall closed as my entire body relaxed for the first time since I had been snatched off the street.

Since they had jammed that needle into my neck.

Since I had woken up bound to a damn chair.

"The name's Maverick," the man said, holding up another piece of chicken to my mouth. "And you are?"

I swallowed quickly and gladly took another bite. "I'm helpless, but I'm not stupid."

He smiled. "Beautiful name. Want some potatoes?"

I couldn't help but snicker. "Mm, yes."

"There we go," he said as he stabbed one and held it out in front of me.

I chewed and swallowed before practically lunging my neck out toward the food. Bite by bite, he fed me. And bite by bite, my stomach stopped waging war against my body. If he thought I was stupid enough to tell him my name, though, he had another thing coming.

No amount of food would ever get me to trust that man.

"So," he said, placing the fork down, "why won't you give me your name? I'm sure it's just as beautiful as you are."

I cased him with my eyes. "Because you're convinced that I'm someone I'm not. What does it matter if you're going to kill me anyway?"

He nodded before he reached his hand out. "Thirsty?"

Suddenly, my mouth felt like cotton. "Yeah."

He pulled a bottle of water back toward him and cracked it open. "Axton can be rough around the edges, but it's for a good reason." He plunged a straw into the bottle before holding it up to my lips. "Drink."

I didn't hesitate. "You first."

He rolled his eyes before taking a gulp and I watched intently. I watched to make sure it didn't do shit to him before I chugged it back.

"There, happy?" he asked, holding the straw back up to my lips. "Now, will you drink? You can't go for much longer without water."

"Axton?" I asked before I wrapped my lips around that straw.

I chugged the ice-cold goodness as Maverick held the bottle firm. "That's the man that's been interrogating you. The big one."

I stopped chugging. "With the shoulders."

He snickered. "Yeah, with the shoulders."

I took one last pull before I sat back. "You guys call being smacked around and starved 'interrogation?'"

"Our form of it, sure."

My gaze held his. "Thank you for the water."

"Thank you for your time."

I wanted to give him my name. For some reason, my body felt drawn to him. Like a moth to a light. But I'd grown up with one of those bug zappers on my porch as a child, and I knew what happened when those little fuckers got too close to the light.

"You feel comfortable enough telling me your name now?" he asked.

I had to admit, I had to force my lips to not move. But those fateful, lumbering footsteps started down the stairs, and all at once, my stomach threatened to eject my entire meal.

"He's coming," I hissed as I tried scooting my chair back.

"No, no. It's okay," Maverick said, standing to his feet. "Don't panic; he's just coming to find me."

My eyes darted around. "He's coming. Please. Turn off the light. You have to turn it off. He's going to get mad."

"Beautiful, it's okay," he said as he placed his hand on my arm.

"Get off me!" I shrieked.

He stumbled back as if I had slapped him with my words. My heart leapt into my throat. It grew hard to see through my watery gaze. My legs locked out and my muscles tightened. Fucking hell, I couldn't breathe.

"The hell did you feed her down here?" the brutal voice asked.

"Axton, stop," Maverick said.

And much to my shock, the man shielded me with his body. He stepped in front of me, blocking my view of the behemoth man that had rumbled down the stairs.

It grew easier to breathe with him standing there.

"Church time," Axton said. "Leave her here. We have to talk."

"I'll be up in a bit," Maverick said.

The man peeked around his body, and I turned my head away so that I didn't have to face him.

So that I didn't have to face my executioner.

"Uh huh," Axton said. "All right, but don't fuck around down here. The guys are already upstairs."

Guys? What guys? Holy fuck, there were more guys.

"It's okay," Maverick said, turning to face me once more, "he's gone."

I elongated my neck and peered over his shoulder only to find that he was right. Just as quickly as Axton had appeared, he was gone again.

"Church? What's—what's church?" I asked breathlessly.

Maverick grinned as his thumb swiped over my chin. "Had some grease on there."

I glared at him. "What is church, Maverick?"

Jesus, I thought his eyes were hazel, but as he stared at me, they looked more green than hazel. "It's a meeting we're about to have where it's revealed that we've fucked up in taking you. So, I'd expect these binds to be off your body in no time."

"Wait, really?"

He tucked a strand of loose hair behind my ear. "Really, really."

"So, so that means I—I can go home? I can—go see my kids? Get back to work?"

"Let's not get ahead of ourselves just yet."

Tears immediately streaked my cheek. "I swear to you, I won't tell anyone. I'm super good at keeping secrets."

"I bet you are," he said as he raised up.

"My kids and their parents trust me with them all the time. I can keep this. I swear, Maverick, I can! Just let me go home!"

He walked toward the stairs. "We'll see one another soon."

"Maverick, please! Don't leave me alone down here! I swear, I won't tell anyone! I'm a good secret-keeper! Maveriiiiiiiiiick!"

But the only sound that answered me was the sound of the door upstairs thudding closed.

Leaving me with nothing except my racing thoughts.

5

MAVERICK

"Maverick, please!"

My cock stiffened as I worked my way up the steps.

"Don't leave me down here!"

"How I wish I didn't have to," I murmured as I got up the steps.

"I swear, I won't tell anyone! I'm a good secret keeper!"

It took all of the energy inside of me to close that door behind me.

"Maveriiiiick!"

I groaned as I shouldered the door closed. Sweat broke out along the nape of my neck and I pressed my forehead against the fucking door. I heard her crying. I heard her sobbing out loud for the first time since we had yanked her off her fucking sidewalk. I wanted to take her into my arms and whisk her up to my bedroom. I wanted to wash her hair. I wanted to clean the piss off her legs. I wanted to run those soapy bubbles all along her skin while I listened to her sigh with relief.

What we were doing to her was wrong.

We have to let her go.

"Goddamn it," I grunted, pushing myself away from the door.

This couldn't go on. We had the wrong girl. I knew we did. I didn't need a fucking church meeting to tell me that. Her eyes told me that. Her voice told me that. The desperation and the lack of psychopathic emptiness in her startling ice blue eyes told me that. It didn't take a profiler like Dante to look at that girl and realize we had the wrong person.

I made my way to the top of the clubhouse before emerging with only one question on the tip of my tongue.

"So," I said as I strolled in and extended my arms out to either side, "we've got the wrong girl, don't we?"

Axton pointed to my chair. "Sit your ass down and shut up."

I grinned as I walked by Wolf, our latest prospect. He held out his hand behind his back and I managed to clap mine against his.

"Now," Axton glowered.

Wolf leaned back and lowered his voice. "Told you something was off about all this."

Axton leveled that man with a death stare. Or at least tried to while Wolf cheekily smiled at him like a little boy who had gotten away with stealing a cookie from the jar before dinner.

"Church time," Axton said, planting his hands into the wooden table in front of us. "Sit."

All of us sat. Except for Dante, of course.

"You have the floor," Axton, our President, murmured before he flopped down into his chair.

The distress on his face told me everything I needed to know about how he felt.

"Right, so," Dante started as he slid one hand into his pocket and used the other to rake through his hair. "Went to the hospital. Tracked down my contact. Of course, he was wildly happy to see me."

A chuckle reverberated around the table, but it did nothing to lighten the mood.

"He got me documents he didn't give me before and—"

"Why?" Wolf asked as he interrupted Dante.

Dante pointed at him. "Good question. When I first asked him for all of the information he had on Rachel Ludick, he originally didn't have any information. That started our runaround for—"

"Just get to the point," Axton groaned.

Dante licked his lips. "I went back and asked him to give me everything he had on the woman, including information from her birth. He didn't understand why that was relevant, so when we finally figured out who we were looking for and tracked down her medical records for information, it didn't make sense for him to give us her birth records. We assumed, originally, that it was because she wasn't born in this area. Easy enough to accept."

I nodded slowly. "Something we all accepted."

"We shouldn't have," Axton spat.

Rocker wiggled his fingers, as if to haphazardly raise his hand. "How do we know that woman downstairs isn't who we're looking for?"

"Yeah," Locker said. "She's the spitting fucking image of The Grim Reaper."

"In her birth records," Dante continued as he pinched the bridge of his nose, "there's something called a birth order. If there is more than one child born, the medical documents lay out what order the children born to that mother were born in."

The room fell silent as Dante raised his gaze to all of us.

"The woman we have downstairs? Whose medical records we obtained thinking she was our gal? She was the second-born in the birth order."

"So, what?" Locker asked. "That means we got some twin out there running around cappin' us all in our asses?"

Dante pointed at him. "Bingo."

"Jesus motherfucking Christ," Rocker groaned.

Wolf smiled as he shifted his sucker into his other cheek. "It just keeps getting better and better."

"God fucking damnit!"

The bellow that left Axton's mouth had nothing on the way the entire room shook when he shot out of his chair. When he balled up his fists. When he slammed them down onto the table in front of us. Drinks shook. Wolf's coffee tipped over. And as a water bottle rolled off the edge of the mahogany table, I could have sworn I saw Axton's eyes glistening.

I couldn't imagine how that man felt right now.

"Shit," he hissed, pacing around the table. "This isn't good. Not good, not good, not good."

"Axton," I said as I stood.

"We have to let her go. We don't have any other choice," he muttered.

I reached out and grabbed his arm. "Axe."

Wolf cleared his throat. "She may understand if we simply tell her what's going on."

Axe stared me down with a death glare. "Let me go."

I shook my head. "I've already built rapport with her downstairs. The food, remember? She let me feed her. She talked with me. We can build on that. We can still get ourselves out of this."

He shoved my grasp away. "Have you been beating her face in for the past two days?"

"No."

He got into my face. "Then, you shut the fuck up."

Yeah, he wouldn't let himself off the hook for a very, very long time for this.

It made me sick to my stomach to think about.

"He's right," Dante said as his voice catapulted itself over everyone's heads at the table. "If Mav's already got rapport with her, he's our best shot at getting out of this without her immediately rushing off to the police."

Axton shook his head. "I'm not concerned about the police."

Rocker scoffed. "Well, ya should be."

"Well, I'm not," Axe gritted, "and neither should you guys. You know we're always a shoo-in with the department around here. Have been for years. We explain what's happened, we pay off the right people, we're good."

"Then, what the hell are you so wound up about?" Locker asked.

Axton turned toward him as his face fell to stone. "What's the first rule of The Road Raiders?"

Locker's gaze fell to his lap, and he folded his hands together. Axton grasped the arms of the man's chair, turned him away from the table, and bent forward. Enough to stick his face in Locker's and snarl.

"Say it," Axton growled.

Locker brought his gaze upright. "Never do harm to those who don't deserve it."

Axton shoved himself upright. "Exactly. Do you think that woman down there deserves this?"

"No."

"Well, at least you're smart enough to answer your own questions nowadays," I murmured.

"Shut up," Locker spat.

I placed my hand on Axton's shoulder. "Let me be her interface for now. Whatever you need her to know, or even say to her, I can do on your behalf. But it's our best and only shot that we've got. We'll need all hands on deck to figure out where in the hell this woman's sister is, anyway."

Axton simply nodded before he stormed out of the room, and I knew that wasn't good. The only other time he had ever walked out of a church meeting before dismissing us was when we had lost our first-ever crew member under his tutelage.

And as he slammed the door behind him, my eye twitched.

"All right, everyone," Dante, our Enforcer, said as he stepped up to the plate, "here's what's gonna happen: we get back into our A-B-C patrol groups and start them back up. As far as I'm concerned, we're back at square one. So, we act as such. We keep up patrols, we keep digging around town for information, and as long as we've got her sister with us in this clubhouse, we know that whoever we run into will be the woman we're looking for."

"That bitch deserves to pay for what she did to Luca," Rocker grumbled.

Dante's gaze sharpened. "Which is why we're gonna find the bitch. No one takes out a president of ours and gets away with it."

"Axton knows that none of us could have possibly known, right?" Wolf asked. "I mean, a twin? It's almost like a comedy sketch."

"And yet, there's nothing funny about any of this," I said flatly. "About beating up an innocent woman for information she doesn't have."

"We can't just let her go, though," Dante said as he slid both of his hands into his tight-ass pockets. "You guys know that, right?"

That rendered the table silent once more.

"As long as she's in our grasp, we have to wait and make sure she isn't gonna run to anyone and everyone who will listen. We're in a precarious position, so we have to tread lightly while watching our backs."

The sea of heads around him nodded, but I could tell they

were all off in their own little world. This was a first for us. We'd never snatched someone off the street that we hadn't meant to take. It felt odd. Wrong, even. And it gave me a stark reality check with my own conscience.

Not enough to leave, of course.

But enough to know that we had to tread lightly, otherwise we'd all go down for what happened.

"A-team, your patrol is up. Run our back roads for two hours, then run the main roads for the other two hours. B-team, you'll switch out with them after with the same pattern, but C-team?"

"Yeah?" Rocker and Locker asked in unison.

"I want you patrolling our delivery routes. I want to make sure none of our outside operations have been compromised by us being distracted for the past few days. By that time, I should have an indefinite schedule of patrol times, routes to take, and things to check off while you're out and about on the road."

I drew in a deep breath. "Guess I'll go break the news to her."

The door slammed open, revealing a very pale Axton. "I can do it."

"Uh, what?" Dante asked.

"Dismiss church and get on with the patrols," Axton called out as he headed for the stairs.

Dante looked at me. "Mav?"

I bolted for the door. "I'll take care of it."

Dante clapped his hands. "Church dismissed, everyone. Get to your jobs. We've got a fuckton of work to do if we want to catch up."

6

AXTON

I tried not to get pissed off at the fact that Mav was perched at the top of the steps. As I stood there in the doorway, I watched as that spotlight illuminated the space around that woman. In the light, I saw everything that I had done to her. The swollen black eye she couldn't use. The ligature marks around her neck from choking off her ability to breathe. The missing fingernails from her scratching at the arm of the chair, trying to break herself free.

I almost wished someone would beat the ever-loving shit out of me.

"Who's there?" she called out.

The tremble in her voice took my breath away.

"Who is it? Mav?"

I swallowed hard as I walked down the last step and into the basement. "No."

Immediately, she recoiled at the sound of my voice. "Please, don't. I swear, I didn't do anything."

I took another step toward her. "I know."

Tears immediately streaked her face. "I'll do whatever you

want. Please, just don't. All I did was eat. I ate like a good girl, I swear it."

"I know."

"Don't come any closer," she hissed.

I paused my movements before an overwhelming stench filled the room. The sound of trickling water accompanied the sounds of her soft sobs, and as she hung her head, I slid my gaze down her body. I watched the dark trail of urine slide down the inside of her leg. It dripped to the floor with a putrid smell that reminded me of how badly we had starved and dehydrated the woman.

"I'm so sorry," she said through her sniffling. "I'll clean it up. I will. Don't worry."

"No, you won't," I said, tilting my head.

She choked out her next set of words in a broken voice that shattered my soul.

"I won't run if you release me. I'll clean it up, and get into bed, and I'll stay there until you need me. Just please, let me go. My wrists, they hurt so badly. I can hardly see. And my ankles. The pee, it... it burns. Oh, God. Help me. Someone, please help me."

I walked over to her and watched her shiver. She shook so violently that I thought her bones might come undone from one another. Her teeth chattered, as if someone had stuck her out in the cold. Everything inside of me froze to ice as I reached down and undid the binding around her wrist. The rope fell away, and as I watched her red, irritated, bleeding skin expose itself to the elements, she cradled her hand against her chest.

"Thank you," she said breathlessly. "Holy fuck, thank you. Oh, God. It hurts so much."

Blood dripped down her arm. It stained her silken white blouse and made my stomach turn over into itself. Jesus, that woman had put up a fight. I undid her other wrist, only to watch more blood drip all along her lap and shirt as she cradled both of them against her bosom.

"Sit still," I murmured as I crouched down.

I swallowed the bile creeping up the back of my throat. I unraveled the rope from her ankles, and the skin that pulled away damn near made me gag. She needed medical attention. Serious medical attention, before something got infected.

My God, what have I done?

"Come with me," I said, scooping her into my arms.

"No, no, no, no! No! Please. Whatever it is, I can do better. I will be better. Whatever it is that you need."

"It's okay," I said, trying to keep my voice as level as possible. "Nothing is going to happen."

"Oh, God. No. Please. Someone help me! Help me! Mav!"

I chewed on the inside of my cheek. "He's just at the top of the steps."

She shoved her hands into my chest, but she was so weak that I barely felt her touches.

"No, no, no. No! Stop! Heeeelp! Someone, help meeee!"

Her blood smeared itself across my clothes. The stench of her urine should have been accompanied by the stench of her feces, but it wasn't. She shook in my arms, trying to roll away from me. And yet, every time I pulled her back to cradle her, she flailed.

Well, as best as she could given her wounds.

"Axe?" Maverick asked as I crested the top of the steps.

I nodded toward the stairs. "We need clean-up down there. And get a bedroom ready for her."

"Should we call a doctor as well?" he asked.

"Yeah."

Mav nodded before he bit down onto his lower lip. I turned the woman away from the harsh sound of his whistling, but it only caused her to scream. I'd never heard a woman make that sound in all my life. It was worse than those horror films Dante always watched late at night when he couldn't sleep. It rang my ears and rattled my brain in its skull, as if her voice were the only strength she had.

"Clean-up crew! Downstairs! Now!" Maverick bellowed.

"Oh, God. What is happ—happening?" the young woman choked out.

I simply started toward the stairs, though, where Dante waited for me.

"What do you need?" he asked.

"Pick a room," I said, walking up the steps, "any room. Whichever one is safer for her. She needs her own space while a doctor checks her out."

"Is she hungry?" he asked, walking backwards up the steps.

I nodded. "Just get her a little bit of everything. Some drinks. Some snacks. Maybe some warm soup. A sandwich. I'm sure she's still hungry."

Dee ushered his arm out toward the first guest bedroom we happened upon. "This one has a little mini fridge that we can keep stocked for her."

"Perfect," I murmured as I turned a hard left into the room.

"What's happening? Someone talk with me, please. What did I do? How can I make it better?"

I didn't know what to say to her, though. Apologies didn't work. Not with something like this. The only thing that I could do was show her, with actions, that she was safe now. I didn't know if it would work. I had no clue if she'd bolt at the first sign of an exit strategy or not. At that moment, I wasn't really concerned about it.

All I wanted was to get her better.

"Please," she whispered desperately.

I perched her on the edge of the bathtub in the ensuite bathroom. "You were right."

She teetered, her tired body swaying side to side softly. "Huh?"

I leaned against the bathroom countertop and folded my arms across my chest. "You were right, you're not the woman we're looking for."

The pathetic look in her eyes immediately turned angry. "I fucking told you so."

"We've still got an issue, though."

"What? You think I'm gonna flee to the cops and talk about the guys that stole me out from in front of my home and tortured me for two days?"

"Yes, but I wasn't talking about that."

Curiosity fled behind her eyes. "Then, what is it?"

I pushed off the edge of the countertop and bent forward. I ran the hot water first, getting it tempered to a temperature that I knew her body would handle. Then, I shuffled around, rummaging through the cabinets until I found what I wanted.

A bottle of peroxide to pour into the water to help disinfect her wounds.

"Answer me!" she damn near shrieked.

I dumped the entire bottle into the bath before I tossed it into the trash can.

"Are you aware that you have a twin?" I asked.

The woman's eyes narrowed before she blinked. It was slow. Deliberate. As if she were trying to put on her best poker face possible while turning over the information inside of her head.

It gave me the answer I needed.

"Figured as much," I said, raking my hands down my face. "Well, it turns out you have one. And that's the woman we're looking for. She's dangerous and ruthless, and until we find her, you're not safe."

I had to admit I had no clue what reaction to expect. Would she hit me? I would have let her. It was the least I deserved.

Would she yell and stomp around and try to leave? Again, it wouldn't have shocked me. There were so many things that flew through my head. So many things I expected her to say, do, or promise. Our deaths, for one. She'd have every right to plunge a steak knife right into my chest cavity.

What I didn't expect, however, was for her to laugh.

"Haaaahahahahahaha."

I paused as I watched her head fall back.

"Haaaaaaah-hahahahahaa!"

My brow furrowed tightly. "Are you—"

She held up her hand and drew in a deep breath as her face turned red.

"BWAAAAAHAHAHAHA! A TWIN! OH, MY FUCK!"

I tilted my head as steam filled the space between us. She shook her head as laughter fell from her lips, and I turned my back as she stripped her clothes off.

"Aaaaaahahahaha! A twin. You guys expect me to believe that! Baaahahaha!"

"It's true," I said as the sound of her clothes plopping to the floor made my toes tingle.

"HAH! Oh, God. That's fucking rich. Fuck you guys. Holy shit, you almost had me there," she said as water sloshed around with her movements.

Dante appeared in the doorway with a tray of food. "Uuuuh... everything okay in here?"

"A twin!" she barked. "God, how pathetic! And I thought I was an idiot! Ahahaha!"

I walked over and yanked the tray out of his grasp. "You got an extra copy of that hospital paperwork?"

Dante crooked an eyebrow. "Yeah?"

I walked the tray of food over to the bathtub and set it down for the laughing hyena we had inherited.

"Get her a copy," I said as I strode out of the bathroom. "She needs to see it. Now."

Her laughter echoed behind me as I made my way out of the bedroom. It was damn near maniacal, and I clapped my hands over my ears until I started down the steps. I couldn't move away from her quickly enough. I couldn't leave her in the dust as fast as I wanted. My hands fell away from my ears as Maverick and the clean-up crew emerged from the downstairs. And as her laughter echoed softly throughout the corridors of our multi-tiered clubhouse in the middle of the fucking desert, Mav simply sighed.

"You told her, didn't you?" he asked.

My gaze got lost over his shoulder. "The clean-up done down there?"

He nodded. "Yep."

"Good," I said, brushing past him, "because I need some time alone to think."

And it wasn't until I got into the basement and closed the door behind me that her laughter finally ceased, leaving me with enough silence for one haunting, stomach-curdling thought to cross my mind.

How the hell am I going to make this right?

7

BRIELLE

I couldn't control my laughter, or the bubbly feeling of "holy fucking shit" that rose up from my toes and infected the marrow of my bones. Even if I wanted to, I couldn't stop.

A fucking twin?

Were they serious with that bullshit?

What a pathetic attempt at an excuse.

The mountainous human being in front of me lumbered away as feeling rushed to the tips of my fingers. I thought it would feel freeing. I thought I'd rejoice. That I'd get up on my feet, shake my ass, and rejoice to the heavens. But the pain was rather excruciating.

And by "rather excruciating," I meant that I would have accepted the big man snapping my fucking neck compared to it.

"Good God," I groaned as I leaned over.

"I gotcha," someone whispered, before they yelled directly into my ear. "Mav! I need some help in here!"

Footsteps sounded quickly down the hallway before I heard his friendly voice. "Gimme the food. You get her."

"Where the hell did Axe go?" the bodiless voice asked.

"They burn," I choked out.

I heard so many foreign sounds. Things clinking and clattering together. Water steamed up from the bath that kept filling. My body shook with the pain radiating up my legs. It felt like someone was trying to pull my toes out of their sockets.

"What's happening to me?" I asked breathlessly.

"Hey, can you look up at me?"

I tilted my head back as far as it could go and saw him. Mav. The guy that fed me that food.

"You," I said softly.

He grinned. "Me. Your hands and feet hurt because your blood is rushing to it all at once."

I swallowed hard. "Who's holding me, then?"

Mav perched beside me. "That's Dante. He's just holding you steady, so you don't fall into the water."

My gaze danced along his baby face. "And the big guy? That was—"

"Axton," Mav said with a head nod.

"Water's ready," Dante said.

Mav scooped me into his arms. "You get the tray of food, Dec. I'll get her into this bath."

I looked down. "But my clothes."

"Do you want them off?"

I peeked up at Mav's face. "Do you usually take baths with your clothes on?"

He placed me back down onto my feet. "We can give you some privacy to get undressed if you wish."

I slowly turned and found myself taking in a tall, lanky man with auburn hair and forest green eyes. He stood there with a tray clutched in his hands with his gaze piercing straight into my soul. My God, he was tall. He had to have been at least six-and-a-half feet tall.

Well, maybe not quite that tall.

But close enough.

"You guys are never gonna let me go, are you?" I asked him.

He answered my question when the stick figure glanced over my shoulder at the man behind me.

"Why don't we take it one step at a time?" Mav asked.

"Answering a question with a question is never good," I said, tilting my head and continuing to stare into those hunter green eyes. "But then again, something tells me you already know that."

Mav was still the one to answer me, though. "I don't have an answer for you. But you should probably reserve your opinions until you speak with Dante. He's got a lot of information you need to hear."

My gaze dripped down the lanky man's surprisingly chiseled form. "And if I still choose to leave?"

Dante moved the tray in his hands a bit, almost as if to lift it up and offer it to me. And of course, he stepped right around my question.

"I'll hand you your food once you're in the bath," he said plainly.

I scoffed. "I'm not undressing in front of either of you. So, both of you go stare at a wall or something until I can get beneath the bubbles."

I watched the two of them as they stared at one another. Were they debating my request? Because it certainly wasn't something that was up for debate. I crossed my arms over my chest and stepped off to the side. I got out of their line of sight, giving them plenty of time to silently make out or whatever the fuck it was they were doing while they held one another's gazes from across the bathroom.

Then, the two of them pivoted on their feet and faced their respective walls.

"Thank you," I said as my hands gripped the hem of my shirt.

My once-pristine white silken blouse had holes and blood stains on it. I clocked them as I pulled it over my head, grunting and groaning with the pain that coursed throughout my body. I turned toward Mav, who stood in a corner next to the bathroom mirror, and I tossed my top onto the counter. I caught my reflection in the mirror as I unhooked my bra, and the bruises alone stole my breath away. I had dark rings around my neck. Bruises on the tops of my breasts. I unzipped my pencil skirt and dragged it down my legs, taking in the bruised indentations on the backs of my thighs from fighting with the chair so damn much. It brought tears to my eyes. Hell. I had been in hell for the last couple of days, and it didn't look like my torturers were going to let me leave anytime soon.

"I see you peeking, Mav," I said flatly, catching his gaze in the reflection of the mirror.

He cleared his throat and shuffled on his feet. "Just making sure you didn't need any help."

"Trust me," I grunted, shoving my urine-stained panties down my legs, "you guys have helped enough."

Standing there, naked, in front of the mirror, I caught a glimpse of what they had actually put my body through. The dark bruises that covered at least thirty percent of my body. The missing fingernails from where I tried clawing my way out of my binds. The pain had subsided in my extremities, but it did nothing for the pounding in my skull.

Maybe I had a concussion.

Maybe it would kill me, and this nightmare would be over.

"Do you need help getting into the bath?" Dante asked.

I slowly turned toward the bubble-filled tub. "If you so much as flinch to turn away from that corner, I'll claw your eyes out."

Mav chuckled. "Feisty."

I stepped into the tub and hissed at the pain. "You don't know the quarter of it."

I eased myself slowly beneath the warm coating of bubbles that popped against my aching skin. My bones grew weak. My skin gave way. It took all of the energy I had to lower myself into those bubbles without collapsing and making a fucking mess. Why couldn't they take a cue out of Axton's book and just leave me the hell alone? All I wanted was to be left with my thoughts.

So, I could find a way out of this fucking place.

"Okay," I said after covering my breasts with soap. "I'm ready."

Mav spun around. "Great. Dante?"

That food tray came out of nowhere, hovering in the air as the skinny man's spindly fingers sat the tray in the corner by my head next to the wall the tub sat against.

I reached over my shoulder for a grape and plucked it off the stem. "Thank you."

Mav shook his head. "No thanks needed. You take all of the time you need. Dante is here to talk when you're ready."

And with one last glance toward Slender Man, he left the two of us alone in that bathroom.

"Right," I murmured as I sank deeper into the bubbles.

"I only have one question."

His voice commanded my attention, even though it wasn't harsh. "And what's that?"

"Do you really want to see the paperwork?"

I tilted my head back and looked up at his upside-down face. "What paperwork?"

"The paperwork that proves I'm right. Do you want to hear it from a stranger? Or would you rather look at the papers for yourself?"

I shouldn't have found it considerate that he asked, but I did. "I appreciate you asking."

"They're just downstairs if you want them. I could leave you alone with them to process and everything."

Alone.

He was willing to leave me alone?

I nodded. "I'd like that."

He pressed up from his perched position on the edge of the tub. "I'll be back in five."

"I'll be right here," I said as I reached for another grape.

I listened as he closed the bathroom door and I waited. I held my breath with that grape in between my fingertips and strained my ears to clock his footsteps. They were quiet. Almost too quiet. Almost as if he were intentionally quieting himself down. But that telltale click of the door told me that he had gotten out of the bedroom and into the hallway.

So, I practically lunged myself out of the tub.

"I have to get out of here," I whispered to myself.

I bolted for the window in the room, my body dripping with water and bubbles. I flipped the lock and tried prying it open, but it wouldn't come unstuck. Grunts and groans did nothing to aid in my lack of strength, and it angered me that I couldn't get the stupid fucking thing open. But when I checked the seal, I noticed that it had been painted over.

"I can fix that," I muttered to myself.

I hobbled over to the sink and threw open drawers. Most of them were empty, which wasn't shocking, but it didn't help my conundrum one damn bit. I dipped down onto all fours and opened the bottom drawers. I peeked beneath the sink for any signs of something sharp that I could use.

And when I found myself staring at a toolbox, I smiled from ear to ear.

"Bingo," I hissed, reaching toward the back of the cabinet.

I moved as fast as I could, flipping the top open and rummaging for something I could use to scrape the paint away from the window frame. I found a small flathead screwdriver that sat perfectly within the palm of my hand, and for the first time in days, hope blossomed in my gut. I pulled myself out from beneath the sink and rushed back to the window. I jammed that fucking thing into the lower window frame and raked it across, taking with it chips of paint that flew into my face and splattered all over my wet body.

Until finally, the window popped.

"Gotcha," I whispered.

I tossed the screwdriver to the floor and threw open the window. The wind kicked up, shrouding my face in fresh air as I drew in a deep breath. Home. I was one step closer to getting home. To getting help. To getting out of that place.

Until I opened my eyes.

"Oh. My. God," I muttered.

As far as my eye could see, there was nothing but desert. Nothing but cracked ground, spewing up dark shadows in the form of caustic cacti and tumbleweeds. Tears lined my eyes as I searched for a road or a dirt path. Anything that I could shimmy down to and run toward. There were no signs of life anywhere, though. No wells of water. No cars sounding in the distance. No people chattering about.

How far away from home was I?

"Nice ass," Dante said.

I gasped as I whipped around and I found the tall, subtle man standing there, clutching a file of papers. His head tilted off to the side, as if he were a father scolding a child who had just got caught with their hand in the candy jar.

Then, he licked his lips as his gaze slid down my body.

"Oh, no you don't," I hissed, trying to use my arms to cover up my body.

His smirk was positively devilish as his gaze came back to mine. "I have the documents you wanted to see."

I jutted my arm out. "Give them to me."

And of course, my tit fell out the second a brisk wind kicked up through the doorway. It puckered my nipple, much to Dante's amusement judging by the hungry look on his face. I quickly gathered my arms back around my body. I stood there, shivering from the cold as goosebumps fled across my nakedness.

"I'll just... leave them here," he said, placing them on the edge of the tub.

Then, without another word spoken, he turned and made his way back into the bedroom.

"Dante?" I blurted out.

He paused, but he didn't turn around. So, I figured I had his attention.

"You guys aren't ever going to let me go, are you?" I asked again.

I hated how weak my voice sounded.

"If you truly want to leave after reading through all those documents, then be my guest," he said, peering over his shoulder. "But if I've read you right, you won't want to."

His words stunned me. What the hell did that mean if he read me right? His words hung heavily in my head as he slipped out of the bedroom and quietly closed the door behind him. Hell, I barely heard it latch before the soft pitter patter of his footsteps practically scurried down the hallway. No doubt, to go tell his butt-buddies about my pathetic attempt at escape. I groaned as yet another cold, forceful breeze kicked up. It caused me to turn around long enough to slam the window closed before I made my way back to the tub. I eased myself into the warm waters, feeling another set of goosebumps race across my body in thanks for relieving my skin of the torturous cold.

Because it only made my pain worse.

"There we go," I said with a soft sigh.

At first, I discarded the folder in favor of the food. My stomach let out an unearthly growl, one that would have gotten the government involved had they heard it. I wolfed down the grapes and wasted no time with the chocolate covered strawberries. But it was the comforting tuna melt with barbecue chips that warmed my gut. The fuller I became, the deeper I sank into the bath until there was no food—and barely any of me—left on the surface.

Then, my gaze panned over my shoulder and found the tip of that folder.

"You shouldn't do it," I whispered to myself.

And yet, I exchanged the empty tray for the file as my curiosity got the better of me.

The front page was a color-coded document of what the different colors of highlighting meant. Pink was urgent, yellow was important, green was good stuff to know but not necessary, and red was simply entitled, *holy shit*.

So, I skimmed the document for the red highlights.

"What the fuck?" I spat.

I went from slowly drifting beneath the bubbles to sitting upright. The very first red highlight mark I had come to was a section of my birthing documents entitled, *birth order*. How the hell they had gotten their hands on my motherfucking hospital records, I had no clue. Had they asked my parents? Dear God, had they done something to my family? Blood boiled beneath my skin. If they so much as laid a hand on—

Birth order: second.

That one word ripped me from my heated trance. Second. Birth order, second. What did that mean?

Did that mean what I thought it meant?

"Let's just keep flipping," I said as I cleared my throat.

The next red highlight I came to was a name. It wasn't my name, however.

"Rachel Ludick," I said softly to myself.

That stopped me dead in my tracks. I blinked a few times, trying to see if maybe the name would change. Trying to see if maybe my brain was playing tricks on me. After all, I had been beaten. Starved. Tortured, practically. Maybe my brain filled in blanks. I swiped my thumb over the name. I spat on the paper and tried to wipe it away. And even though the paper curled up, fiber by fiber, the name didn't disappear.

Rachel Ludick.

When I was adopted, it was shortly after I was born. I knew the extent of my adoption. My parents never tried to keep it from me. They answered any questions I had, and one of my impending teenage-hormone-addled questions was whether or not my birth mother had named me before they did.

Want to know what they named me?

"Rebecca Ludick," I whispered to myself.

I leaned up, pulling my entire torso out of the water as I furiously flipped through the pages. I came upon pictures. Black and white pictures of a woman smiling into a security camera that looked exactly like me but wasn't me. Pictures of her holding a knife to a man's throat. A picture of her just after she had tossed that man's body to the floor. She was covered in blood, holding the knife above her head, and even though she had her face angled down, it didn't take a genius to read the curl of her lips.

To see the smile of her crow's feet.

To see the confidence of her posture.

She was enjoying what she was doing.

And she looked just like me.

"Jesus fucking Christ," I said flatly.

As much as my brain screamed at me to stop, I kept reading. Maybe I enjoyed the torture. Enjoyed the pain. But the more I read, the more my heart broke. We looked exactly alike, and yet the more I read about this woman, the more I sided with the guys that had taken me. This woman was sadistic. She was as cunning as she was evil. Her torture tactics alone made the guys' tactics seem like child's play, and bile crept up the back of my throat. I clutched the papers with a death grip as I leaned my head over the edge of the tub. My stomach heaved and hoed, clinging to the food it so desperately needed while bile spewed from the back of my throat and onto the floor next to the tub. My entire body quivered with fury as those black and white photos emblazoned themselves onto my brain. My knuckles turned white as I gripped the edge of the tub. My body strained, then shook. Strained, then shook. Strained, locked out, then shook some more. And the entire time, her name rushed through my mind.

Rachel.

Rachel Ludick.

Holy fucking hell, I had a twin sister named Rachel.

And she was a murderer.

Fucking hell, Dante was right.

8

———

DANTE

"How bad was the rest of the clean-up?" I heard Mav ask as I made my way down the stairs.

Axton harrumphed. "Little piss never hurt anyone."

I heard Mav munching on something crunchy, and I would have rather he knocked me the fuck out. I couldn't stand listening to that man eat every chance he could.

He always ate so damn loud.

"You know," I said as I made my way into the kitchen, "it may be worth it, having her looked at by our doc."

"Already on it," Axton said flatly, "that peroxide I dumped into her bath is only going to do so much."

"When's the doctor supposed to be here?" Mav asked.

"Which one did you call? We've had a few on call over the years," I said.

Axton stayed silent, however. He sat there at the kitchen table with his legs outstretched and the frame of the wooden chair he sat on begged for mercy. Every movement caused the chair to groan. Watching him fold his arms over his chest as he stared out the kitchen window above the sink felt more like watching an act of God than a struggling man at rest. The wind kicked up quickly, a tactic the Chihuahuan deserts of Texas that surrounded us were used to throwing. It was part of the reason we stayed safe out there. Because hardly anyone could get to us.

And even with the whistling of the wind by the window that kicked up a small storm of sand pelting against the clubhouse, he continued to stare.

Empty.

Angry.

Mindless.

"You couldn't have known," I murmured, easing myself onto the chair next to Axton.

He scoffed. "Tell that to her bruises."

Mav leaned against the countertop and folded his arms across his chest. "You can't blame yourself for—"

Axton leapt out of his seat as if someone had set him on fire. "I beat an innocent fucking woman within inches of her life!"

"Give me a bit more credit than that," her angelic voice said as it echoed down the hallway. "It was hardly inches."

Axton whipped around with a kind of shock on his face, which was odd, because I'd never seen that man shocked. And yet, as I slowly stood—sipping my Coke in one hand as I traced my fingertips along the top of the kitchen table with the other— he stood there in absolute silence.

With eyes that grew wider with every step that woman took into our kitchen.

"Axton," the woman said with a soft nod of her head.

Axe's hardened stare along her face froze him in place. However, I couldn't stop staring at the robe I had silently hung for her in the bedroom next to the closet. I was glad she had found it, because dear fucking heaven it made her legs look positively delectable.

"Eyes up," she said as the heat of her gaze fell against my forehead.

I slowly crawled my gaze up her body until I clocked the frustration on her face. "Be clearer next time, then."

I could have sworn I saw the faintest shadow of a grin upon her rosy, red cheeks before she pulled her hand out from behind her back and slapped the weight of that file into the chair Axe had been occupying.

"Question," she said.

Mav pushed off the countertop. "Answer."

She pointed down toward the documents. "How many people are looking for this woman who looks just like me?"

Mav cleared his throat to respond, but she held up her hand.

"Axton?" she asked.

I had to admit, the exchange was intriguing. So, I perched my hip on top of the kitchen table, took a sip of my Coke, and settled in for the ride.

"Our rival crew is," Axe said once he found his voice. "She was originally employed by them when she crossed us. They're also searching for her."

"Why?"

"That's confidential."

She smirked. "Within an inch of my life. Those were your exact words. I think that deserves at least a few answers, don't you think?"

Mav barked with laughter. "She's spunky. I like her. Can we keep her?"

"Isn't that your plan anyway?" the woman asked.

Goddamn it, she was intriguing. She knew how to read a room.

I liked that in a woman.

"Maverick," Axton said hotly.

"Hey," he said, pointing to the back of the man's head and looking over at me, "that's not a no, Dante."

I chuckled before taking another sip of my drink. "No, it is not."

"So..." the woman asked, holding out her arms. "Care to answer?"

Axe clicked his tongue. "They're searching for her because she's gone rogue. She killed one of their prospects."

The woman tilted her head. "She killed your president, too. Right?"

Axton simply nodded.

"You know," the woman said as she took a step closer to Axe, "I read a lot of information in that file Dante gave me."

"Good," he said flatly.

She tilted her head back to keep his stone-cold gaze in view. My God, it was almost comical how much he dwarfed her.

"Apparently, she had a great deal of health issues when she was first born," she said. "Bilirubin struggles. Heart struggles. Breathing struggles. All sorts of struggles because of her umbilical cord getting wrapped around her throat."

"I know what's in the document," he grumbled.

"Apparently," the woman continued, "she also bounced from foster home to foster home because of it. No one wanted such a sick child. No one wanted all of those medical—"

"I know what's in the fucking file, Rebecca."

The woman giggled. "You think that's supposed to be my name? The one in the file?"

I peeked over at Mav, and even he looked shocked.

"So, that's not your name," Axton said before he drew in a deep breath through his nose, "good to know."

"My point is," our nameless woman said as she stalked around him, clasping her hands behind her back, "it could have been either one of us. Either one of us could have ended up in her situation. And I have to admit, that tickles a part of my heart you probably wouldn't understand."

Her statement sucked the air out of the room as Axton's back straightened. He cracked his neck, most likely digesting the fact that she had essentially just called him a heartless psychopath.

And if anyone knew Axton like we did, they'd know that wasn't the least bit true.

"Axe," I murmured.

He slowly turned to face her. "What's your point?"

"My point is," the woman said as she stood in between Mav and Axe, "is that I want to help."

"Help," I said.

She turned her attention toward me. "Yes, I want to help because you were right. If this stuff is happening outside, there's no telling who else might end up thinking that I'm her."

"It's more than possible," Axe murmured.

The woman drew in a deep breath. "No doubt my parents have already gone to the police, though. And the only way you'll get them to back off is if I call them and tell them that I'm fine."

"No," Axe said hotly.

"She's not wrong, though," Mav said, pushing away from the kitchen countertop. "If they've got police searching for her, it's only a matter of time before they come knocking on our door. You know we're always one of their first pit stops."

It was enough of an argument for me, so I slid my hand into my pocket. I pulled out my cell phone, unlocking it with one swift motion before I pulled up the phone dialer. And the entire time, I felt Axe's death stare on the top of my head.

"Dee," he said curtly.

I rolled my eyes as I held my phone in my hand. "Just let her call off the dogs, then we can go from there."

"I'm the President of this palace, not you."

I slowly stood to my feet and took a long pull from my Coke, draining the rest of the can. His head arched back, taking in the last four inches I had on him as I crumbled the can in my hand. I tossed the damned thing over his shoulder, sinking it into the trash can right by the entryway that always sat with its lid open because Mav never fucking closed the damn thing.

Then, I approached Axe and cloaked him in my shadow.

"You're our President, yes. But I'm our Enforcer, which means part of my job is making sure we've got the manpower to defend what comes our way. We don't right now. You and I both know that. So, we call off the dogs."

Mav jutted his head in between us. "It's the only option we've got, and you know it, Axe. Just one phone call. Less than thirty seconds so it can't be traced, like always."

"Like always?" the woman asked. "What are you guys? Some sort of super-secret spy group?"

Axe yanked the phone out of my hand and turned to face the woman.

"Your name," he said.

She snickered. "What?"

He handed her the phone. "You get a phone call; we get your name."

"That's not how this works," she said as she reached for the phone.

He pulled it away from her, holding it over his head. "Your name for the phone call. Otherwise, you can take your chances out in the desert while we pack our things."

"Making a run for it? That's your plan if this doesn't go down well?"

Mav grinned. "We're thirty minutes away from the Mexico border for a reason. We'll get there before you get back to the nearest city."

"And before you ask, no," I said as the woman whipped her head toward me. "The closest city isn't yours."

She swallowed hard before she snatched the phone out of Axton's hand. "Brielle."

"Brielle... what?" I asked.

Her face fell flat. "Lancaster. Now, shut up so I can make this phone call."

Brielle Lancaster.

A beautiful name for a beautiful woman.

"Remember, no longer than thirty seconds," Axe said as he took a few steps back from her. "But if you feel it's going to exceed that time—"

She held up her hand before holding the dialed phone to her ear. "I've watched enough police procedurals to know why."

Mav's smile was nothing short of evil. "She's really spunky."

She was in for a ride with him if she kept that shit up.

"Shut up, all of you," Axe commanded.

And as Brielle turned her back to us with my phone stuck to her ear, I stared the back of her head down. Ready to lunge the second her thirty seconds were up. Because I didn't care who she was, what she had gotten herself into, or who she resembled. We had a family to protect. Brothers to keep safe. Money to secure.

A set-up I wouldn't allow some "spunky" girl to ruin with her basic profiling skills.

Where did she pick those up, anyway?

9

———

BRIELLE

Come on, come on, pick up the phone.

Why the hell weren't they picking up their phone? You'd think that with their daughter missing, they'd pick up any phone call that came their way.

Unless, of course, no one knew that I was missing yet.

"Hi! You've reached the voicemail box of—"

"Shit," I hissed as I hung up the phone.

I barely looked at the screen before those Slenderman fingers of Dante's came into view. He quickly plucked the phone out of my grasp, and I whipped around long enough to watch him flip it over. Off came the back cover before he tossed the battery into the trashcan from across the room. It sank with a heavy *thunk* as I stared at him with wide eyes, watching as he slid a thin, barely-there card out of the back of the phone as well.

"What's that?" I asked.

He strode toward the kitchen sink, tossed everything in, and turned on the water.

"A SIM card," Dante said flatly. "Mav?"

"Already on it," he said, handing me a new phone.

I looked at his outstretched hand precariously. "You're going to let me try again?"

He grinned. "You'd be surprised how many of these we've got."

"Take it or leave it," Axton said with a grunt.

I shook my head as I took the phone from Maverick. "Thank you."

While Dante cleaned up his mess, I dialed my father's number. If Mom hadn't picked up, then maybe he would. The phone rang in my ear, haunting me with that monotone sound as it rattled around in my head.

One ring.

Two rings.

Three rings.

"Come on!" I yelled at the phone.

Then, the heavens finally let me catch a fucking break.

"Brielle, please tell me that's you."

"Brielle," Dante said as his voice appeared behind me, "lovely name."

I shot him a look over my shoulder. "Don't hang up, Dad, it's me and I need you to listen closely."

"Did you just call Mom?" he asked frantically. "Where are you? Hold on! HONEY!?"

"Twenty seconds," Dante said.

Frustration bubbled over. "Dad, I don't have time. Listen to me."

Rustling sounded on the other end of the line. "Sweetheart? My God, is that really you? Where are you? We can come and get you. You never showed up to work and—"

I gritted my teeth together. "I don't have a lot of time, so listen. I'm safe. I'm fine. But I can't come home. Not yet, anyway."

"Why?" Dad asked. "Where are you? What's going on?"

"Twelve seconds," Dante murmured.

"Who's that counting? Who's with my baby!?" Mom practically shrieked.

Her voice brought tears to my eyes. "Did you guys know that I had a twin sister?"

The phone went deadly silent before Dante's voice whispered along the shell of my ear.

"Ten seconds."

I swallowed hard. "My twin sister has done some really bad things, you guys, and there are people out there that think I'm her. I'm safe, but you guys have to call off the police if you've called them."

Mom's voice grew angry. "Why?"

"Five seconds," Dante murmured as his hand hovered over the phone against my ear.

I closed my eyes. "Because after not telling me that I had a twin sister, you owe this to me. Don't you think?"

"Three," Dante said.

"Sweetheart," Dad said as his voice cooed into the phone, "just tell us where you are, and we can—"

I sighed heavily. "I love you guys. I'm safe, I promise, but I'll be safer when she's caught. And if you love me at all—if you feel guilty about this, at all—you'll stop your search."

"And we're done," Dante said, plucking the phone from my hand.

"I love you guys so much!" I called out quickly.

Before he hung up the phone and started dismantling it like the other one.

"Oh, God," I whispered as tears lined my eyes.

"Axton?" Mav asked.

Slowly, something crept into my view. The movement out of my right peripheral made me jerk, but as I whipped my head toward the foreign object, I found yet another phone lingering around for me. The fingers that grasped it were thick. Red. White around the knuckles from clasping the phone so hard. And as I traced the bulging muscles and veins attached to the arm outstretching the cell toward me, I found my abuser attached to it.

Axton handed me another phone.

"That's not smart," Dante warned.

Axton didn't respond, though. Hell, he didn't even flinch. "Thirty seconds. Call them back."

I swallowed hard. "Why?"

He picked up my hand and placed the phone against my palm. "Because family is everything."

I had to admit his words shocked me. "Thank you."

"Don't thank me," he said, pulling up the dialing application on the phone. "Just call."

And I did exactly as he asked.

"Brielle!?" Dad practically shouted into the phone.

"Honey," Mom said breathlessly, "why can't you tell us where you are? You're worrying us."

"We can't call off the police until we know without a shadow of a doubt that you're safe," Dad said.

I shook my head. "There's nothing to be afraid of. I'm fine. And believe it or not, I'm with the only people on this planet that I could possibly be safe with."

"Nonsense, that's with the police," Mom hissed. "And we aren't calling them off. You're obviously in trouble. You've been kidnapped!"

Even Dad grew frustrated. "Who has you? Are they standing around you? Monitoring the call? We can come up with a code word. Something to tell us that you're in distress and need help."

I rolled my eyes. "You guys, there are bad people out there that believe I'm my twin sister. But the people I'm staying with for now are keeping me safe. They know the situation more intimately than the police ever will. That's why I'm safe with them."

"But if we come and get you," Mom said curtly, "then we can inform the police of what you and they know. They can keep you safe."

"Fifteen," Dante murmured.

I closed my eyes. "I need you to do something for me."

"Tell us where you are and we'll do anything," Dad said.

I scoffed. "Fine, then don't. I'll talk to you guys—"

"Wait!" Mom exclaimed.

I paused. "Yes?"

"What do you want us to do?" Mom asked.

"You're not seriously considering this," Dad said flatly.

"What is it?" Mom asked between gritted teeth.

I cleared my throat. "I need you to call the school and fill them in on what's happening. I can't lose my job; it took me forever to get it. Just tell them that I'm caught up in something my twin sister is throwing down, and until she's caught, I have to stay hidden so that there's no mistaking me for her."

"Because it's already happened? Is that what you're getting at?" Mom asked.

"She's smart," Mav murmured as the guys hovered around me.

I nodded. "Exactly. That's how the kidnapping happened. They thought I was her until we found the information proving that I'm not."

"Oh, God," Mom said with a soft whimper.

"Five seconds," Dante whispered to my left.

"Call the school, then call off the police. If anything, they should be looking for my twin sister, not me. And until she's caught, I'm staying as safe as I can, and you guys don't get to dictate how that's done."

"Three," Dante said.

"To hell with this!" Dad exclaimed in the background. "I'm going to get my fucking daughter!"

"Two," Dante murmured.

Tears dripped down my cheeks. "I love you guys so much."

"I'll call them both, I promise," Mom whispered.

"What if she's under duress!?" Dad yelled in the background. "What if they're making her say it!?"

"We should have told her," Mom said flatly.

"Have I ever given you guys a reason not to trust me?" I asked.

"One," Dante said.

I moved away from the man and held up my finger.

"Nu uh," Mav said as he stalked toward me, "that wasn't the deal."

I shook my head. "They aren't on board yet. We're still in trouble. Just give me a second."

"Who are you talking to!?" Dad bellowed.

I put them on speakerphone and held it out for the guys to hear. "Have I ever given you guys a reason not to trust me? Answer the question!"

"No," they said in unison.

"Then, trust me now. I'm safe. I'm more than safe, actually, and until this is resolved, I have to stay off the radar. For my own good. For the good of my students. For the good of you guys. If I step out and people think I'm her, I'm dead. That's how bad she is. So, please, just do what I ask. For my sake, okay?"

Axton reached for the phone, but I pulled it away.

"Okay!?" I yelped.

"Okay, okay," Dad said.

"We've got it," Mom said.

"I love you guys," I said before I hung up the phone.

Then I tossed it to Dante, and he booked it for the sink. "That was stupid of you."

Mav simply shook his head as he raked his hands through his hair. "For all we know that call was being traced."

"Chances are, not likely," Axton said, staring me down.

I looked up into his brooding brown gaze. "Thank you."

He shrugged. "Least I can do. But now, we've got to get to work. Make yourself at home."

Dante scoffed from the sink. "We're just going to leave her here?"

Axton lumbered out of the kitchen. "No, idiot. Get the patrols out. You know, do your job. And Mav?"

The cheeky man stared me down with a devilish smile. "Make sure she feels at home? I can do that."

Axton came over and placed his hand on Mav's shoulder. "No hinky shit, got it? Doc's on his way, and he'll be here in a few minutes to look her over."

Mav tossed me a playful wink, and a shiver worked its way down my spine.

"No promises, boss man."

"Great," Axton murmured as he turned and left the kitchen.

Leaving me with so many more questions than answers.

"Doc?" I asked when Axton and Dante finally left the room.

Mav pivoted toward me, his gaze falling upon my body like a dog in heat. "Guess so."

"You guys just... have a doctor on speed dial for all the women you capture and torture?"

He snickered. "Trust me, what you went through wasn't nearly—"

I blinked. "Go on, don't be shy. Finish that sentence."

He clicked his tongue as he pulled a kitchen chair to my side. "I'll sit with you until Doc gets here."

"Thanks, I guess."

He shrugged. "Or, I could leave. Give you some privacy. If that's what you'd prefer. But Doc can be a little..."

I slowly turned to face him. "A bit what?"

He bobbed his head side to side. "Eccentric?"

"I have no idea what that means."

"Boys!" someone exclaimed down the hallway. "I hear I've got a patient!"

Mav thumbed over his shoulder. "That would be Doc. Hold on a second."

My brow stitched together with confusion. "Wait, you guys really just call him 'Doc'?"

"Coming, Doc! She's in the kitchen!" Mav exclaimed down the hallway, leaving the kitchen.

I wasn't sure what to expect. I held out my hands and found skin scraped away from my wrists. I peered down at my ankles and found bruises already formed. Skin, already exposed to the elements. Jesus, I hadn't even looked in a mirror. I had no fucking clue how bad off I was. And as my attention turned to my injuries, a dull ache pulsed all across my body.

As if my entire form vibrated with frustration.

"Ugh," I groaned, leaning my head back.

"She's in here," Mav said.

"Ah, hello," a gentle voice said as the chair next to me raked across the floor, "what's your name?"

I slowly leveled my head on my shoulders. "Brielle."

"What a lovely name," the gentle white-haired doctor said as he wiggled his fingers at me. "Why don't you give me one of those ankles so I can take a look?"

"You're not gonna take my vitals or something first?"

Doc grinned as he dipped down and gently picked my leg up into his lap. "You don't show any signs of a panicked state. Your breathing is registering as normal. You've got your arms wrapped a bit tight around you, but it hasn't impacted your ability to focus. If I take your vitals, I'm probably going to find that they're slightly elevated because of the intense situation you've found yourself in, but it won't be anything that shocks me."

Mav chuckled. "He's good, I promise."

"Like your word is supposed to mean something," I muttered to myself.

"Well," Doc said, placing my ankle down and picking up the other one, "the skin removal is topical. Doesn't feel nice, but

I can give you some Tylenol with codeine to help with the pain."

"I appreciate that, thank you. Will it help with the headache I've got going on?"

He placed my ankle back down gingerly. "Now is where I'm going to check your vitals. You ready?"

"Bring it."

Out came that tiny flashlight from his white jacket pocket. He clicked it on and shined it on my eyes while simultaneously asking me to follow his finger. The light blinded me at times, but it didn't make me flinch. Hell, it didn't even make the headache any worse.

"Good news," Doc said as he clicked the light off and pressed his two fingers to my neck, "you don't have a concussion."

"We never thought she did," Mav piped up and walked over to the refrigerator. "Drink?"

"Would love one, thanks," Doc said as he kept clocking my pulse with the watch on his wrist.

"Brielle?"

"Oh, so you care about that now?"

"Water, it is," Mav said.

"Like I said, a bit elevated. But, given the tense situation—"

"You mean, the fact that they snatched me right from in front of my home?" I asked flatly.

Doc slowly turned his head over his shoulder. "You guys really getting into it this time?"

Mav snickered and handed Doc his drink. "You have no idea."

And when he handed me the glass of ice water, I could have sworn I saw something akin to guilt flash behind his eyes.

"Thanks," I said, quickly taking the drink from him.

"It's the least I can do." I side-eyed him as he sat down, but

Doc stayed on course. He checked me, head to toe, for any sign of something he had to fix. He checked over my wrists and ankles one last time before slathering this comforting salve over my irritated skin. Then, he wrapped it all up in gauze that felt as if it had been crafted by the clouds above our heads. With every sip of water that I took, the pounding in my head subsided. Water had never tasted so divine, and by the time I had drained my glass, Mav was up on his feet getting me another one.

"Here. Drink all you want," he said as he slid another drink toward me.

"Don't mind if I do," I said breathlessly, reaching for the cold plastic cup.

"You should get her some food, while you're at it," Doc said as he stood from his seat.

"What would be best at a time like this?" Mav asked.

"Anything that is nutrient dense. A salad with some chicken. Or steak. Some vegetable soup. Something like that."

Mav smiled from ear to ear as he reached into the back of the fridge. "Veggie soup coming right up."

I didn't like how nonchalantly they were talking about me and my circumstance. Did Doc really know what the hell was going on? Well, of course he did. I had blurted that shit out, and not once did the older man flinch. Did he just not care? Was this a normal thing for these guys?

God, what kind of trouble was I really in?

"All right," Doc said as he stood to his feet and jammed his hand back down into his bag, "I'm going to leave this with you. It's a ten-day supply of Tylenol with codeine. Take one in the morning and one in the evening, at least ten hours apart. And after five days, if you're still uncomfortable enough that regular Tylenol doesn't do the trick, have the guys call me again. I'll bring some more around."

His words terrified me. "I'm—I'm going to be here for more than five days?"

Doc looked cautiously over at Mav. "I'll send you my bill."

Mav chuckled, placing something in the microwave. "You know you're always paid before you get back home. Thanks again, Doc."

"Anytime."

"Wait," I said, reaching out and snatching his forearm.

"Nice reflexes. That's a good sign," Doc said as he stared down at our connection.

"Don't I need a hospital or something?" I asked.

Please take the hint. Please take the hint. Please take the hint.

But he simply pulled away from my grasp. "If you did, those men would've called you an ambulance. You're going to be okay, all right?"

The man wasn't eccentric, he was a fucking idiot. "Thanks for your help."

"Anytime," he said, moving back toward the front door, "and like I said, after five days, if regular Tylenol isn't keeping things in check, have the guys call me."

"We will!" Mav called after him as something touched down against the kitchen table.

I slowly turned toward the steam rising up from the bowl in front of me. Inside, there was this creamy sort of broth with hunks of potatoes floating around in it. Peas and corn. Carrots and onions. It was a regular garden variety fest in that bowl of soup.

And it smelled divine.

"I know you want to go home," Mav said as he held a spoon beneath my gaze, "and you have my word that we'll take you home once we know what's going on and whether or not you're safe."

I snatched the spoon out from his grasp. "Do me a favor?"

"Anything."

"Don't talk to me anymore."

And as I slipped my spoon into the soup, a heavy sigh fell against my ears. Not my sigh, though. Maverick's.

A sigh filled with so much guilt that it almost made me want to forgive him.

Almost, anyway.

11

MAVERICK

God, she was gorgeous. Her pin straight black bangs covered her forehead, framing her icy blue eyes in a way that tugged at my cock. Her delicate waist poured into a set of hips I wanted to mark with my teeth, and heat pulsated throughout my body. I briefly heard Dante toss the soaked cell phone into the trashcan before gathering the bag out of the waste basket, and off in the distance Axton barked orders out on the front porch.

The instant we were alone, however, I locked my gaze with hers.

"So, *Brielle*," I said as I walked over to her, "care to be escorted to your—"

She brushed past me without so much as a look. "Leave me alone."

I nodded as she knocked into my shoulder. "I can do that, too."

Her angry footsteps carried her up the stairs before the creaking of the floorboards above me tilted my head upward. I drew in a deep breath as the pounding of her feet made me shiver. I'd get her beneath me. I'd get a taste of those luxurious curves before she left our clubhouse. She had every right to be pissed, though, especially with her parents. And if we were being honest for a second, I felt for her. None of the other guys would; they enjoyed burying their trauma beneath mounds of fuck you's and bullets. I mean, having a sibling betray you was a harsh reality to swallow. It sucked the air right out of your sails whether you knew them well or not.

My older brother did it to me several times.

And not once did my parents ever believe me when I told them what was happening.

"Where'd she go?" Dante asked.

His voice ripped me out of my trance and I turned, only to find him sticking his head around the corner from the hallway.

"Well?" he asked.

I pointed toward the ceiling. "Upstairs. Most likely to the room we set up for her."

His gaze raked down my body. "She has every right to be pissed. Don't take it personally."

I shrugged. "I'm not."

He chuckled as he disappeared back down the hallway. "Yeah, you are. So, suck it up."

I barked with laughter. "Noted, asshole!"

I couldn't just stand there, though. Not when our beautiful little houseguest was in such distress. And with nothing else to do until my patrol shift that evening, I decided to go in search of her. I decided to follow my nose and track her scent like a wild animal before I showed up at her closed bedroom door.

Since I was right about where she ended up.

I grasped the doorknob, turned it softly, and tossed the door open. I found her in the bedroom, gazing out the bay window, sitting there with her legs curled up to her chest. Well, as closely as she could get them to her chest with those luscious tits of hers. God, what I wouldn't have given to plant my face in between them and have her smother me whole. She had the body of an angel, and all I wanted was to sin with it like the devil I had become. She still donned that silken robe, and the way it fluttered around her thighs made my mouth water. I wanted to flick my tongue along her curves, dancing it softly against her skin the way that robe kept doing. Never in my life did I ever think I'd be jealous of a piece of silk, yet there I was, unable to control the throbbing of my cock as the sun shone down against her features.

The sheen of her legs tickled my balls. The way her toes wiggled as she lost herself in deep thought made me want to lick them, just to see what her reaction might be. What I wouldn't give to sink myself into her just once. Just enough to feel her warmth wrap around me. Just to feel her juices marking my balls as hers. She was breathtaking with that thick body of hers. She had this cute little waist that called to my palms, teasing me as I leaned against the doorframe of her bedroom.

"Pretty picture for a pretty girl," I said in the hopes of getting her attention.

But as she stared out at the world, it didn't matter that my words made her blush. It didn't matter that the rich red color made me damn near growl with feral need. It didn't matter that I saw a soft smile tick her cheek, despite the fact that she fought to bury it.

All that mattered was that she couldn't look at me in the process.

"Are you kidding, Dante!?" Axe exclaimed downstairs.

"We're fucking working on it!" Dee yelled back.

The shadow of her smile faded as a twitch took over her eye, and I quickly stepped into her room. My hand motioned out behind me, closing the door softly as it muted the sounds of their voices. The two of them continued to face off downstairs as their muffled voices fought to be heard through the extra insulation we had placed behind the plaster walls when renovating the clubhouse a few years back.

And the quiet got her to finally speak.

"Thanks," she said softly before breathing out a sigh of relief. "Their voices carry."

I snickered. "Don't I know it."

That got her to peek over at me. "Are you guys really going to keep me safe? Or did I just lie my ass off to my parents?"

I shrugged. "Not like they haven't been doing that to you for your entire life."

Her stare grew watery before she quickly tossed her gaze back out the window. No one should cry alone, especially someone like her who had gotten caught up in an innocent game of "kill the bitch." I walked over to her and perched on the edge of the bed facing the bay window. I linked my hands together and let them hang between my legs, watching as the air conditioning brushed her black bangs away from her forehead.

I clocked a small scar near her scalp. "Yes."

She sniffled. "Huh?"

"Yes," I said as I pushed myself up from the bed and walked toward her, "we're really going to protect you. Especially since you're not the woman we wanted in the first place."

She shook her head. "All my life, I felt like I've never been wanted. Even by my own parents sometimes. So, it's sort of ironic that the same principle is about to save my life."

"Never?" I asked.

She had officially piqued my curiosity, but she didn't take the bait.

"Anyway," she said with a burdened sigh, "thanks for checking up on me. I'll probably just stay up here, though, if that's all right."

I shrugged as I sat down at the other end of the bay window

seat. "We said to make yourself at home, and we meant it. If that means locking yourself down in here, then that's fine."

"But…"

"No buts," I said with a shake of my head.

She flicked her gaze down my form before gazing back out at the desert surrounding us. "Thank you."

I leaned back against the frame of the window. "You know, families can cover up the most insane things sometimes."

She nodded mindlessly. "Mhm."

"And family secrets can kill if one isn't careful."

She peeked over at me. "That's one way to put it."

"You deserved better than what they gave you, Brielle."

She wiped her eyes. "You think so?"

I reached out and settled my hand on her bare knee. "I know so. You deserved the whole truth. You deserved to know your truth, and you deserved to have it acknowledged."

She looked down at our connection. "What did your family cover up?"

I cleared my throat and removed my hand. "Just some touching that shouldn't have happened, that's all."

Pity filled her stare, which meant it was my turn to divert my gaze. I couldn't stand that shit, the pitiful glances when they figured out that I had been diddled as a kid. It was in the past. I had left it behind. It didn't affect me, didn't hinder me, and it no longer haunted my dreams. Their stares did, though. All those pathetic, weakling little stares that reminded me of just how scared I'd been every time my brother came into my bedroom at night.

How angry it made me every time I felt his fingers race through my hair.

"I'm so sorry, Maverick," Brielle whispered.

I quickly stood to my feet. "It's in the past, and I left them behind for a good reason. Just know that you always have options."

She stood with me. "Mav?"

I turned toward the door. "Let me know if you need anything."

"Mav."

I started for the doorknob. "We can get you a mini-fridge in here as—"

When she took my hand, however, the warmth of her touch stopped me dead in my tracks. She planted her hand on top of mine, stopping my want to rip that door open and book it for the stairs. Vulnerability. That was one thing I hadn't expected from her. From the bruises that stared at me every time she picked her gaze up from the floor all the way down to the broken skin and ligature marks around her wrist and ankles, she had somehow found the strength to touch one of her assailants.

At that moment, I knew she was stronger than any of us would ever be.

And all I wanted was to feel her palm against my bare chest.

"Thank you for being so kind to me, even in the beginning," she said, brushing her thumb along the top of my hand.

I couldn't turn to face her. My eyes burned too much. "I knew something was off. I knew something wasn't quite right."

"Mav, look at me."

I blinked back my tears. "Brielle, this really isn't—"

"Please?"

I'd never be able to resist a pleading woman, especially her. She captivated me. She had crawled beneath my skin so quickly and so swiftly that it shocked me. Her touch held me hostage. The way her finger stroked my skin sizzled the tip of my cock. But it was her soft, reassuring, angelic voice that moved me.

So, I turned to face her as she continued tracing faceless images with her thumb against the skin of my hand.

"Yes?" I asked, staring into her sparkling aquamarine eyes.

"Thank you," she said as she stepped closer to me. "I need you to hear me when I say that."

I nodded. "I hear ya."

Her stare held mine as the pulsing of her breath fell against my face. Her fingers shifted, finding the slats of mine before she locked our touches together. My heart leapt into my throat. My cock hardened against the zipper of my jeans. If she did anything else—if she touched any other part of me—I'd be a goner. I'd never be able to contain myself.

And I wasn't sure what that said about me as a man.

"Be careful what you wish for," I said, lowing my voice.

"Trust me," she said as she closed the distance between us, "I always am."

She stood onto her tiptoes. As I watched her face come closer to mine, I gripped that doorknob for dear life. Jesus Christ, I could have taken the fucking door off its hinges had I allowed my body to move. I had to stay still. Stay put. Even as I watched her lips gravitate to mine. Even as she placed so plump, pillowy soft lips against mine, I held my ground. I couldn't be like my brother. I couldn't just take what I wanted. That rule was for savages. That rule was for psychopaths. Brielle deserved better than that.

"Mav," she whimpered against my lips.

And as much as I wanted to toss her onto that bed and claim her with my cock, logic won out.

"You need rest," I murmured as I placed my hands on her shoulders.

I pressed a chaste kiss to the tip of her nose before softly twirling her around. Her body needed to recuperate, and the last thing she needed was to get caught up in yet another torrid affair. The gauze wrapped around her wrists and ankles glared like high beams on a night drive as I led her to the bed. She climbed in without another word, without a single sentence of protest, and I wondered how upset she was with me. But, as I tucked her in, inching that comforter up her body, a soft smile crossed her face.

Before she wiggled down into the deep expanse of the mattress.

"Mmmm, thanks," she said softly.

I brushed her hair away from her blackened eye. "Rest as long as you need. The guys need me downstairs, anyway."

She peeked her black eye open. "You could climb in with me, you know."

I chuckled. "Cheeky, cheeky. But, maybe some other time. Once you're healed."

She groaned as she buried her face into the pillow. "You make good points."

"So I've been told."

I didn't want to leave her, though. I wasn't ready. She had me magnetized, and her body refused to give up its control over me. So, I sat there. I rubbed her back and slid my fingers through the ends of her hair, working out knots as her ragged breathing slowly morphed into a slow, rhythmic pulsing. Her body relaxed, sinking into the depths of the bed as she shifted back onto her side. A broken breath escaped her lips. Her eyes squeezed shut as her hand flopped over her head. And as she laid there with her lips slightly parted, I had to resist every single urge to press a kiss to her pillowy lips.

"Sleep well," I whispered, standing to my feet.

And I hoped that she did.

If nothing else, so that her body could heal from the wounds we had inflicted upon such an innocent body.

12

DANTE

My phone buzzed in my pocket as I sipped my coffee. The night had been long, with fruitless patrols and nothing to report.

And Axton wasn't happy.

"Who the fuck is calling you at an hour like this?" he grumbled.

I snickered and pulled my phone out. "It's ten in the morning."

He groaned as his head fell back. "Fucking hell, did any of us sleep last night?"

"No," I said plainly as I answered my phone, "this is Dante."

A familiar voice came alive. "Dee? It's Roger. I need a favor."

"Roger?" I asked, turning to Axton.

That got his attention, and he leapt to his feet before striding toward me with that determined look on his face.

When Roger called, there were jobs to be had.

And when there were jobs, there was payment.

"Listen, I can't talk long. Got a hell of a morning in front of me," Roger said, shuffling around on the other end of the line. "So, you guys interested in some protective services?"

I'd never seen Axe nod his head that fervently. "You know we always are."

"Good. You heard of the charity ball taking place next week?"

"Of course, of course," I said as I turned to Axe, whose stare would have burrowed a hole through God himself, "have you not already booked protective help for the masses?"

"We did," Roger said as something dropped on his end. "Fucking Christ."

"But?" I asked.

"But," he said with a grunt, "the police only allotted two guards for the entire night. Two. For the whole fucking thing."

I chuckled. "I told you to stop asking the police for a protective guard. They never take those events seriously."

"So, you'll do it? I can put you and your guys down?"

"For our regular price, plus fifteen percent for having to organize so quickly."

Axe's grin grew wild as Roger huffed in my ear.

"Fifteen percent? Seriously, Dee?" he asked.

"Seriously," I said as a chuckle emanated from my mouth. "A week isn't a lot of time for prep work, and you know how much goes into what we do."

He paused for a second, but I knew he'd cave.

And cave he did.

"Fine, fine," he said with a heavy sigh, "I'll have contracts drawn up and ready for you to sign once you guys get here."

"Perfect, we will see you in a week, then. Shoot me the basic details so my men can scout the venue and get some good vantage points going."

My phone buzzed against my face. "Already done. Thanks a ton, Dee. I appreciate it."

"Anytime, Roger. See you soon."

"See you soon."

I didn't even get the phone hung up before Axe snatched it out of my hand and opened the text. I stood there as he swiped over the message with his eyes, and the frown on his face gave me pause.

"What is it?" I asked.

He peeked over at me. "Just a hunch."

"Well, we all know about your hunches. Let's hear it."

He tossed my phone back to me. "Since when has Roger ever used the police department for protection?"

I shrugged and looked down at the text for myself. "It's happened on a few occasions."

"Okay, let me phrase that another way: when has Roger ever used the police for something as important as his charity balls?"

That gave me pause. "All right, what are you thinking?"

Axe clicked his tongue. "I'm thinking that it's a big ass coincidence that we snatch the wrong girl off the street, make asses out of ourselves while trying to double back, and all of a sudden, we've got a paying job from out of nowhere that just so happens to take our sights off that bitch's bounty."

I eyed him carefully. "You think Rachel's behind this?"

He shrugged. "I think we'd be stupid to think about anything else right now."

He was right, though. It was a hell of a coincidence.

"You've got a plan rolling around in your head," I said as I stared at the furrow taking over Axe's eyes. "Spit it out."

He heaved a heavy sigh. "Maybe it's nothing, but maybe it isn't. Maybe this is just a way for us to make some money to appease the guys for now, but maybe this is something more. And if it's something more, we should be prepared, right?"

I nodded. "Right."

He turned to face me. "You think Brielle would want to accompany you to the charity ball?"

I blinked. "You're not serious."

"Think about it," he said, closing the distance between us. I'd never seen him so locked into an idea in all the years I'd known him. "If this is nothing, then she gets a nice night out and we don't look like the shitheads we currently look like. But, if Rachel is there? She'd never suspect that we'd take Brielle to that event. What if we throw her off with her own fucking twin?"

"You act like she wouldn't know she's got a twin."

"Even if she does know, would she expect that twin to show up on your arm to an event like that?"

I cleared my throat. "I see your point, but there's one small hiccup."

"What?"

I pointed to the ceiling. "Who's convincing her to do it?"

And when Axe smiled, I rolled my eyes as I backtracked down the hallway.

"Fine, fine. I'll go talk with her."

"Good man," he said.

I shook my head as I made my way up the stairs. We didn't have much time to prepare our services for the coming ball, which meant I certainly didn't have the time to coach her through every single little thing she was going to need to know. I stood in front of her bedroom door, wondering if it was smart. I mean, I knew Axton wanted that woman in our clutches, but dangling Brielle in front of her?

Hadn't Brielle already suffered enough?

"Brielle?" I asked as I eased her bedroom door open. "Can we ta—?"

Her soft snores hit my ears and it gave me pause. The door eased open, showcasing her shoulders as they moved slowly up and down. A soft smile graced my face as I strolled into the room. The comforter molded to her curves, showcasing the slope of her waist as I perched on the edge of the bed. I reached out and placed my hand on her arm, smoothing it softly up and down.

Fuck, her skin was so soft.

"Mmmm, mm," Brielle groaned as she shifted in bed.

I yanked my hand back, figuring my stroking had disturbed her. But instead of waking up, she simply rolled over. She swiped her hand out and I watched it knock against my knee before she shuffled. Moved. Her legs kicked and she wiggled like a glorious little worm toward my body, her hand outstretched for something. So without thinking, I placed my palm on hers. And as she curled her fingers around my skin, her body stopped moving.

She stopped once she had me in her grasp.

"You could be the death of us, you know," I muttered.

I couldn't bring myself to wake her up. I knew that I needed to ask her, but not while she was getting some much-needed rest. The gauze on her wrists were twinged with a yellow sort of fluid that made me sick to my stomach. Her eyes, blackened and still swollen from the swings Axe took at her.

Jesus Christ, what had we done to her?

"Dante?" she asked groggily.

I drew in a curt breath through my nose. "I don't mean to wake you, but your gauze needs changing."

She picked up her wrist and brought it to her narrowed, sleep-crusted eyes. "Fuck, you're right."

"Do you know where your gauze is?"

She thumbed lazily over her shoulder. "Bathroom, I think."

I patted her hip before I stood. "I've got it, you just lay there."

"You, okay?"

Thank fuck I had my back turned to her when she asked. "Yeah, just coming to check on you. You slept all through the night."

"I'm still tired."

"Then go back to sleep," I said as I entered the bathroom.

She was right, all of her supplies were sitting right there on the countertop. I snatched the bag up from the surface and made my way back out to Brielle. I perched back on the edge of the bed and took her wrists into my lap. With my leg crooked beneath my other one, I cradled her hands as I unwrapped the gauze, watching her delicate skin come into view. It was seeping, and mangled.

Jesus, she deserved better than that.

"Sssss," she hissed, "ouch."

"Sorry, sorry," I murmured as I casted the unsavory gauze off to the side. "It sticks sometimes."

"It's okay," she said softly.

I slathered her exposed skin in some cream before I rewrapped her wrists. One by one, with her arm outstretched to me and her eyes boring a hole into the top of my head. I counted the circles around her wrists in my head, wrapping it the exact same way Doc had wrapped it the day before. And after both of her wrists had been taken care of, I scooted back a bit and patted my lap.

"Time for your ankles," I said.

"I can do those, if you need to go," Brielle said.

I slowly picked my gaze up, locking it with hers. "Give me your ankles, Brielle."

She swallowed hard as she shifted, sliding her cold feet into my lap. I worked diligently, trying my best not to pop fucking wood right there in the bed with her. She had no idea how beautiful she was, with her sloping curves and her thick, shining hair just begging to be pulled. Every sound that fell from her lips was a sound I wanted her to make with my cock in her mouth. Every movement she made had me wondering what her soft skin might feel like undulating against my own. It took all I had to keep myself in control as I finished wrapping both of her ankles. Cleaning her up, so that she could get some rest.

And as I stood from the bed, I still couldn't find the words to ask her to the ball.

"Need any medicine?" I asked.

Brielle closed her eyes as she nuzzled down into the pillow. "I think it might be smart to take some, yeah."

I thumbed over my shoulder. "I'll go get you something to drink, you sit tight."

"Dante?"

"Yeah?"

She looked up at me with those big doe eyes, and I knew that I was a goner. "Thank you."

I turned toward the door and made my way into the hallway. "I'll be back with your drink soon."

I had to get out of there. I had to leave her alone. Because if I stood there another second, breathing in the air she breathed and watching my fingertips dance against her skin, I'd become the biggest sinner this world had ever seen. I'd take her as mine, pinning her beneath me, and I wouldn't stop until she begged me for mercy.

And we had too many things to focus on besides me getting my cock wet.

13

AXTON

I had no idea how much time had passed. As I sat there, staring at the wall in a dining room that never fucking got used, I twirled my lukewarm beer bottle in my fingertips. The scraping of the glass against the finished wood battered around inside of my head. Sleep was hard to come by, with cat naps turning into twenty-minute intervals of peace before something else fell apart. Four days. We were five fucking days out from the charity ball, and Dante still hadn't asked Brielle a damn thing about it.

And we were no closer to figuring out who the fuck Rachel really was.

Dante peeked his head around the corner. "Axe, you got a second?"

"No," I said plainly.

He thumbed over his shoulder. "I just need you to come look at—."

"No," I said, whipping my gaze toward him.

He patted the wall with his hand. "All right. Well, come find me when you're ready to do something productive. Yeah?"

I could've strangled him for that snarky remark. But I let

him live as I watched him disappear around the corner and out of sight.

I didn't even get resituated back in my chair before Mav came in, though.

"Hey, you got the schematics for the ballroom, yet?"

I sighed and closed my eyes. "That's a Dante question, not a me question."

"He said to come ask you."

I drew in a deep breath through my nose. "Let me guess: the schematics are what he's wanting me to look at?"

"What?" Mav asked.

I waved my hand at him. "Nothing. Give me some time and I'll come view everything."

"Uh, I'm still not following."

"Mav?" I asked as I panned my gaze toward him.

He nodded. "Get lost? Got it."

"Thanks," I said flatly.

But I barely got my focus and train of thought back before the dam burst.

"Hey Axe, we're out of spices in the pantry."

"Axe, I found something on our patrols last night."

"Axe, can you take a look at this?"

"Axe, can you come and—"

"Leave me alone," I said flatly.

"But, Axe, we need t—."

I shot to my feet and balled my fists up at my sides. "Leave me the fuck alone! I'm trying to fucking think!"

Between the bitch and the ball, we were all much too distracted. And the longer we floundered, the more convinced I became of Rachel's involvement in all of this. If she was going for us being distracted, then she had achieved what she wanted. We were distracted. We were focusing on things that didn't mean shit. We had completely stopped our hunt for her in exchange for a paying job to get the guys off our backs about how long it had taken to track this bitch down, and if I were a betting man, then somewhere, Rachel was celebrating her victory over us.

We had to keep our heads in the game.

Which meant I had to provide an example.

"Fucking hell," I groaned as I shoved myself out of my seat, "time to go find D—."

BA-DUM BA-DUM, DUM!

"Ah!"

The second I heard Brielle's yelp, I took off like a bat out of hell. Six leaps and bounds were all it took for me to get to the stairs, and then I lunged my way up them. Three at a fucking time.

"Brielle!" I bellowed. "Are you okay!?"

"I'm fine!" she called out. "I'm fine. Just... just lost my balance!"

I careened down the hallway, making my way toward her door. "Stay still. Let me come in there and help you. What do you need?"

"I really am fine," she said as I threw her bedroom door open.

I didn't see her in the room, however. "Brielle, where the fuck are you?"

"Ah, shit," she hissed.

My ears perked up as my gaze leveled off toward the bathroom. "Brielle?"

"What?"

"Do you need any help?" I asked, closing the bedroom door behind me.

She groaned. "No, Axton. I don't need help taking a fucking shit."

She punctuated her sentence with the slamming of the bathroom door. But it didn't deter me.

"Are you sure?" I asked as I stood at the foot of her bed.

She snickered. "Yes, I'm sure that I don't need a four-hundred-pound brute helping me on and off the toilet."

"Three sixty, actually."

"Whatever. You can go now."

I didn't want to, though. So, I simply sat down on the edge of the bed and waited.

"I don't need company, either!" she called out.

A grin tugged its way across my face. She sure as hell was a fiery one. Full of life. Full of strength. Determination unlike anything I'd ever seen, except for in my men.

We were gonna catch hell for keeping her around.

The toilet flushed and the sink turned on. I heard her lumbering, favoring one side over the other as the bathroom door rushed open. She stared me down, eyeing me hotly with that intense glare of hers. But, when she took a step into the bedroom, her legs collapsed.

"Oh, no you don't," I grumbled, rushing to her side.

I wrapped my arms around her, catching her just before she tumbled to the carpet. Without another word spoken between us, I scooped her into my embrace and walked her back to her bed. I settled her in the small indentation her body had left behind on the mattress, then managed to pull the covers over her body before she snatched them from me.

"I've got it," she murmured.

"I know you do," I said as I sat back down on the edge of her bed.

"What are you doing?"

"Can I get you anything? Food? Water? More medicine?"

She shook her head. "I'm fine, thanks."

But her stomach growling out told me a very different story.

"Are you sure about that?" I asked.

She shook her head and rolled her eyes. "It's fine. I'll come downstairs and—."

I stood to my feet. "No, you won't. I'll be back in a bit with some food."

"Axton."

"Brielle."

She chewed on the inside of her cheek. "You really don't need to do this."

"I know."

"So, why are you?"

I shrugged. "Because I don't know how else to apologize."

She studied me for a long time after I spit that out. But, to my shock, she caved.

"I could use a drink to take some more medicine. My legs ache," she said softly.

I nodded before I headed for the bedroom door. "Give me twenty minutes."

It didn't even take me that long to throw something together. A bit of grilled cheese, some soup to dip it in. A soda and some ice water, in case she wanted some variety. It had been days since I'd felt that useful. Since I felt like our efforts were geared toward something worthwhile. And as I carried the tray of food back up to her side, I relished the relief that crossed her face when she took her first bite.

"How many cheeses did you use for this?" she asked.

I reached for her medicine and popped it open. "Three."

"Mmm, mm, mm, so good. Thank you, Axton."

I smirked as I dumped two pills into my palm. "Here, take these. You should be good now that you've got some food in your stomach."

She took them from me, and the soft scraping of her fingernails against my skin sent a cascade of shivers down my spine. I watched her part those soft, shimmering lips of hers before she tossed those pills back, taking them like a champ. She barely chased them down, for fuck's sake!

I wondered what that mouth could do to other things.

"How are you feeling?" I asked, breaking the silence in the hopes that my cock would stay put.

She took a bite of the soup and her eyes fluttered closed. "Oh, God, Axton. This is amazing."

I drew in a deep, sobering breath. "I'm glad you like it."

"Fuck," she whispered as she took another large bite of her grilled cheese.

I twirled my fist into the comforter to keep my lid from blowing. "Can I get you anything else?"

She groaned as she dipped her grilled cheese into her soup and took a bite. "Dinner. You can bring me this exact combination for dinner."

I chuckled. "Consider it done."

"Jesus," she moaned.

I had to get out of there. I'd never be able to contain myself if she kept making those kinds of noises.

But I didn't want to leave her side.

"Uh, Axe?" Wolf asked from beyond Brielle's closed door.

I stood to my feet and cracked my neck. "What?"

He jiggled the doorknob, but I was quick to put a stop to that.

"Don't you dare open that door. What do you want?"

I heard him scoff. "Well, whenever you've got some free time to spare us, Your Majesty, you're needed downstairs if you're done distracting yourself up here."

I growled as I charged the door, ripping it damn near off its hinges, swinging it open. "What the fuck did you just say to me?"

But, instead of being met with Wolf's face, I was met with his footfalls as they backtracked away from the door.

"Downstairs when you've got free time to spare us, Me Lord!" he shouted at me.

Oh yeah, we were about to catch hell from our guys over this shit.

14

———

BRIELLE

I woke up one morning and felt... surprisingly better. The sunshine streamed through the windows of the room that the guys had put me in, and as I swung my legs over the edge of the bed, the telltale pain that used to waft up to my hips was no longer present. I looked down at my ankles and saw that my gauze was clean. I picked my wrists up, studying them for any sign of leakage, but found none.

Maybe I was finally turning a corner.

"Shower time," I whispered to myself.

It helped, taking the gauze off in the shower. It didn't stick to my skin that way. I shed my clothes and turned on the water as hot as I could stand it, ready to cleanse my life of the burdens it had picked up along the way. The steam overwhelmed the room as I slipped inside, drenching my gauze with water so that I could unravel it from my body and see what was beneath. And to my relief, the skin had healed over, covering the raw and irritated wounds with skin that now needed time to heal.

It felt good, not to feel pain with every step that I took.

"Oh, yeah," I groaned as I stuck my head beneath the flowing hot water.

I wasn't sure how long I had been in bed, but it was long enough for me to feel like I was caked in a layer of dirt and sadness. I grabbed whatever soaps and shampoos I could find. I scrubbed myself from head to toe, twice. While the conditioner that I was shocked to have found sat in my hair, moisturizing it after days of neglect, I took the liberty of stretching out my sore muscles. I raised my hands above my head. I bent down and tried to touch my toes. My back cracked and my joints popped, as if my body were settling back into its original groove.

It felt good to feel good again.

I showered until the water ran lukewarm. I knew the guys would be pissed, but I didn't care. I deserved that shower, as far as I was concerned. And they owed me, big time. But all good things had to come to an end, so I rinsed out the conditioner and turned off the water.

Before wrapping a towel around my body and heading back into the bedroom.

"Well, well, well," Mav said as he stood next to my bedside table, "what do we have here?"

I watched the stem of a sucker he had in his mouth wiggle with every word.

"Morning, Mav," I said, standing there in the entrance to the bathroom.

He raked his gaze down my body and I enjoyed how hungry he looked. "Heard the shower kick on and I figured I'd come up and see if you needed help."

"That's very kind of you, thank you."

His stare raked back up. "But I can see that you're obviously feeling better."

I gripped my towel with one hand and held my other one up for him to see my wrist. "Skin's healing up nicely, too."

He popped that sucker into his other cheek. "Perfect."

I walked over and perched at the foot of the bed, only for

him to quickly join me at my sides. Our thighs pressed together. His shoulder seated next to mine.

I couldn't help the goosebumps as they fled across my body, starting at my nose, and flooding my body all the way to my toes.

His warmth was simply... delicious.

"How are you really feeling, though?" Mav asked and nudged me softly.

I shrugged. "I'm honestly feeling okay. I didn't even need my second dose of medication last night to get to sleep."

He smiled, and it lit up his boyish features. "Good. That's very good. We've been wondering when you'd turn a corner."

"Well, consider it officially turned."

He chuckled as he patted his hand on my knee. "I'll be sure to let Dee and Axe know."

That is, before he splayed his fingers against my knee and squeezed it softly.

"Mav?" I asked cocking my body to face him.

"Yes, Brielle?"

My eyes danced between his. "Do you think—."

He tilted his head and cocked his body toward mine, fully facing me. "Do I think what, Brielle?"

I swallowed hard. "Do you think that my sister... knows about me?"

He reached out and tucked a strand of hair behind my ear. "I don't know."

"Have you guys been able to figure out much about her yet?"

His hand slid behind my head, cradling it in his palm. "We're working on it."

"Is there anything you can tell me? Anything at all?"

He smoothed this thumb underneath my eye. "Looking much better."

"Don't change the subject."

"Does your eye still hurt?"

I shook my head softly before I nuzzled against his hand. "No, it doesn't."

He smiled softly. "Good."

His thumb trailed along my skin, exploring my face. His gaze danced around, as if he were drinking me in, and I found myself entranced by the soft motions. His thumb traced my lower lip. It made my knees quiver where I sat as his gaze studied my mouth. I parted my lips softly, wanting nothing more than for us to pick up right where we left off.

But instead, he dropped his hand and nodded. "I'm glad you're on the mend."

I couldn't stand it any longer. He smelled delectable, and those muscles? Jesus Christ, I had dreamt for days about what his body might feel like pressed against mine. He walked with confidence and talked with grace. He cared, genuinely cared, about how I was doing. He harbored no guilt because he had never been a guilty party in my eyes, and all I wanted was to melt into him and never let go.

"Brielle," Mav murmured.

My body must've taken control of my conscious mind, because when he said my name, I realized how closely I had leaned into him. I realized how much I had scooted against him.

"Jesus," I whispered as I leaned back, "Mav, I'm s—."

But he caught the back of my head with his hand and held me there. "Just tell me no."

My gaze searched his. "What?"

He leaned closer, his breath pulsing against my lips. "Just tell me now and I'll leave you be. That's all you have to do."

I darted my tongue out and softly licked his lower lip. "And if I don't want to?"

He moved like lightning streaking its way across the sky. One second, we were millimeters away from kissing, and the next, I was on my back with his knee shoved in between my legs.

"Maverick," I said breathlessly.

He hovered over me with darkened eyes that screamed for more. "Say no."

I kept my mouth shut as he ground his knee against my naked pussy.

"Just say no, Brielle," he whispered.

I moaned softly and rolled my hips against his knee. "Yes, Mav."

"Fuck," he hissed.

I released my towel, allowing it to fall away from my body. "Oh, yes, Mav. More."

"Goddamn it," he growled. "I won't be able to stop if you let me."

"Then, don't," I whimpered. "Because all I want is to feel good for a while."

And as his lips crashed to mine, robbing me of the very breath from my lungs, I grasped his shirt and pulled him closer.

Anything to feel his body seated against my own.

15

MAVERICK

"Fucking hell," I growled as she ground her juicy pussy against my knee.

I lost it. I lost control of myself. The second that little begging sound fell from her lips, the animal inside of me rattled around in its cage. I threaded my fingers into her hair. I encompassed her mouth with mine as my tongue raked across the roof of her mouth. She moaned for me, bowing her back and pressing those delicious tits of hers into the slats of my chest. Jesus, she tasted divine. Like the sweetest apple plucked from the most beautiful tree in all the land. Her hands twisted into my shirt, drawing me closer as my lips swelled against hers. I teased her, sliding my tongue along her teeth and feeling her quiver against me.

Then, the smell of her womanhood pierced my nostrils.

"Help me forget, please," she gasped. "Just for a little bit."

And she sure as fuck didn't have to tell me twice.

Her hands raced to my hair, and I didn't flinch. I didn't even panic as she gripped my tendrils and slid her fingernails along my scalp. For the first time since leaving my family's side, I felt free. Free of the confines and the shackles that my nightmares kept hooked around my body. Free from the shame and the pain of what my brother had done to my body. I couldn't get enough of her. I couldn't get enough of the safe haven her body had created for mine. Her legs shook as she pressed herself against me. I slid my arm beneath her back, pulling her closer to me as I sat back on my haunches. Her body molded perfectly to mine, filling the spots I left behind as she moved with me. Our tongues collided. Our teeth clattered together. That little minx sucked on my lower lip, and I swear to hell on high, I damn near blew my load. And as I stood to my feet, I bent down long enough to grip the backs of her thighs.

Before hoisting her against my body.

"Mav," she gasped down the back of my throat.

I growled as I spun her around, pinning her to the first available wall. A growl worked up the back of my throat, letting loose as our tongues fought for dominance. Her knees trembled against my body. Her ankles locked around me and I slid my tongue down the expanse of her neck. The heat of her pussy battered my skin through my jeans, teasing my cock as it pressed heavily against my zipper. And oh, how her smell grew. How it thickened and permeated the room around us, broadcasting a carnal need we both had swelling between our bodies.

My hands explored her, cupping her tightening tits as I felt her nipples pucker against my palms. I gripped the globes of her ass and rolled my hips into hers before I pulled her away from the wall. Freeing her from the prison I had pinned her against. She groaned as she clung to me, burying her fingers into my hair as a gasp fell from her lips. And the second I felt her collapse against me, the second that wall fell away from her back, she climbed me like a fucking tree.

Before she drew my lower lip back into her mouth.

"Good God," I grunted.

"Mmmm, so good," she whimpered.

A growl bubbled up from my gut. It fell into her mouth as we collapsed to the bed at my side, her body bouncing for my viewing pleasure. I wanted those legs of hers wrapped around me. I wanted her thighs molding to my hips. And as my mouth fell to her neck, I sucked in patches of skin and nibbled on the sweetness of her presence.

"Oh, fuck," she moaned. "Mav, yes."

My hand inched down her torso. "Mmmm, so good."

Her legs parted for me. "Oh, shit."

I slid my hand up her robe and found her bare pussy waiting for me. And fucking hell, the smell of her womanhood was too much to handle.

"I have to taste you," I grunted as I rushed down her body.

And before she got a word in edgewise, I had her legs tossed over my shoulders as my tongue slid up her slit.

"Uuuuugh-mm," she groaned and wrapped her hands up in the comforter of the bed.

I flicked her swollen nub with the tip of my tongue. "God, you taste so good."

"Mav," she whimpered, "please. Don't stop."

And again, she sure as fuck didn't have to tell me twice.

16

BRIELLE

My hips bucked and my toes curled. Electricity shot through my veins at lightning speed. As my eyes rolled into the back of my head, my hands flew into his hair from the sheets. I wanted him closer. I needed him flush against me. That body. Those muscles. That cheeky little chuckle of his.

I felt its rumbles against my clit before he came up for air.

"Sounds like someone's enjoying themselves."

I groaned. "Shut up and finish the job."

He kissed the inside of my thigh. "Yes, ma'am."

My eyes bulged as his tongue flattened out against my clit, but it had nothing on the feeling of his finger slipping inside of my pulsing entrance. My jaw unhinged in silent pleasure while he crooked it behind my swollen mound, tickling it from one side while his tongue lapped against the other. I gasped for air. I raked my fingernails along his scalp as another finger filled me up. My walls collapsed. My legs locked out. My back arched so deeply that I thought it might snap like a fucking twig.

And as my orgasm crashed over me, I barely got out his name.

"Mav—er—Mav, God. Shit. Fuck, fuck, fuck."

"Yeeeeah," he damn near growled as he slid his arms beneath my thighs. "Get that pussy over here for me."

"Ah!" I yelped.

He didn't stop. Even as ecstasy rocked my body, he pulled me steadily closer. He sucked my clit between his lips and slid that tongue along its oversensitive tip, like I hadn't just seen Jesus. Silver stars burst in my vision as I stared up at the ceiling. My limp body became his to control and my thighs wrapped around his head like a headband. Hearing him lapping up every droplet I had to offer him stirred something within me. Something primal. Something hungry.

Something that I hadn't entertained in years.

"Oh, God. It's coming. It's coming. Mav. I'm gonna—I'm gonna—ooooh, my Gooood."

He slid two fingers back into my entrance and pumped them quickly. "That's it. Come for me, beautiful. Let me hear those sounds of yours."

All I could get out was a whimper, though. "Oh, shit."

I spiraled. The room tilted on its own axis as the ceiling became the floor. Pleasure, unlike anything I had ever experienced, sizzled through my veins, and sent dollops of sweat dripping down to the nape of my neck. I panted for air as my voice caught against my vocal cords. Mav lapped me up from slit to clit, drinking me down as if I were the only source of nourishment he had.

Then, once my body finally collapsed back to the bed, he rushed up my body.

"Open wide," he taunted, rolling me over on top of him.

I salivated at the thought. "Looks like someone's eager."

He fisted my hair and dragged my face to his. "Wouldn't you be if you were in my situation?"

I grinned. "What makes you think I'm not already?"

He chuckled. "That's my girl."

My heart slammed against my chest and my lips fell to the crook of his neck. Hearing his soft groans and muted grunts churned my gut while my tongue traced a trail from his pulse point to his pelvis. His stiffened cock throbbed against my skin. Precum slicked the spots it bounced against as my curves rumbled along his chiseled muscles. His abs called to my fingertips. His thighs flexed with glee as I hovered my warm breath over its tip. His cock stood at attention, already leaking and I marveled at the vein bulging beneath his girth.

But just as I wrapped my hand around its base, a knock came at the door.

"Just ignore them," Mav said, wrapping his hand into my tendrils.

I giggled. "My pleasure."

The knocking continued. "Don't make me pick this lock."

I paused. "Can he really do that?"

Mav groaned. "Fine, fine, just give us a sec—"

Before he even got the phrase out of his mouth, I heard something tinkering. Mav scrambled in a mad dash to get to his clothes while I did the only thing that came to mind. I grabbed the comforter, rolled my body over, and managed to cover myself just as the doorknob twisted. And as Mav tucked his pussy-soaked cock quickly into his boxers, the door swung open.

Revealing a less-than-enthused, Dante.

His blank stare fell onto me, pinning me to the bed as I held the comforter close against my naked body.

"Care to join?" Mav asked with a grin, hopping back into his jeans.

I shot him a look. "Shut up, Maverick."

He bit his teeth at me playfully before snatching his shirt off the floor. "And here I thought you liked my sounds."

His stare against my face grew fierce. "Axton wants to see you, Mav."

He turned to face me before holding out his arms. "Duty calls, beautiful."

"Don't work too hard," I said with a smile.

He snickered and slipped between Dante and the doorframe. "I can't promise that, but I can promise a sequel if you're interested."

"Mav," Dante said flatly.

"All right, all right," he said, disappearing down the hallway, "I'm going."

And not once did Dante's glare waver from my face.

"Yes?" I asked as I sat up.

His gaze flickered down the rest of my covered body. "Glad to see you're making yourself at home."

"I was told to."

He blinked, and for a split second, I thought he had something that he wanted to say. But if he did, he didn't let it slip through those fish thin lips of his. Instead, he simply closed the door behind him before his barely-there footsteps headed toward the stairs that Mav had descended only moments before.

And the entire time, I wondered what in the fuck he meant by his words.

"Asshole," I murmured as I flopped back down onto the mattress.

As I laid there, wanting to die of embarrassment, thoughts of my twin sister consumed me. Heat burned my cheeks at the anger I still held toward my parents for never telling me. All my life, I'd felt this hole in my heart. Like part of me had never truly been there. I talked to imaginary friends as a child, praying that one day they'd come to life, so I'd be less alone as an only child.

I was never an only child, though.

"My God," I whispered as I closed my eyes.

I'd seen that shit on the news all the time, those expose pieces where twins were reunited after so many years apart. I had always been so drawn to them. So enraptured with the idea that, somewhere out there, I had a sibling looking for me. Searching for me. Wanting me to come into their life. I fantasized about it as a teenager. Fantasies where my sibling showed up at the front door, ready to become one big, happy family.

No wonder I had felt incomplete my entire life.

For all the years I had been alive, I never felt adequate. I got straight A's all throughout high school, but it wasn't enough. I graduated at the top of my class, but it didn't fulfill me. I worked with children that would otherwise be sacrificed to a brutal public school system, and yet I found myself questioning my life's work at times. But now, I understood why.

Because an entire chunk of my life had been missing.

A chunk that shared my exact DNA.

CRASH, THUD!

"Aaaahhh!" I shrieked, scrambling to get to the other side of the bed.

I heard his voice before I saw his looming, shadowed profile. "Do you want to help?"

I swallowed hard as Axton's voice fell heavily against my ears. "What?"

He stalked closer, coming all the way to the edge of the bed. He stared down at me, raking his gaze along my comforter-covered body as his nose wrinkled in disgust.

At least, I thought it was disgust, what with the deep furrow of his brow and the disapproving look in his stare.

"Do you want to help us or not?" he glowered.

My head tilted. "Depends on the help. Why?"

He didn't hesitate. "There's a party we've been asked to provide protection services for."

My eyebrows slowly rose. "Seriously?"

"Helps us bring in residual income as a crew."

"Who do you provide protection to?"

He shrugged. "Elitist assholes with too much money."

"Ah."

"And in exchange, it provides us with a chance to rub elbows with those that have connections to make our lives easier."

I didn't even want to ask what that meant. "How exactly would I be helping, then?"

He drew in a deep breath. "We have reason to believe that your sister might be there. We think seeing you will throw her off enough for us to catch her."

"Which means releasing me."

"Yep."

I chewed on the inside of my lip. "Formal event?"

He nodded. "Uh huh."

"I don't have anything like that to wear."

"Leave that to us."

I scoffed. "You think you can just go out there, buy me a dress, and have it fit perfectly?"

"It's a talent of mine, yes."

You know those moments where you become a slave to your own memories? When your brain decides to throw a temper tantrum and remind you of things you were better off not knowing in the first place? As Axton loomed over me with those predatory eyes of his, my brain decided to hide itself. It didn't matter that I was intrigued with this talent of his. It didn't matter that I felt safer than I had in days. It didn't matter that he was on one side of the bed and that I was on the other.

I guess, the only thing that mattered was his presence.

"Wake up, bitch."

I remembered back to the first time I ever heard his voice. It had been accompanied by a kick to my chair that startled me awake.

"Ah!" I exclaimed as my head ripped up.

Before the pain that shot through my skull caused me to lean over and vomit onto the floor.

"Disgusting bitch," he growled as he fisted my hair.

"No!" I exclaimed as he ripped my head back, forcing me to stare up at him.

"Shut the fuck up and listen," he snarled. "You've committed sins you have yet to atone for, so consider me your God. Do you wish to confess?"

I whimpered. "What am I confessing?"

The crack of his first slap against my face jolted me out of my own trance, but when it did, I found that Axton was no longer standing in front of me. No longer did he loom over me like the brutal man his scars boasted him to be. Instead, my body trembled as I searched for him.

Before finding him perched on the edge of the bed near my head.

"Axe," I whispered as a tear slid down my cheek.

He cleared his throat. "All you'd do is wear a nice dress, some heels, and you'd mingle. Dante will go with you as your date and—"

I blinked. "Dante?"

"Yes, Dante. He's the one that coordinates security jobs like this, so he'll be the easiest date for you to slip in there with."

"Seriously? That man's ready to gnaw my muscles off my bones."

To my shock, Axton laughed. He barked with it, actually, and the sound disarmed me. "He blends in well with that kind of crowd, believe it or not. He doesn't stand out and wears a tux well enough to hide who he really is."

I nodded slowly. "So, what happens when you catch my sister?"

"We hand her over to who wants her."

"Is that another thing you guys do? Bounty hunting or whatever?"

He stood to his feet. "Getting your sister off the street and into the hands of those who want her is the only way for you to get back to your life. So, are you in or out?"

I noted how he dodged the question, but I didn't call him out on it. In fact, I didn't hesitate at all when I answered him.

Which shocked even me.

"You should know that green is my color," I said as my back straightened.

"The point is to blend in," he said, starting for the door, "not stand out."

"Awww, and here I thought you weren't capable of paying someone a compliment."

That actually pulled a genuine chuckle out of him. "I'm capable of many things, Brielle."

"Like what?"

And when he peered over his shoulder, the devious look in his eye made me squeeze my thighs together.

"Don't ask for an answer you're not ready for yet," he said.

Man, he really knew how to keep a girl on the edge of her seat.

17

DANTE

I hadn't worn my tuxedo in ages. In fact, I was stunned to see that it still fit. I'd put on some muscle mass since originally commissioning it from across town. I slid my hands down my white button-front shirt as I clocked the position of my ankle gun. I had to make sure there was enough slack in the legs to cover that damned thing up, but it didn't look too bad.

"At least the pants break at the right place," I murmured to myself.

My hands slid along my leather belt, disappearing beneath the tailed black tuxedo jacket. I played with the knife holsters on my hips, counting both of them on either side of my body. My palms gravitated up to my breast jacket pocket where I checked to make sure my taser was both accessible and charged, ready to fire.

Then, I drew in a deep breath before winking at myself in the mirror.

"Let's do this," I murmured.

I was ready to wrap-up this open-ended contract. We'd had this damned thing on this bitch for much too long, and she honestly made us look bad. Bounty hunting was all about precision and opportune timing. However, if a contract was held onto for more than a month or so, it made the holder of the contract look like an incompetent ass wipe. Plus, it kept us from taking other bounties, which meant our pockets ran dry with each day that passed. No matter where we turned or what we did, this bitch had ruined us. She took our President. She fucked with our money. She dodged us at every turn and taunted us with a fucking contract we couldn't fulfill no matter what we did.

Four months on a contract was long enough.

She died tonight if I got my hands on her.

"Boy, am I jealous of you," Mav said, poking his head into my bedroom.

"Is she ready?" I asked as I fucked with my black tie one last time.

He smirked and leaned against the doorway with his arms crossed over his chest. "She is, and you should see her in this dress."

I rolled my eyes. "Well, I'm ready when she is."

"Axton was right," she said as her voice fluttered into my bedroom, "you do cut nicely in a tuxedo."

"I've had it for a while," I said as I fucked with my onyx cuff-links and turned to face her, "but I'm glad it... still... fits."

Brielle held her arms out before giving me a soft turn. "So, what do you think? How did Axton do with the eyeballing? Because I swear, I wasn't sure I believed him when he said—"

My gaze devoured her presence. "He's got a few tricks up his sleeve."

The slope of her waist and the way it blossomed into a decadent set of hips made my fingertips tingle. The way her broad shoulders gave way to her perfect little handfuls of breasts called to my palms. The strapless black dress she donned dripped down her body, all the way to the floor. And the slit up the left side of her dress exposed her long, shimmering leg, all the way up to her hip bone.

I had to draw in a deep breath to contain myself.

"So?" she asked. "What do you think?"

I walked over to her and offered her my arm. "I think I'm ready to go if you are."

She smiled as she linked her arm with mine. "As ready as I'll ever be."

Mav playfully sniffled as he dabbed his hand at his nonexistent tears. "So beautiful. My little babies, all grown up."

"Shut up," I said, gazing down at Brielle.

She peeked up me. "If I didn't know any better, I'd say you were talking to me with all that staring you enjoy doing so much."

A grin ticked the edge of my lips. "You'd like that, wouldn't you?"

All she did was toss me a wink and I damn near caved. I understood why Mav had caved so early and so quickly to her. She was delectable. A sarcastic delight to have around. Plus, she was very easy on the eyes.

So easy that I had to draw in another deep breath to keep my cock from giving me away.

Focus. There's a job to do.

As we descended down the stairs, I let out a piercing whistle through my lips. The bodyguards for the night gathered at the front door, dressed to the nines in their all-black suits fit for a job like the one we were about to tackle. We needed to blend in while still announcing our presence. No leather cuts and spiked bats for us that evening. With our guns on our hips and our personal weapon stashes hidden on our bodies, we all took to the parking lot. Most of my men climbed onto their bikes and sped off into the distance, carving out a path for us to drive.

And as I led Brielle toward my bike, Black Beauty, her jaw dropped.

"Wow," she said breathlessly as her fingertips danced along the shining black paint, "I've never been in one of these before."

I took her hand and helped her onto the back of my bike. "Always a first for everything."

She giggled and hiked up her dress to get comfortable on the leather seat. "Dante?"

"Yes?"

"What if something happens to me tonight?"

Immediately, I leaned forward, placing my face so close to hers that I felt her breath pulsing from her ruby red lips against my face.

"I'll die before something happens to you tonight. Understood?"

She drew in a broken breath. "Yeah, I hear you."

"Good."

I swung my leg over the bike, situating myself against the seat. I heard her shuffling around with her dress, and out of the furthest corner of my eye, I saw the dollop of excess fluid against her inner thigh. I swallowed down a groan bubbling up the back of my throat. I cranked the engine and allowed the vibrations between my legs to distract me.

But it had nothing on the heat of her body as she wrapped her arms around my waist.

"Is this okay?" she asked.

I revved the engine. "It better be, because it's how you'll hang on."

"Will you go slow at first? You know, so that I can get the hang of it?"

My balls tingled with need. "Of course."

"Thank you, Dante."

Her sweet little voice wrapped around my head and damn

near held me hostage. I kicked off toward the road, keeping myself a few miles under the speed limit. The way she clung to me stiffened my cock. The way her thighs blanketed me from behind swirled my head with all sorts of salacious thoughts. Me in my black tuxedo, and her in her black dress, soaring with me toward this gala on the back of my black bike. There was a seductiveness to it all that caught me off-guard. A warmth that seemed to melt the icy cage around my heart.

I forced myself to focus as we blazed a trail toward the gala location.

With the wind in my hair and her hands gripping my belt, I kicked it up a notch. I bumped things up to the speed limit, and the faster we went, the harder she clung to me. Her fingertips curled against my clothing. Her thighs clamped down against the outside of my legs. Hell, even her cheek pressed between my shoulder blades as she rested it against me.

I felt powerful with her holding me like that.

"You good back there?!" I called out to her.

"This is incredible!"

"It really is, isn't it?!"

"It's so freeing, Dante. I don't know why I haven't done this sooner!"

"Just needed to find the right person!"

"Weeeeee hooooo!" she exclaimed.

The thing you had to understand about the life I led was that, in order to do what we do, most things had to be compromised. Family had to be left in the dust, which wasn't too hard for me in the first place. Friends had to fall to the wayside, which again, wasn't too hard for me. I had been a quiet child. One that kept to myself and never really made friends. I preferred to watch people instead of interacting with them, especially my drunkard father.

But that was another story for a different day.

Anyway, the point was, the life I led had a tendency to be isolating. Happiness was harder to come by with the dark looming so closely over our heads. Don't get me wrong, I utilized the darkness to my benefit. I slunk around in it as if it had been my first home, and some of my brothers might argue that the darkness was, in fact, my first home. As Brielle laughed, however, that bubbly sound made my heart skip a beat.

Something it hadn't done in, well, ever.

"Focus on the goal, Dante," I muttered to myself.

"What was that?!" Brielle asked above the sound of rushing wind.

"Nothing! Just talking myself through the evening!"

"Ah!"

I had one goal tonight, and that was to get this twin of hers in custody so that we could deliver her to the contract holder. I was ready to get paid. Hell, we all were. The trick would be making sure none of my guys killed her before we could ante up on our end of the deal. Six mil was nothing to shake a stick at, and yet that was what we stood to gain with turning her in. A cool six million, split between all of us, netted us a little over six hundred thousand.

Enough to keep all of us going strong through the end of the year, and then some.

"All right," I said as I eased into a parking space in front of the hotel, "we're here."

"The party is at a hotel?" Brielle asked.

I slid off my bike, put down the kickstand, and offered her my hand. "It's in one of their ballrooms, yes."

She slid her palm against mine. "That makes a bit more sense."

I linked her arm with mine and ushered her into the building. With a nod of my head, my guys let us through, though I noticed that Rocker got a bit too ballsy staring at Brielle's ass in her dress. I shot him a look, letting him know that I was watching him, and that seemed to straighten his gaze out long enough to clock the people behind us and ask for some identification.

Which freed us up to go through the side entrance to the ballroom.

"Wow," Brielle said breathlessly, "this place is incredible."

I patted her hand with mine. "It *is* one of their nicer rooms."

The vaulted ceilings gave way to black chandeliers with flickering lights mimicking firelight. The marble floors had black skating through them to match the glimmering lights, and the marble pillars providing support all the way up into the rafters sparkled with the lights that shone down from above. Heels clicked across the floor in all directions, accompanied by women dripping with their most expensive items. Jewels and diamonds. Gemstones and tailor-made rings. Men showed off their watches and gabbed on about their tailored suits. Silver trays rushed about by silent figureheads donning black-and-white outfits to blend in with their surroundings.

And as I walked the outer perimeter, checking in with my guys while I escorted Brielle around, I felt it.

Her sister was there.

"Keep an eye out," I muttered as I leaned down to the shell of her ear. "I feel her presence."

Which only made her stiffen before her head set itself on a swivel.

Gazing in every direction she could while I kept my eyes peeled for any sign of that murderous bitch.

18

BRIELLE

I kept his pace, easing around at his side as he skirted the edges of the ballroom. I clung to him, turning my head every which way, taking in the unfamiliar sights, sounds, and smells. Caviar on crackers passed by us and I did my best not to wrinkle my nose. I couldn't stand the smell, much less whatever it may have tasted like.

"Not a fan?" he asked.

"Hmm?"

"Caviar. I take it you're not a fan?"

I shrugged. "Well, I've never been around it."

"And now that you are?"

I grinned up at him. "I think I'll stick with sushi, thanks."

"Ah, another sushi lover. Good to know."

"Why?"

He shrugged, but he didn't offer any sort of explanation, and that piqued my curiosity. I went from paying attention to my surroundings to paying attention to him and the way he focused on the world around him. Dante was the most unassuming of them all, with those shimmering natural reds mixed into his chestnut hair and those hunter green eyes of his. His height made him stand out, sure. He was at least a head taller than everyone else in the room, and if I had to take a guess, that was most likely the reason why we were sticking to the shadows.

I swear, with all these men in black suits, I would have absolutely pegged them for cops. I mean, they had earpieces, for fuck's sake!

Uncanny.

"Dante!"

He paused at the sound of his name as I peered over my shoulder.

"Dante, there you are. I was wondering when I'd catch you."

An older man in a navy-blue suit with a light pink button-front jogged up to us.

"Mr. Calvin," he said with a nod of his head.

The man stopped just shy of us and held out his hand. "I wanted to thank you personally for providing the security for our fundraising event."

"It's not a problem, Mr. Calvin."

"I swear, it gets risky sometimes with this many big diamonds and jewels in the same room."

"It's my pleasure," Dante said.

"Dante, is that you?"

A woman's voice appeared next, and I didn't know why it made me bristle. Dante quickly shook hands with the man before a tan-skinned woman in a skin-tight red dress came up to us. Her curly brown hair fell well past her shoulders. The diamonds glittering around her neck held my gaze hostage. They sparkled in the light of the chandeliers, and I couldn't help but admire her stiletto Louis Vuitton red bottoms.

Of course, they matched her dress exactly.

"Long time, no see," the woman said as she slid her gaze

down Dante's body as if I wasn't standing right the fuck there with my arm linked with us.

"Has it been?" he asked.

"I was wondering if they'd hit you guys up for protection for the event. I'm glad they did."

"So am I."

The woman giggled. "And why's that?"

Dante shrugged. "I always like getting paid for what I do best."

The woman's face fell, and I couldn't help but giggle. I looked down and curled my lips over my teeth, but it wasn't enough.

"And what do you think is so funny?" the woman asked curtly.

"I'd be curious to know that as well," Dante said.

I slowly looked up at him, and when he tossed me the slightest wink, I leveled my head on my shoulders.

"I just think it's funny that you intentionally gloss over the fact that someone has accompanied him to this gala because you believe you're better than me. But I can promise you, your spiky heels don't make you better than me."

The woman's eyebrows rose as she turned to face me. "You speak as if you see yourself as competition."

"I promise you, there is no competition from what I'm seeing."

Music started up in the background as the live band took their place on stage. The woman scoffed as she looked me up and down, and I couldn't help but straighten my back with pride. Fuck her and whatever horse she rode in on. She didn't get to hit on my date just because she thought she was better than me.

"Care to dance?" Dante asked.

I smiled up at him. "I'd love to."

"Well, when you get bored, Dante," the woman said as she brushed past him, "you know where to find me."

"I do," he said as he started for the dance floor, "at the pound."

My jaw hit the floor when he spun me around. I laughed with delight as my dress fluttered out, only for him to spin me back into him. His arm wrapped its way around my waist. He held my right hand up into the air before cradling it against his chest. He placed my palm on top of his beating heart as he continued to survey the room high above my head.

I couldn't help but place my ear against the lower part of his chest.

"You know, I've never really been a big dancer," I said.

Dante shrugged. "I get by at these events. Appearances are important at things like this."

"I can only imagine."

He didn't say anything else, so I didn't push the matter. Mostly because I felt myself melting into his embrace. The more we softly rocked side to side, the more it lulled me into a trance where all I knew was him. All I knew was his comforting strength wrapped around me, pulling me closer with every sway. He dipped me back, allowing my hair to just barely grace the ground as I stared up at him. His green gaze sparkled with mischievous delight, and I had to admit, I was curious to know what he was thinking about.

Jesus, what are these men doing to me?

"Brielle?" Dante asked, bringing me back up onto my feet.

"Yes, Dante?" I asked as I gazed up into his face.

"You look gorgeous tonight."

I blushed beneath his stare. "I'd say you do as well, but I'm sure you get that all the time."

He brought my hand to his lips to kiss. "Ready to do another patrol with me?"

My hand trembled when he caressed my skin with his lips. "Ready whenever you are."

His body froze, and I ceased my movements alongside him. The music continued to play as people danced around us, but I had no idea why in the world he had stopped. Had I stepped on his foot? Was something wrong with one of his guys?

"Come with me," he said, picking me up off my feet.

I scoffed as he damn near tossed me over his fucking shoulder. "Not like I have much choice right now."

A door slammed open before I found myself in a bathroom. He placed me back down onto my feet and the panicked look in his eyes shocked me to my core.

"She's here, isn't she?" I asked.

He ripped the door open and poked his head out, looking both ways before slamming the door closed again.

"Dante, talk to me," I urged.

He flipped the lock before spinning around to face me. "She's here, and I don't want you in the crossfire."

My entire body vibrated with fear. "But—I didn't see anyone?"

He gripped my upper arms. "I want you to stay here until I come back for you. All right? Can you do that for me?"

I shook my head. "No, I came here to help you. What can I do? How can I help you g—"

He clapped his hand over my mouth. "You can help by staying here until I come back for you, understand?"

I nodded quickly as my fear consumed me. I wanted to help. I wanted to do whatever it took to piece my life back together. Maybe my sister wasn't the terrible person they thought she was. Maybe she had just gotten caught up in something way over her head. It happened, you know. Like the predicament I had found myself in only days ago.

There were so many questions that I wanted to ask Dante, but he answered them before I could spit them out.

"No, Brielle," he said as he pulled his hand away from my mouth, "no one will get to you. No one. You hear me?"

I swallowed hard. "But what if—"

"No one," he growled.

My eyes watered over. My lower lip quivered as the reality of the situation dawned upon me. She was there. My twin sister was there, and she had seen us.

Wait, had she seen us?

"Dante, I'm scared," I whispered.

He wiped my tears away with his knuckles. "Which is why you need to stay here. Lock the door behind me and don't you dare let anyone in."

I grabbed his wrist just as he pulled away from me. "Wait."

"The longer we wait, the more we risk—"

"Just... Can you give me a second?"

I looked up into his face and committed every single part of it to memory. The little scar he had that cut right through his left eyebrow. The slight crookedness of his nose that reminded me of all those Rocky Balboa movies my mother always watched during her Sunday rerun marathons. I reached up and cupped his cheek, relishing the way the heat of his skin penetrated all the way down my arm.

"Come back to me, okay?" I asked softly.

I expected an answer. Or possibly a sarcastic, "I can't promise shit" kind of thing. But instead, I got something so much more... delectable.

"We can seal that with a kiss if you'd like," he whispered as his lips hovered over mine.

"That's a pretty strong promise. Sure you can ante up to it?"

He cupped my cheeks and pinned me to the bathroom wall. "You have no idea what I can ante up to, gorgeous."

"Then, why don't you stop being all talk and actually do something about it?"

Something flashed behind his eyes. Something dark. Something carnal. Something... devious. His eyes danced along my body, as if to clock every single movement that I made. I stood tall, though. I straightened my back and let his brain put together whatever inferences and connections it would. Because I knew he was searching.

He was looking for any sign not to proceed.

"Any luck?" I asked.

His growl answered me just fine, but it was the way he crashed our lips together that tossed all deals out the window. The second our tongues connected in a sensuous tango that stole my breath away, I locked my arms around his neck. His dexterous hands and long, strong fingers roamed my body, cupping my tits and sliding down my bare leg as the slit of my dress gave way. His heat made me quiver. My pussy jumped as I ran my fingers through his soft, unhindered locks. I gripped his tuxedo jacket and pulled him closer, feeling his girth pressed against my clothed warmth.

And when his hands gripped my hips, he hoisted me off the ground.

"Oh," I squeaked.

"Now," he said, his gaze darkened, "wrap those legs around me and hang on."

"I'd say that's much more than a kiss, D—"

He gripped my cheeks and squeezed them until my lips puckered. "Be a good girl for me, hmm?"

It was a whirlwind of sensations that led to the only thing that mattered. As he hiked up my dress and pulled my thong off to the side, his juicy cock slid between the wet folds of my entrance. My head fell back against the wall, causing his lips to attach to my pulse point. His tongue flicked rhythmically along my sensitive skin. I reached out for any part of him that I could grasp, any tendril of hair or piece of clothing that helped to ground me as his mouth alone tossed me into the heavens. I groaned when his thick tip slipped inside of me with a pop. The electric sensations that overtook my body forced a heavy high into my skull. I hissed as he filled me, his face sinking into the crook of my neck while he kissed and tickled my exposed collarbone with his tongue.

He seemed to stroke every single part of me at once.

But nothing could have prepared me for the ecstasy of his movements when the pad of his thumb found my clit.

"Oh, God," I asked shockingly.

"Now, what do we have here?" he murmured.

"Shit," I choked out, grinding my pussy against his hand.

"Goddamn it, you're so tight for me."

"Dante," I moaned.

"Say that again."

"Dante."

"Again."

"Fucking hell, Dante, please don't stop."

His lips found the shell of my ear. "That's what I like to hear, sweet girl."

Every time he pumped himself into me, his thumb swirled around my clit. His cock filled me to the brim as my quivering walls collapsed around him. They held on tightly, refusing to let go of the comforting heat he pushed throughout my body. Silver stars burst in my vision as his face meandered down my body, planting itself firmly into my tits. He groaned and growled, sucking in patches of skin, and nibbling on them as if I were the snack voice of the evening. I'd never felt so beautiful. So wanted. So... free. Sensations rushed across my body, pulling goosebumps up from the edges of my skin as his cock overwhelmed me. My body betrayed me and my juices dripped down his balls. They smacked against my bare ass, coating me in my own mark as the buckle of his pants clinked against the bathroom floor.

But there was no beauty like the sound of his voice shivering for more.

"Shit," he hissed as his broken breaths came in short pants, "you feel so good."

My jaw unhinged. "Dante. Oh, fuck. Please. A li—a little more. Harder. Deeper. Oh, God. Fuck. Just like that. Just like that, Dee."

The sounds of skin slapping skin filled the air around us as my pussy clamped down around his cock. He picked up his head and wrapped his hand around my throat, squeezing against my pulse points. My eyes rolled into the back of my head. The feral sounds that fell from his lips filled me with a high I couldn't explain. My toes curled as my walls milked him for all he had. My entire body locked out, held hostage by the ecstasy coursing through my veins. His predatory stare, locked with mine and a twisted grin sank against his cheeks. He watched my every movement. He stared me down with every roll of my eyes and every buck of my hips. I was his little puppet, and he was my marionette master, pulling my strings and pushing every single button until he had the reaction that he wanted.

He had caught his prey.

And I'd let him catch me again if he ever gave me the chance.

"Fucking Christ, sweet girl," he grunted.

His hips stuttered when his attention finally pulled away from me. My body collapsed, spent from the orgasm that had barreled through my body. He pinned me to the wall with his body, and for the first time since laying my eyes on him, I felt his strength. As his body held me up with no help from my own, I got a small glimpse of what his lean, taut form was really capable of. He didn't bat an eye while he held me there, suspended before him. He didn't lose a bead of sweat down his brow as his hands cupped my ass cheeks so that he could hold me up and finish himself off. I let him contort me in any way he wished. He pinned my hands above my head and bounced me up the wall with his pelvis, sinking me down the whole of his girth every single time.

Then, his body finally caved to mine.

"Oh, fuck," he said breathlessly.

Feeling him fall against me slammed my heart against my chest. His hands planted onto the wall on either side of my head, and I kissed his cheek as his own descended to my shoulder. He shivered as he stood there, his cock still filling me up as the evidence of our debauchery leaked from between my legs. And as my lips reached out for him, falling against his shoulder, I felt the last threads of his hot arousal pour into my body.

Marking me as his territory.

"My God," I said breathlessly.

"Come here," he murmured, gathering me into his arms.

He pulled me away from the wall and I fell limp in his embrace. He walked me over to the sprawling marble bathroom countertop before perching me on top of it. He peered over the crown of my head into the mirror behind me, straightening his tie and shoving his cock back into his pants. And as I sat there, still trying to get the room to stop tilting and twirling on its own axis, his words dawned on me.

"...so, that means if I'm not back in twenty, use this phone to call the only number in the contacts."

I forced my gaze to focus, and I found him standing there, looking as if nothing had happened. His cheeks weren't flushed.

He hadn't broken out in a sweat. He wasn't panting hard, or even panting at all. His clothes were pristine, as if I hadn't even touched him. There was no makeup anywhere on his shoulders or his chest. There was no wrinkling from where I had grabbed him and crushed my lips to his. There was no evidence of me at all. Just some dirty little secret to be kept away from the world.

It made me feel so fucking inadequate, and the swell of emotion shocked me.

"Brielle, did you hear me?" Dante asked.

I took the phone from him. "Whose number is it again?"

He backed away and repositioned my dress over my legs. He slid his hands down my thighs in little spurts at a time, as if he were dusting me off. He pulled the piece of fabric over my leg, hiding my thigh away from the slit that had given us such easy access early.

It... sort of made me feel like he didn't want to see them.

"It's Axton," he said as he turned toward the door. "He'll know what to do if you have to call."

I cleared my throat. "Twenty minutes, you said?"

He unlocked the door and slipped out. "Yep, and not a second over. Got it?"

I nodded mindlessly as I stared down at the phone. "Yeah, yeah. Got it."

"Lock the door behind me."

"Uh huh."

"Brielle."

The harshness of his voice almost brought tears to my eyes. "I hear you, Dante. Just go."

And without another word, he left.

As I sat there with his cum still dripping down between my thighs, I stared blankly at the basic-ass cell phone in my hand. A flip phone, of all things. I scoffed and hopped off the bathroom counter. I grimaced at the way his mark dripped down my legs.

Nothing but a cum dumpster, I suppose. I took note of the time before setting the phone down. I rushed to the door and locked it back, heaving a sigh of relief as I did so.

Then, all I had to do was wait.

What the hell do I do in a bathroom for twenty minutes?

I walked over to the paper towel dispenser and pulled some out. As I cleaned myself up, or tried to at least, I counted down the seconds in my head. I discarded the paper towels and went straight for the folded washcloths on a wall-mounted holder next to the sink. Unsanitary as fuck, if anyone asked me about it, but they smelled clean. Bleached, even.

I ran it under some warm water, rubbed some soap into it, and cleaned the rest of myself up.

"Come on, Dante, where are you?" I muttered to myself.

Ten minutes had passed. Then, eleven. Then, twelve. And not once had I heard a thing. There was no commotion. No gunfire. No crossfire to even speak of. At the very least, I expected a scene to be caused. Yelling, or a bullet nailing one of the chandeliers, or something! There was nothing, though. Nothing outside of the faint live music playing in the background while the soft murmurs of conversations passing by filtered through the locked door.

I damn near convinced myself that Dante had lied to me.

Until a knock came at the door just shy of the eighteen-minute mark.

"Thank fuck," I said as I flipped the lock on the door. "I was getting worried that—you're not Dante."

I found myself staring into the face of my carbon copy. "No, I'm really not."

My heart froze in my chest. "What have you done with him?"

She shoved me into the bathroom before slipping inside. "I need to borrow your clothes, *sis*."

I scrambled to steady myself onto my feet. "I won't ask you again. Where the hell is D—"

I didn't even get my question out, though, because the second I righted myself long enough to face her, the last thing I saw was her fist.

Then my entire world went dark.

19

DANTE

I closed the bathroom door behind me and waited. I stared down the hallway, watching. Waiting. If she had seen us, then she had seen Brielle, which meant I had to get her somewhere safe. Somewhere with no back exit. Somewhere behind a locked door.

Like the bathroom.

Click.

"'Atta, girl," I murmured, pushing off the wall.

"Attention everyone," I said as I strode down the hallway, "we have lift-off. I repeat, we have lift-off. Copy?"

"Copy," Rocker said.

"Copy," Locker said.

"Position?" Wolf asked.

"North-face, the bar. She's wearing a—"

"I've got eyes on her," Rocker said quickly. "Near the stage, left of the band."

"I'm headed your way from the backside," Wolf said.

I halted my tracks as I stood at the entrance back into the ballroom. "Be on alert. We can't allow her to leave, nor can we allow her to cause a disturbance. Got it?"

"Got it," everyone said in unison.

"Rocker, you still got eyes?" I asked.

"No, she slipped backstage. Pursuing now."

"I'll follow around and catch that other exit back there," Wolf said, panting.

"And whatever you guys do, do not panic," I said curtly.

I watched Wolf part the crowd as he headed for the stage, but I stuck to the perimeter. I walked along the outer edge of the room, keeping a keen eye trained toward the stage. This woman was trained. She knew how to duck and run like a professional, which meant I had to treat her like one.

"Rocker?" I asked.

"Still no visual," he said gruffly.

My gaze panned toward the kitchen. "Is there anything that links the kitchen with the back of the stage?"

"Not that I can see," Rocker said.

"Darkness does, though. There's a hallway back here," Wolf said.

"Shit," I hissed, heading for the kitchen. "Keep your eyes peeled. She doesn't get out of here tonight."

I checked my watch. I'd already been gone for six fucking minutes. I cursed beneath my breath and shouldered my body into the swinging kitchen door. I damn near ran over one of the guys with a tray of champagne, but he did a damn fine job of diverting himself without spilling a drop.

"Sorry, what's your name?" I asked.

He looked me up and down. "Raylen."

I nodded. "Sorry for the intrusion. Good dodge."

He snickered. "Thanks. You need anything?"

"Did you see a woman come back here at all?"

He shook his head. "No one's allowed back here except workers and staff."

"I know."

"I'll keep my eyes peeled, though?"

I patted him on the shoulder as I brushed past him. "You do that, thank you."

"What's she wearing?!"

I ignored her question as I threw open closets and looked for any sign of her. Long hairs that had been left behind while she booked it. Anything that had been knocked over and not cleaned up. I looked above my head at the grating system for the HVAC. The damned vents alone could've shielded her as she crawled through them. But none of the grates were hanging from their hinges.

"Backstage is clear," Rocker said.

"So are the dressing rooms," Wolf said.

"Locker?" I asked.

He grunted before his voice sounded. "Fucking hell, it's like she disappeared. The bartender doesn't even remember clocking a woman that looks like her."

I turned back around toward the kitchen entrance into the ballroom. "This is what she does for a living, of course she's good at it."

"What now, boss?" Locker asked.

I checked my watch. Fucking hell, fifteen minutes had passed. "Lock down the venue."

"On it," Rocker said.

"Locker, take your rifle and get to the roof. If she leaves, plug her."

"Oh, hell yeah," he said.

"And Wolf?"

"What's up?"

"The second one of these guys has eyes on her, you tail her ass. I don't care whose car you gotta steal in order to make it happen. Once we find her, don't let her out of your sight."

He chuckled. "Perfect. I'll head out to the parking lot and do some scoping."

"Uh, sir?" someone asked.

I turned around and found a pimple-faced kid with an oversized chef's hat on.

"Yeah?" I asked flatly.

"Do you need something? Because if not, I need the burner your ass is on."

I peeked behind me and found that I had leaned against an industrial stove. "Of course."

"Thanks," the young man said with a strange look on his face.

I scanned the kitchen one last time before heading back out into the ballroom. I had to get back to Brielle. I had three minutes before my time was up, and I needed to get her out of there.

So, I kept a cool head while walking back across the venue before I knocked rapidly on the door.

"Brielle?" I asked as I kept knocking. "Open up, it's me."

The lock clicked before the door inched open, and those fearful little eyes peeked around the corner.

"Is everything okay?" she asked.

The tremble in her voice broke my heart, but I had to admit, I was relieved to see her unharmed.

"Yeah, everything's fine. I'm going to take you back."

She inched the door open a bit further. "Did you catch her?"

I pressed my hand against the door and opened it the rest of the way. "The guys are on it. But right now? My priority is getting you somewhere safe."

She slid her gaze down my body. "You really think she's gonna hurt me, don't you?"

I found it odd that she asked such a question. "Yes."

She still didn't seem okay, though.

"Brielle?" I asked.

"Yeah?"

"Are you okay?"

She snickered. "Well, I've never been ditched after sex before. But I suppose a girl can get used to anything in a dress like this."

She slid her hands down the silken black gown, and something felt off. The hairs on the nape of my neck stood on end. I peeked my head into the bathroom and surveyed the scene, not sure what I was searching for, but searching, nonetheless.

Until she linked her arm with mine.

"And you're sure you're okay. No one came by and bothered you?"

She giggled. "You're such a worrywart. No, Dante, no one came by to pester me. I mean, a couple of women weren't pleased that the bathroom door was locked. But, you know, that's just sort of par for the course."

Talkative. "Right."

She ushered me out of the bathroom, not the other way around. "Are you okay, though? You seem... tense."

I studied her with intention. "Just worried about you."

"Well, I'm as okay as I can be. I'm nervous, but that's normal."

"I suppose so."

"And you're sure she's not here?"

I shook my head. "I'm not sure of anything right now."

Maybe it was just post-coital bliss. Maybe my senses were much too heightened, and I was reading into things too much. I took one last look over my shoulder before the bathroom door closed, and there wasn't even a hint of a shadow anywhere. No one else was in that restroom, except for her.

Brielle.

And yet, the hairs on the nape of my neck didn't settle down.

"Come on, let's get you out of here," I said, patting her hand.

"Lead the way, handsome," she said.

Something she had never called me before. Even after we had sex.

Something was very, very wrong.

20

AXTON

"I'm about to go to that fucking party myself," I growled.

I slammed my silent cell phone down against the conference table on the top floor of the clubhouse. I turned around, staring out toward the darkness of the desert and a multitude of stars twinkled in the sky. Something was wrong. I felt it in my bones.

Something had happened to my men.

"That's it," I muttered, snatching my phone up. "I'm going to that party and yanking them out of there."

The last update from Dante had damn near been an hour ago when he initially told me he had spotted her. I charged out the door and rumbled down the stairs. I patted my pockets, making sure I had my keys and my wallet along for the ride.

But just as I entered the front foyer, I heard Dante's bike pull up.

"About mother fucking time," I murmured to myself.

"That what I think it is?" Mav asked, bolting in from the kitchen.

I sniffed the air. "Roast beef. Again?"

He shrugged. "What? It's my newest serotonin food."

"Can't you pick something that doesn't smell like shit?"

"It doesn't smell like shit. I made it personally this past weekend."

"Well, what you make smells like shit," I said flatly as the doorknob turned.

And when the door flung open, Dante stood there with Brielle on his arm.

There was a look on his face, though.

"Well, well, well," Mav said as he took a bite of his nasty ass sandwich, "how were things at the charity event?"

"It came and it went," Dante said, ushering Brielle inside.

Mav whipped his gaze up to me and I froze. The phrase. He had thrown out our phrase. Luca had originally put that into motion with our group. A code phrase for anytime trouble was right behind us. I stared Dante down as he nodded his head. His smile told me he was fine, but his stare told me something was wrong. And when I looked over at Brielle, I watched her head swivel around. Left to right. Up and down.

As if she'd never seen the place.

"It came and it went?" Mav asked.

Dante nodded. "Yep, pretty uneventful charity event, if you ask me."

I narrowed my eyes. "You told us you had found her. Yet, I don't see her with you. What the hell happened? Bad intel?"

Dante shook his head and dropped his arm, releasing who we thought was Brielle. But clearly, he didn't think that was her. And honestly, neither did I.

So, where the fuck was our girl?

"I saw her. She was there, all right. But by the time we established a perimeter, she was gone," Dante said.

"Fuck!" I exclaimed.

Mav chewed on the inside of his cheek. "We may not get another opportunity like that."

With my back turned, I pulled my gun off my hip. I

whipped around and pointed that damned thing straight at that woman's fucking head, but I turned around only to find that she had beat me to the punch. She held out two guns, one in each hand, and as she leveled them at both Dee and Mav, I stilled my gut.

"Hello, Rachel," I said.

She practically spat at me. "That isn't my name."

Mav shook his head and continued eating, as if being held at gunpoint by the deadliest woman we'd ever pursued wasn't enough to shut off his stomach.

"Not what your medical records say," he said with his mouth full.

"Didn't your mother ever teach you to chew and swallow before you talk?" she asked flatly.

"No," Mav said with a smile.

"You fucking bitch," Dante growled.

"Awww, how sweet," she said as she cocked both of her guns, "he's trying to flirt."

I walked toward the woman until the barrel of my gun sat against her forehead. "Where is she?"

"Where's who?" she asked with a smirk.

I cocked my gun as well. "Brielle. Where is she?"

The woman grinned wildly, and I almost pulled that trigger. Watching her bloody body drop to the ground would have been the highlight of my fucking evening.

But we had to figure out what in the fuck she had done with Brielle.

"He won't ask you again," Mav said.

The woman giggled. "I swear, it's like taking candy from a baby with you guys."

"Where is she?!" I bellowed.

The damn bitch didn't even flinch. "You ask such boring questions. Anyone got any better questions?"

"Yeah, I do," Dante said as he turned to face her. "What the fuck do you want?"

She shrugged. "Needed a way out of that venue. I swear, you boys are relentless."

His shadow cloaked her. "I didn't ask what you wanted. I asked what you want now. Right now. Right this second."

She smiled up at him. "You could've plugged me the second we got outside. You knew who I was. Or, at the very least, you had an inkling. Right?"

I looked over at Dante. "Is she telling the truth?"

He swallowed hard. "I wasn't sure."

"Fucking hell," I hissed.

The woman nearly cackled, she was so entertained. "So, with that little inkling in the pit of your gut—"

Dante interrupted her, though. "That goes both ways. You could've done away with me the second you got onto the back of my bike with that knife on your left hip, but you didn't. Why come all the way here?"

And when she didn't answer, I answered for her.

"Because you're out on a contract trying to get paid," I said.

She slowly panned her empty gaze over to me. "The three amigos have a lovely little contract that I simply can't ignore. After all, a woman can do a lot with three mil a head."

I'd never seen Dante's face get as red as it did at that moment. Even Mav dropped his sandwich to the floor and placed his hand on the butt of his gun. I was fuming. Every single ounce of blood in my body boiled at once. Who in the absolute hell had a bounty out on us?

And how the fuck did we not know about it!?

"Axe," Mav warned.

I dropped the gun and placed the barrel right against that bitch's crotch.

"Hey now," she said with a grin, "don't tease me with a good time."

"I won't ask you again," I said as I damn near shoved it up her fucking pussy. "Where. Is. Brielle?"

Dante grabbed that woman's hair, however, and yanked her head back. "Who took the bounty out on us?"

"Dante," Mav said curtly.

"Oh," Rachel groaned as I slid the barrel of my gun up to her chest, "I bet she loves being manhandled by you."

Dante dipped down with his teeth gnashed together. "Answer my fucking question, you useless bitch."

"Now," I said, pressing my gun to her heart.

She giggled like a fucking schoolgirl. "You mean, the man who can read everyone like an open book doesn't have the faintest clue as to why someone would want them dead? You're slipping, Dante."

"Tell me!" he bellowed.

"Dante," Mav said, yanking his grip out of the woman's hair.

Her head whipped up and her fiery gaze connected with mine. "What's the best way to throw someone off their game?"

"No more games," I said, raising the gun to her head, "tell us where Brielle is."

Dante answered, though. "A distraction."

Rachel smiled so broadly that it made my fucking stomach flip. "A bit slow on the uptick, but at least he got there. Right, Axton?"

"Who took it out?" Mav asked.

She peered over at him, moving only her eyes. "I suppose whoever wants you distracted."

Dante glowered. "I can think of only one person that would be."

And when her smile overtook her face, I knew.

She was the one that took the bounty out on us.

"Brielle," I said flatly, "where is she?"

"Tsk-tsk-tsk-tsk-tsk," she said, having the audacity to click her tongue at me, "your little play toy? Oh, she's fine."

"Spit it out," Dante snarled as he grabbed her arm and spun her around. "We don't have any more time for your games. Who the fuck are you taking us to in exchange for Brielle?"

The woman's eyebrows rose. "Guess you're not slipping as much as you let on. Risky, risky."

Dante scoffed. "It's the oldest play in the book. It's not like you're revolutionary. You take us, you capture her, and then you trade us for the bounty and set her free. So, who are you taking us to?"

"What makes you think I'm going to set her free?" Rachel asked.

"You will never get your fucking hands on her," Mav snarled.

And that was when I heard tires rolling over the pressed dirt of our parking lot outside.

"That's my cue," the woman chirped as she quickly holstered her weapon. "Now, if you'll just make your way outside with me, you guys can zip tie each other's wrists together and climb into the back of that van."

I loomed over her as my teeth gnashed together. "Not until you tell us—"

She pulled her gun back off her hip at such lightning speed that by the time she pointed it at my feet, it was already too late. The crack of her gun sent Dante flying into me, tackling me to the ground. The smell of gunpowder filled my nostrils. Mav growled before another bullet popped off. And as Dante scrambled to his feet, he grabbed my leather jacket and helped me up.

"I'm gonna kill her," Mav growled as his trigger finger twitched.

"No!" Dante exclaimed, slamming his arm against Mav's, making him drop his gun.

"What the fuck!?" Mav exclaimed.

"I swear," the woman said with a deathly smile on her face, "this is better than cable."

"Enough," I grunted.

Dante and Mav looked over at me as I drew in a deep breath.

"We'll do as you ask, so long as you take us to her," I said.

"We're going to what?" Dante glowered.

I whipped toward him. "If she's dead, so is Brielle. If you haven't picked up on that yet, then it's your own damn fault for being so fucking blindsided. You, out of all of us, should've seen this coming. Why didn't you?"

The woman snickered. "Maybe it has something to do with the sex he had tonight."

I wanted to choke Dee out. "Are you fucking kidding me?"

Mav chuckled. "I knew when you walked in on us that—"

I slowly panned my gaze to Mav. "You fucked her, too?"

He shrugged. "You told her to make herself at home, so she did... on my face. What do you want from me?"

Red dripped over my vision as I slowly turned back toward the woman with the gun.

Who still wore Brielle's dress.

"We'll play ball," I said, placing my gun back into its holster on my hip, "but you take us to her. Immediately. Otherwise, we kill you and everyone else we can get our hands on before we're gunned down."

The woman winked at me as she holstered her gun again. "Good boy. Now come along, gentlemen. We don't want to keep anyone waiting."

My God, there was no telling what she had done with Brielle. For all we knew, her body had been discarded back at the charity gala. I couldn't stomach the thought. If Brielle was dead because my men thought with their dicks more than their brains—

"Come on!" I bellowed and Dante and Mav stared at me like I had lost my fucking mind. "Let's go! Or I'll be the one to put bullets in you."

"Ha-HAH!" the woman barked, throwing open the van doors and holding up the zip ties. "I can see why she likes you guys. Here."

And as I caught the zip ties against my chest, I knew only one thing for certain.

The second I got to wherever the hell we were headed, everyone who stood in the way of Brielle was dead. I promised I'd keep her safe, and I meant it. I promised her she'd be safe with us, and I meant it. She'd come back home, she'd go back to her life, no matter what I had to do in order to make that happen.

Even if it meant me giving my life for hers.

BRIELLE

My head ached. My body burned. Jesus, it felt like someone had run me through a fucking wood chipper. I tried to pick up my hanging head, but the ache in my joints kept it from leveling out on top of my shoulders. There was one thing, though. One thing that completely disarmed me.

There was silence.

"Hello?" I called out.

The sound wasn't very loud, though.

"Hello?!" I asked as I tried again.

God, my mouth was so dry. Why the hell was it dry?

As I moved my jaw, the ache shot down my neck. Jesus Christ, why the hell did I feel so terrible? I peeked one eye open and found myself staring down at the floor. A marble, tiled floor.

Holy fuck, was I still in the bathroom?

That woke me up. Despite the pounding in my head, I found myself perched on the tank of a toilet. My gaze focused long enough to find that one of my tits had almost slipped out of my strapless bra. The flimsy thong I wore had sat against my body long enough for Dante's mark to dry out, leaving it crunchy and hard against my skin. But I realized why my wrists hurt so fucking much.

They were bound with rope and tied to my goddamn ankles.

"Help meeee!" I cried out.

Something tugged at the edges of my lips. Something muted the sound of my voice. I moved my tongue around, trying to free it from its heaviness. However, it kept raking against something that felt almost cloth-like. Something damp dripped down my neck. It slithered toward my chest, making me grimace while the smell of Dante's cologne still hovered around me.

Did rich people not use the fucking restroom?

Did they just not have fucking bladders or something?

"Somebody! Help me!" I cried out.

There was no one, though. No music filtered through the door. No soft sounds of laughing and gossiping hit my ears. Hell, the bathroom had those automatic lights that clicked on and off whenever someone came in or left, and it took my eyes forever to adjust to the pitch blackness. Fear consumed me. If Dante didn't know that I was missing, then no one did.

Or maybe Dante was in trouble.

Which meant I was useless to him.

Maybe I've always been useless.

Tears streaked my cheeks. I tried to work loose the binds around my wrists, but the pain was excruciating. I had used a great deal of makeup to cover up the marks Axton had left behind in their faux-pas interrogation practices, and I felt my tears and my sweat carrying it away from my body. The pain made me groan. I doubled over, allowing the drool from my pried-open mouth to drop onto the toilet seat that my feet clung to for dear life.

Then, the bathroom door whipped open, and the light clicked on.

"Help!" I yelped as I tried my best to shield my eyes. "Someone, help me! I'm in here!"

Lumbering footsteps raced my heart. Holy fuck, they had found me. That was Axton. That had to be Axton. The canter was exactly like his. Heavy and slow, with a soft lilt that—

"Well, lookee who's still here."

The voice didn't belong to Axton, however, and that whipped my tired, throbbing gaze back open. I looked up into the burn scars the man used for a face and found that he wasn't wearing a brown leather jacket like the guys did, but a navy blue one. I shook my head and tried to scoot back against the wall. How I would've given anything to *osmosify* right through that painted plaster and pop out on the other side.

"Don't you fucking touch me," I warned.

But the lumbering man simply grinned before he picked me up and tossed me over his shoulder.

"Let go of me!" I shrieked.

He spanked my ass so hard that I yelped.

"Ah!"

The man chuckled. "If you're a good little thing for me, I'll give you more than that."

I kicked my bare feet in an attempt to throw him off, but it was no use. Every time I kicked my legs, it tugged at my wrists and shoulders so badly that I almost wished I were dead. I floated through the air, feeling that man's callused hands running up and down my naked skin. Bile crept up the back of my throat. It dripped through the gag in my mouth and ran down his leather jacket.

Until it finally dripped its stinging efforts onto his hand.

"You stupid bitch," he hissed.

"That's what you get, you stupid son of a—"

"Shut up," he said flatly.

I saw it coming that time. I watched him tilt me before he

swung me into the doorframe of the bathroom. I braced myself for the darkness. For the pain and possible concussion that would follow me the second my skull bashed into that painted wood. And when my temple connected, the night pulled me under. Taking me home, as if we were best friends.

Until it relinquished me back to a world where I no longer wanted to exist.

I didn't dare speak, though. My head pounded and my vision shook with each throb. My shoulders felt as if they had been set on fire and doused with gasoline. My hips screamed at me for a hot bath. The tires beneath me rattled with every divot we hit, and I bit down onto my tongue to keep from making any sort of sound.

I didn't want anyone knowing that I had woken up.

I couldn't think straight, though. With my head rattled and something dripping down the side of my face, I knew I needed a doctor. The nausea alone told me I was in big fucking trouble, but I had no way to get away. I was practically naked. My body had been rendered useless from the pain and the torture of the underbelly world around me. I had no idea what was going on, or what would happen to me, but I almost wished for death. I was a helpless, witless woman who had no business playing ball with the people I had found, and I no longer cared what happened to me.

So long as they were okay, and my twin sister got what was coming to her.

Then, the van stopped. It didn't slow to a stop, like at a stop sign or something. I mean, the brakes slammed down and my body rolled into something cold and hard. I grunted as my back tensed. I struggled to catch my breath.

Until I heard the most angelic voice.

"Brielle?" Dante asked.

I gasped. "Dee?"

"Holy shit, Brielle? Are you in here with us?"

Tears rushed my eyes. "Mav."

Something scooted across the floor before warmth penetrated my forehead, and I yanked myself back.

"It's just me," Axe said.

Tears flooded my cheeks as my head ached with pain. "Oh, God. I thought you guys were—I thought she—"

"It's okay," Dee said softly, "it's all right. We're gonna get you out of here."

Axe slid his fingertips along my forehead. "You're okay. We're right here, Brielle."

I wiggled myself around, shuffling closer to him before I laid my head in his lap. I never thought in a million years I'd want to be anywhere near him, much less in his lap, and yet his presence comforted me. Silent tears fell to his jeans beneath my cheek. His hand slid through the knotted tendrils of my hair, laced with the hairspray it took to hold my updo in place all night.

"I thought you guys were dead," I said through my gag.

"We gotta get that thing out of her mouth," Mav murmured.

"Yeah, once we free ourselves," Dee said.

"Free? What's wrong? Are you guys bound up, too?"

The doors of the van ripped open. "Zip ties are good for that kind of thing."

Axe growled almost immediately. "Get her covered up. Now."

"I'm gonna need your pretty little girlfriend for a second," that bitch said.

"Oh, hell no," I murmured.

"Get her," she said with a wicked smile on her face.

"Get your hands off her. Don't you touch her!" Mav bellowed.

I tried to wiggle away from the hands grasping for my body.

"Don't fight them, Brielle," Dee said. "Just let us handle this."

I whipped my head up. "So, you want me to just go with them?!"

Sadness filled his gaze. "It's our only shot."

So, I stopped fighting. I let whoever the fuck was trying to get to me grab my ankles. I yelped as they slid me toward the edge of the van before yanking me up by my arm, and it was then that the motherfucker with the burns on his face came into view.

"I need something to cover me up," I said plainly.

He tilted his head. "Or what?"

Someone grabbed my hair and yanked my head back. "Ah!"

My sister's upside-down face came into view. "Shut that fucking mouth, or I'll kill one of them just to prove my point. Got a preference for who should die first?"

I wanted to pretend none of it had happened. That I was living a ferocious nightmare and once I woke up, I'd be home. In my bed. With my alarm waking me up to get ready for school. Unfamiliar sights and sounds swirled around me as a bitter cold breeze kicked up, ratcheting up my pain levels. I couldn't help the way my nose wrinkled. The way my body trembled and gave way to the pain I had battled for days.

"Please, just let me go," I choked out through my sobs.

I'd never been so embarrassed in all my life.

"Well, well, well," she said as she walked around to my front, "here we are. Older sister, and younger sister."

My eyes widened as I drank her in. That pin straight black hair. The bangs that covered her big ass forehead. Those icy blue eyes that held absolutely no emotion behind them. I traced my gaze down her broad shoulders. I clocked her lopsided tits, floored that even her chest had developed exactly like mine.

Jesus, it was like looking into a damn mirror.

"Not too much to look at, I'll give her that," she said as she slid her gaze down my form.

Axe scoffed. "One look in the mirror should tell you that."

As if someone had pressed a button, she whipped around. Her hand flung through the air, and I lunged for her before the back of her hand ever approached Axe's face.

"Don't you fucking dare!" I yelped.

But the crack of her hand against his cheek was the only sound that answered me.

"Stay still, you little cum dumpster," Burnface hissed.

"What the fuck did you just call her?" Dante asked with that chilly voice of his.

Rachel turned back to me and closed the distance between us. She gripped my chin, and I tried pulling away, but the man behind me fisted my hair and straightened out my gaze. She held me steady as a smile crept across her face. A smile that lit up her features exactly the way mine did.

I didn't like being her twin.

"Maybe you are a bit... feisty," she said as she tilted her head. "Good. Means you're not a complete waste."

She pushed my head off to the side and I held back my whimper of pain. How the hell I ever thought I could help that woman was beyond me.

Just more ways for me to feel stupid while standing there fucking naked in front of the whole ass world.

"I'll accept my payment now," Rachel said as she peeked over my shoulder at the man holding me against him.

"Leave us be," the man said, "and we'll send it."

Rachel giggled. "I wasn't born yesterday. Transfer the money now, and when I've got it, I'll leave."

They stared one another down for the longest time before the man behind me relented. My body shuffled with his movements while he pivoted and swayed, and the entire time I kept my stare locked with my men. With Axton and the growing bruise on his cheek. With Dante and the anger seeping from his entire being. With Mav and the red-faced worry that filled his body as he continued to struggle against the zip ties.

Then, Rachel's phone lit up.

"Perfect," she said, tucking her phone into her bra.

Then, she turned to me.

"Thanks, sis. I really owe you one."

"NOW!" Axton bellowed.

22

———

AXTON

Thwip! Thwip! Thwip! Thwip!
POW, POW!
BOOM!

"Aaaaaaaahhhhhh!"

Dirt puffed up in small clouds of dust as bullets sank into the ground around my feet. Brielle's shriek rose above the chaos as the men who had followed us came out of the woodworks. Joules appeared on the roof of the abandoned warehouse, sinking .50 calibers next to Rachel's feet. Rocker and Locker came out with their goofy asses, twirling their guns around on their fingers as they pegged men left and right in the knees.

While the three of us sawed our zip ties off against the rusty van that had transported us.

"Aaaaaaahhhhh!" Brielle screamed.

The second my hands freed themselves, I charged her body. Her shivering, trembling, quaking form. I wrapped my arms around her and sprang to my feet. Bullets sank into the ground where we once stood, and I barely managed to scoop her against me before she flailed her feet.

"Let me go, you son of a bitch! Fucking coward!"

I gripped her hair and yanked her gaze up to mine. "Brielle, it's me."

She immediately stopped fighting and tears sprang to her eyes. "What's going on? What's happening?"

I pulled my knife out of my back pocket and flipped open the blade. "Hold still."

Her eyes widened. "Wh-wh-wh—what are you doing?"

"Freeing you."

"What?"

I slid the blade beneath the rope that bound her wrists to her ankles. With a flick of my wrist, the rope gave way to the sharpness of the metal. I grasped, and her arms fell free. She groaned and her head lobbed itself against my chest. She struggled to catch her breath as I stroked her hair with one hand and managed to pop open the restraints around her ankles with the other.

Then, I shrugged my coat off and wrapped it around her.

"Stay put," I said as I laid her down.

She quickly grabbed my wrist. "Where are you going!?"

"We could really use your help out here, Axe!" Mav bellowed.

I smoothed her hair away from her forehead. "Whatever you do, don't leave this van."

"But Axe. I—"

"Promise me."

She nodded quickly. "I promise."

"Good girl. I'll be back."

I planted my hands into the cold, hard, metallic van floor and shoved myself out in one fell swoop. My feet touched the ground before I whipped around, slamming the doors closed with my hands. Bullets whizzed by my ears. Men cried out for their mothers as they fell to the ground, bleeding from orifices I never thought blood could reach. Everything moved in slow motion. Everything smelled like blood, death, and gunpowder.

Until I saw that bitch running.

"Dante!" I roared as I pulled both guns off my hips.

"I see her!" he exclaimed.

"Come here, you stupid fuck!"

I turned toward the sound of the voice and didn't hesitate to tear two bullets through that nasty-colored navy-blue leather jacket. Leather had no business being any other color than what it was supposed to be, in my opinion. I mean, who the fuck was so pretentious that they dyed their fucking leather?

"Pussies," I murmured as their dead bodies hit the ground.

A bullet clinked off the side of the van and Brielle's shriek pulled me out of my hate-fueled trance. I whipped around, aiming both of my guns outward before Mav came up behind the motherfucker. I watched that bullet escape from between his eyeballs. Blood and brain matter splattered to the ground as the man dropped to his knees. No matter how many lives I took, that dead stare would never leave my mind. And as I watched the man look over at me with that blank stare, I aimed my gun at his chest.

Before putting a bullet in it just for good measure.

"You good?!" Mav called out.

Something glinted out of the corner of my eye. "Don't stop until all of those fuckers are dead."

He grinned wildly. "My pleasure."

He turned on his heels and headed for the first man he saw, and I got the sincere pleasure of watching him tackle that man to the ground. But the glinting out of the corner of my eye didn't stop. Even with chaos raining down, I managed to find the time to look down into the dirt. There was a phone sitting there. Just beneath the shade of a tree we had parked beneath. And even with my men barking out orders to those around them, it didn't stop me from scooping the damned thing up.

Before I realized what I was looking at.

"Oh, hell yeah," I said as a wicked smirk crossed my cheek.

One touch of the screen, and I realized the phone hadn't locked itself yet. The interface was black with neon blue letters, and the green checkmark beside a six-million-dollar transfer made my fucking mouth water. It couldn't be. There was no fucking way she'd be that stupid.

And yet, the proof was in the pudding.

"All right, then," I murmured as I hung my guns from my fingers and started typing with my thumbs, "let's see how you like... this."

I ducked behind the van to get away from the barrage of bullets. Someone had spotted me in the shadows, and that meant I had to get away from the van. I had to pull the gunfire away from Brielle, unless we all wanted something irreparable to happen, and that sure as fuck wasn't happening on my watch. I waited for the transaction to take. I waited as that money transferred from one bank account to another. And when that green checkmark popped up, I tossed the phone to my feet.

Before plugging it with two bullets.

"Take that, bitch," I glowered.

"Jesus Christ," Dante hissed as he came around the back of the van, "the hell are you doing back here?"

I grinned. "You guys will figure it out in a couple of hours."

He blinked as he fired a bullet over his shoulder. "Whatever. You gonna ask?"

I aimed my gun around the corner of the van as footsteps trickled up the left-hand side. Brielle whimpered in the back, scrambling around to try and get away from the noise. She shrieked when I pulled the trigger, since I didn't have mufflers on my guns like Dante did. And when I heard the telltale sign of a lifeless body dropping to the ground, I smiled.

"So, how the fuck did the guys know how to find us?" I asked.

Dante patted his back pocket. "Silent alarm. I set the guys up with it. It broadcasts our location to their phones with an emergency—hold on."

He peered around the right side of the van and let loose enough bullets to level a fucking elephant. Then, he slammed the guns against his hips, reloading them with the magazines protruding from his tailor-made leather holster.

"Nice," I said.

"Anyway, when it broadcasts to their phone, it makes this sound that—"

I held my finger up. "Hold on."

"Come here, you cowards," someone growled.

I stepped out from behind the van, ready to drown that motherfucker in his own blood. But before I had the pleasure, the man's eyes widened. A bullet pierced through his chest from behind, spewing blood from his mouth that he coughed onto my jeans.

"Jesus fuck, Mav. Really?" I asked when the man collapsed onto the ground. "I'm gonna have to wash these damn things again."

Mav shrugged as he held his gun at his side. "You need to wash a lot of things, in my opinion."

Dante sighed as he came out from behind the van. "Silent alarm. Makes big noise. Broadcast's location."

I reached out and patted his shoulder. "Good call. You get a raise."

"Thanks," he said with a snicker.

"We need to burn this place and get the fuck out of here," Mav said as he charged toward the back of the van. "I've already talked to Joules, Wolf, and Rocker. They're going to stay behind and get rid of the bodies."

"They'll need a van to do it, so it might as well be this one," I said.

Mav threw open the doors. "Brielle? You back here?"

"Mav!" she squealed.

The van rocked with her movements as she rushed to get into his arms. She clamored toward him, throwing her arms around his neck, and tucking her nearly naked body against his. He hoisted her into his arms before he backed away from the van. And then, it hit me.

"Actually, I have a better plan," I said as I peered across the lot we had been abandoned in, essentially. "She rides shotgun. Blaze!"

The man jogged past me. "Already on it. Gimme a few seconds and it'll be up and running."

"What will be up and running?" Dante asked.

I pointed. "That."

With bodies littering the ground at our feet, I watched our clean-up crew drag them toward the van. Brielle cried softly against Mav's shoulder, a sound I hoped to never hear again so long as I lived. It broke something inside of me. Something cold and hard. She didn't deserve to cry like that. To be exposed to the masses while blood splattered all around her.

She was better than that.

She was better than the life we led.

"Holy shit," Dante said breathlessly.

"Where are we going?" Mav asked impatiently.

I pointed to the short, white bus that had been abandoned at whatever defunct junk yard we had found ourselves in. Blaze already had himself tucked up underneath the vehicle, checking things over with that keen eye of his. If anyone could fix that thing and get it to run, it was him.

"How long!?" I called out.

Blaze slid out from beneath the chassis. "Ten, fifteen minutes!?"

"Perfect," I said as I turned to Dante. "Let's help the clean-up crew get those bodies in the back of the van."

"What do you want us to do?" Mav asked.

My gaze scanned over a shivering Brielle. "Get her away from the van. Maybe take her over next to Blaze. Once he's got that thing cranked up, throw her in the bus and come get us."

"On it," he said as he brushed past me.

"Wolf," I said as I reached out and grabbed his arm before he passed by me.

"What's up, boss man?"

I slowly looked over at him. "When you get this van across the border, light that son of a bitch on fire. We can't have our DNA anywhere near this thing."

He wiggled his eyebrows. "Sounds like Daddy gets to have some fun."

I rolled my eyes and released him. "Just do it."

"You know I will, boss man."

Damn near twenty minutes passed by before we all got into our respective vehicles, and not a siren was to be heard. Good. Well, not good, because that meant those assholes were intent on killing us and leaving us for dead. But good because the last thing we needed was to content with the fucking police. I climbed into the driver's seat of that bus with Dante and Mav riding in the seats behind me. Blaze took up a spot near an emergency exit window, where he perched with his guns at the ready. I watched as the clean-up crew pulled out of the junk-yard with the van full of bodies. I saw Joules and Jax use any tools they could find to toss the dirt and sand around, covering up the blood stains their bodies left behind.

And when every last one of my men was free from the junk-yard's confines, I stepped on the gas.

"Let's get the fuck out of here," I growled. "And someone get Doc on the phone!"

Pulling into the dirt parking lot of the clubhouse rushed a feeling of relief through me that damn near made me nauseous. We were working three steps behind our enemy, and I hated that feeling. The entire time, that bitch had been one step ahead of us. Planning. Conniving. Setting things up so that she bene-fitted from everyone else's chaos.

I hated people like that.

Without a word, I parked the bus. I tore up from the driver's seat and made my way for Brielle. She sat there, slouched in her seat with my leather coat still covering her body, and she stared mindlessly out the window.

"Ready to go inside?" I asked.

But all she did was lean her body in my general direction.

"Good girl," I murmured as I scooped her up.

"What do you need us to do, boss man?" Blaze asked.

I cradled Brielle against my chest. "Let's get this bus back to our workshop. It could be useful to us."

"Oh, hell yeah," Blaze said, eyeballing the driver's seat, "a new project."

"I'll go with him, just in case," Dante said as he cocked his gun.

I nodded. "Good idea. Mav?"

He completed my thought process. "Check in on the clean-up crew. I got ya. And Doc should be inside the clubhouse wait-ing. He sent me a text."

I drew in a deep breath before walking past him. "Thanks, appreciate it."

"Anytime."

With one last nod of my head, I carried Brielle off that bus. She didn't say a word as we headed for the porch. There wasn't a sniffle or a sob. No words were exchanged, and no whimpers were heard. Her spent body laid there in my arms, completely vulnerable to me when at one point in time, she couldn't even stand to look at me.

I made myself a silent vow at that moment.

You'll never be scared of me again.

"Is that my patient I hear?" Doc called out as I walked us through the front door.

"Come with me upstairs, she needs to lie down."

I heard him shuffling quickly down the hallway. "Lead the way, then."

I carried her up the steps and made my way toward her room. Well, in my mind, it was her room. She had found a home within it. It brought her comfort and solace. I mean, she had christened the bathroom for herself, anyway. As far as I was concerned, that would always be her bedroom.

"Here we go," I grunted as I laid her down in her bed, "safe and sound."

She just laid there, though. Immobile. Unwavering.

As if she were frozen in time.

"Guess that's my cue," Doc said, placing his massive medical bag down at the foot of the bed. "Miss Brielle?"

She didn't respond, though.

"Miss Brielle, if I could get you to sit up for me, I'm going to check you for a concussion. You've got a pretty good-sized knot on your head, and it's deeply bruised."

It killed me, watching her stare at the wall like that. Her

gaze, blank. Her face, immobile. Her body, refusing to even acknowledge the fact that someone was talking.

What had we done to her?

I cleared my throat and backed toward the bedroom door. "Doc's gonna look you over, Brielle. But, in the meantime, if you need any—"

"Get in bed with me."

Doc chuckled, but her command whipped me around in my spot.

"What was that?"

She sniffled. "Please. Just—for the appointment. Doctors have always made me so fucking nervous. I won't keep you long. Just until he's done. I swear."

How could I say no to such a request? "Fair enough."

"You're good to go anytime, Doc. Just don't make me sit up if I don't have to. My head hurts so bad," she said softly.

"Of course," Doc said as he crouched down to her level, "we can do the exam from this angle."

I kicked off my boots before crawling into bed behind her. She pressed herself against me, angling that plump ass of hers until it sat directly against my pelvis. I had to swallow the growl percolating up the back of my throat. I had to restrain my hands that wanted nothing more than to slide between her legs and stuff her holes. But as she reached behind her, she grabbed my wrist, pulling my arm across her waist.

"Just for a few minutes," she whispered.

"Of course," I murmured as I slid my leg between hers. "However long you need."

"Now, Brielle," Doc said as he pulled out that little flashlight of his, "you need to tell me, on a scale of one to ten, how much this hurts. Okay? I'm going to flash this light in your eyes, but only for a second."

She nodded softly. "Okay."

"You ready?"

"Yeah, yeah, I'm ready."

I held her tightly as that telltale click echoed across her room. And it didn't take long before she tried to crawl her way into my ribcage to get away from the assault.

"Fuck, fuck, fuck. Doc. Stop. Please," Brielle begged.

"Turn it off," I growled.

Doc clicked the light off. "All right, you're going to feel my hands on the nape of your neck. Don't be alarmed, but I do want you to tell me if you experience any sort of topical pain while I'm poking around. Okay?"

She sniffled. "Okay."

God fucking damn it, I knew she had a concussion.

"Anything?" Doc asked as he wrapped his fingertips around to the back of her neck.

"Nothing," Brielle muttered.

He danced them up and down the back of her head. "What about now?"

"Not really. The headache overrides it."

"Where's the headache?"

She picked up her hand and swirled it around toward the front of her skull. "All around here?"

"Is it shaking your vision?"

"Uh-uh."

"Good, good," Doc said as he stood and stretched his arms above his head.

"So?" I asked.

"Oh, I'm not done," Doc said, "I just needed a stretch."

"Right," I murmured.

The appointment went on, with Doc checking her from head to toe. He looked at her bare wrists and ankles, tilting her joints as far as she'd let him so that he could get a good look at the healed skin and the fading bruises.

"She looks healthier overall. More nourished," Doc said mindlessly.

"They've been trying," Brielle said breathlessly.

"Good. That's good," Doc said as he repositioned her legs. "I'm going to test your joints and make sure there's no other phantom pains anywhere that we need to address."

I helped ease Brielle onto her back. "You okay?"

She nodded and gazed up at me. "Yeah, I'm okay."

"You need anything?"

She reached out and grabbed my hand. Well, my thumb. She wrapped her hand around my fucking thumb, and my heart melted.

I knew that as long as she was with us, she'd always hold me hostage.

"All right, Doc," Brielle said as she squeezed my thumb, "let's do this."

I braced myself. I waited for the shrieks of pain. For the blood we hadn't seen. For the wounds we hadn't clocked. I brushed her hair away from her forehead while her stare stayed connected with the ceiling. And fucking hell, I had to resist every single urge that I had to dip down and kiss her.

Just to keep her from worrying so damn much.

"Well, I've got good news and bad news," Doc said after about twenty minutes.

"Bad news?" I asked.

"What's the good news?" Brielle asked.

"The good news," Doc said, perching himself on the edge of her side of the bed, "is that you're going to be just fine."

Brielle sighed with relief, almost as if she didn't believe she would have been.

The thought broke my heart.

"And the bad news?" I asked.

Doc clicked his tongue. "You don't technically have a concussion, but I need you to treat yourself as if you do."

"I'm not following," Brielle said.

"Concussions are rated on a scale of one to ten, based on their symptoms and how bad the trauma is. You've gotten socked in your head pretty good, but none of your symptoms are near that level one threshold."

"That still sounds like good news, Doc," I said.

He held up his finger at me. "The problem is that if you experience any other sort of trauma—a bump that's too much, or being shook up too much, or another little whack to the head—and you're going to need a hospital for your concussion."

"Ah, that's the bad news," I said flatly.

"So," Doc said, pressing his hands into his knees and standing, "Doctor's orders are to rest for the next week."

Brielle bolted upright. "The next week!?"

Doc nodded. "One week, in bed, very little movement or jostling."

She looked between me and Doc. "I can't stay here another week. I have a family to get back to. A home. A job. Goddamn it, you guys, I have a fucking career to get back to!"

"And you will," I said as I helped lay her back down, "but even if you were on the job right now, you know they'd send you home."

She hissed up at me. "My job wouldn't have abducted me and kept me prisoner in a fucking basement."

Fucking hell, the mess we had created with her. I wasn't sure I'd ever forgive myself.

"You're right," I said.

Tears lined her gaze. "Thanks for coming, Doc."

He patted her head. "I know it isn't the news that you wished to hear, but it is going to do you a great deal of good. You'll rest, you'll recuperate, you'll eat lots of good food that I'm sure Mav wouldn't mind whipping up for you at the drop of a hat—"

"You got that right," I muttered.

"—and then you'll be on your way home, I'm sure. Right?" Doc asked.

I felt his stare boring into my forehead, and I raised my gaze to meet his. "Right."

He nodded, but that pointed look of his didn't fade. "See? Told you so."

Brielle drew in a broken breath. "Do I need any medicine?"

"Did that Tylenol with codeine treat you okay?"

"Yeah, it did. I've still got a couple left, too."

"Well, stop taking them," he said as he jammed his hand into his bag. "Codeine increases brain bleed risks in those with compromised brain tissue, which you've got."

He plopped a bottle of extra strength Tylenol on her nightstand.

"That's it? Tylenol?" I asked.

Doc snapped his bag closed. "Unfortunately, not much takes away a concussion headache. Most pain medications are laced with things that increase bleeding risks, so we can't give her those until she's better. Acetaminophen is about the only thing that she can take that won't come with any serious risks."

"I'll take it, then," Brielle whispered.

I reached my hand up. "Thanks, Doc. We really appreciate it."

He shook my hand as his face finally softened. "Anytime, day or night. You know the drill."

"Can I ask one more question?" Brielle asked.

Doc paused. "You can ask as many as you'd like."

Her cheeks flushed a deep shade of crimson, and I thought something was wrong. But, before I could grill her on what was happening, the question she blurted out stopped my heart in my chest.

"What about sex?" she asked quickly.

Doc blinked. "What about it?"

Brielle shrugged softly. "Is that... off limits? You know, with the whole 'no jostling around' thing?"

I slowly raked my gaze up toward Doc, who simply stood there with a calm and collected smile on his face.

"As long as it isn't too strenuous for you, sex is just fine," Doc said.

Brielle drew in a deep breath. "Okay, good to know."

"Anything else?" he asked.

She buried her head into the pillow. "No, that's all."

I thumbed over my shoulder. "You can see yourself out?"

A smirk ticked his cheeks. "I may stop by the kitchen and see if Mav has whipped anything up. But, yes. I can see myself out."

"Thanks," I said, settling back down next to Brielle, "payment will be in your account—"

"—before I get home, I know, I know," he said as he wrapped around the bed and slipped out the door. "And Brielle?"

"Yeah, Doc?"

"I mean it when I say rest, okay? Don't make me meet you at the hospital because you wouldn't listen."

She snickered. "I'll do my best Doc."

"That's all I can ask."

I expected her to kick me out of the bed once Doc closed the door behind him. So, I started to shift. I unraveled my arm from around her and pulled my leg out from between her gloriously comfortable thighs.

And to my shock, she grabbed my wrist and tugged me back.

"Just a few more minutes," she whispered.

"Are you sure?" I asked.

She nodded softly; her hair splayed against the white pillowcase. "I'm sure. I just... don't want to be alone right now."

It didn't take her long to drift off to sleep. As I settled back down next to her, drawing in the scent of whatever she used for shampoo, it took every single shred of self-control inside of me not to flip her over, pin her down, and take that pillowy ass of hers as mine. She was so beautiful and smelled so divine. She was a hell of a firecracker, too. Always willing to get into trouble and rarely ever complaining about the consequences. I knew she wanted to go home. She had to have missed her family throughout all this time. But we couldn't relinquish her. Not until we knew she was safe. Not until we knew that the bitch still running around out there wouldn't come after her simply out of spite.

So, I held her. I held her and felt her rocking against me with soft movements that eventually ceased. And after ten or so minutes, she was out like a light. I couldn't sleep, though. Not after what had happened. My mind raced with all sorts of thoughts. All sorts of what if's and different nightmares that could have come straight from a scenario like the one we had found ourselves in.

No matter what, though, I knew one thing for certain.

I sure as fuck wasn't leaving her side until she was ready to kick me out.

The sun sank beneath the horizon, filling her bedroom with rays of darkness. Stars hung low in the sky beyond her bay window, and I found myself gazing out over the endless, cracked ground of the desert. There was a beauty to the old, weathered peace we got out there. The clubhouse had taken years for us to build, and there were still things we wanted to do with the place. It served its purpose, however. It kept us concealed, it kept us safe, and it kept us off most people's radars.

Which meant that bitch of a twin couldn't have found us without the stunt she pulled at the gala.

The soft rapping against the door made me draw in a deep breath. "Come in, Dee."

He cracked the door open. "You awake?"

"Does it sound like I ever fell asleep?"

He inched the door open more. "She sleeping?"

I rolled over and looked over at him. "Has been for a few hours now."

"And... you're not?"

"Waiting for you."

He chuckled as he peeked his head around the corner. "Awww, didn't know you missed me so much."

"If I had something to throw right now, I would."

He smiled, for once in his fucking life. "Just wanted to let you know that everything has been taken care of. The guys are home safe, everyone's settling in, and Mav thinks it's smart to have church in the morning."

"Me, too. See everyone at ten."

"I'll let them know."

"And Dee?"

He paused. "Yeah?"

"Get some rest. Some actual rest. Because we've got a lot to do to dig ourselves out of this hole."

His sigh told me everything about his state of mind. "You got it."

And as he closed the door, I rolled back toward Brielle, pulling her closely against me and drifting off to sleep.

23

———

MAVERICK

"How the fuck did this happen?"

"No one pulls the wool over Dante's eyes, he had to have known something was up."

"Hey, you leave him out of this. They've been juggling a lot."

"Yeah, like getting their dicks wet."

"Hey!" I barked as I walked into the room.

The men immediately quieted down, and I went and stood at the head of the table.

"Has anyone seen Axton yet?"

And right on cue, he came prancing into the room with his fingers soaring away over his cell phone screen. I scoffed and folded my arms across my chest. He was already fifteen minutes late to church, which was something none of us did. When a church time was set, you fucking showed up.

It didn't look good that our own fucking President was late.

"Care to join us?" I asked flatly.

He pressed a button dramatically with his pointer finger before smiling up at us, and when he did, our phones buzzed.

Screens lit up in pockets. Ringers poured their music into the room at a rapid pace.

"What the hell, Axe?" I asked.

He slid his phone into his pocket. "Check your phone."

"Four hundred thousand dollars!?" Rocker exclaimed.

My eyes widened as I ripped my phone out of my pocket. I didn't even have to open the screen to see the notification, though. It was from my bank. A deposit for exactly four hundred thousand dollars.

"Consider it your yearly bonus," Axton said, shoving me out of the way.

I didn't even care that I stumbled and almost hit the fucking floor. "Where the hell did you get this money?"

The guys were too busy high-fiving one another to pay attention to my question.

"Axe?" I asked.

The guys settled down when he raised his hand into the air. Everyone fell silent before he slowly lowered his hand toward the table, and every single man in that room took their seats. It was amazing to me how he could command a room. How just the smallest flick of his wrist had all of us falling in line. No one was shocked when Luca picked him as Vice President. No one was shocked when he seamlessly transitioned us from Luca's reign to his.

And as he stood there with a proud grin on his face, he drew in a deep breath.

"Everything got fucked yesterday," he said plainly.

Blaze scoffed. "You can say that again."

"Everything got fucked yesterday."

Dee chuckled. "Someone's in a good mood."

He peeked over at Dee. "You mean, four hundred big ones aren't reason enough to celebrate?"

"You got to her money, didn't you?" I asked.

Axe peered over at me from over his shoulder. "She dropped her phone when she took off. Or maybe it slipped out of her pocket. But it hadn't been on the ground long enough for her phone to lock itself back up. So, I found a new home for her money."

"Hell yeah," Jax said with a broad smile.

"So, does this mean we can finally talk about what the fuck that bitch got out of all this?" Dee asked.

Jax snickered. "Outside of six mil?"

I shook my phone at the guys. "Which we obviously have, so that's not it. This woman isn't stupid. She's never been this sloppy. So, why start now?"

Joules finally opened his mouth. "Maybe all of this revolving around her twin sister threw her off?"

Dee shook his head, though. "Gotta have a soul for something like that."

Blaze cleared his throat. "She got all the way back here before Dee knew something was up for real. Was she trying to scope the layout of this place?"

Axe shook his head. "She never got past the foyer before she exposed who she was."

The table fell silent before Dante's face ignited with angry red.

"Oh, no," he glowered.

"What?" I asked as I stepped out of the shadows and up to the table. "Spit it out."

Dee quickly stood. "Protocol. She was sniffing out our protocol."

Axe furrowed his brow tightly. "That would mean she's working with those assholes."

"Do you really think she'd work with Pilot?" Joules asked.

Axe shrugged. "It sure as fuck looked like she was working with them last night."

"It makes sense," Dee said as he tilted his head. "I mean, think about it: she sees an opportunity to cash in on our bounty while also scoping out how we respond to immediate hostage situations."

I shook my head. "To what end, though? What's the point in knowing our protocol if she knows we're just going to change it after the fact?"

No one had an answer. Hell, not even a suggestion. Even Dee flopped back down into his seat and pinched the bridge of his nose. He was the best of us in these situations. The profiler. The people-reader. If anyone should have been able to answer that question, it was him.

And he had nothing.

"So," Wolf said as he rubbed his hands up and down his thighs, "you mean to tell me that this bitch is running around out there, free as a damn bird, and we've got no clue what she wants, no clue where she is, and no clue what her endgame is?"

"Yep," Dee said breathlessly.

"The fuck are we supposed to do with that, then?" Jax asked.

I raked my hands through my hair and turned away from the table.

"Take a breath, Mav," Axe said flatly.

That made me angry, though. "We promised to keep her safe!"

I spun myself around and pointed my finger in Axe's face.

"We gave her our word, man! And look at what our word got her!"

"You think I don't know that!?" he roared as he threw his hands into the air. "You think I'm just gonna go about this all willy fucking nilly and not give a damn about what this is doing to her? About what it's doing to all of us?!"

His voice rang in my ears. It pounded my head as he

hovered over me with anger in his voice. I'd never seen him like that before. Scrambling. Fearful. Worried.

Then, the heavens parted for us.

"I think I know what she's after."

All of us turned at the sound of her voice. We turned toward the door and saw her standing there, draped in a long shirt and a pair of sweatpants. Her hair sat tangled against the crown of her head. She yawned as she rubbed her eyes, and I rushed toward her. I tucked a loose strand of hair behind her ear before she threaded her arms around my neck, and her hug was so warm and so comforting that I almost forgot where I was.

Until Axe cleared his throat. "Come on in, Brielle. Everyone?"

The guys mumbled their names as I walked her to the head of the table. "You okay to do this?"

She nodded softly as she cupped my cheek. "I know what she wants, Mav."

"What does she want?" Axe asked, standing behind her.

She turned toward the head of the table and found all eyes on her.

"We're ready when you are," Dee said, looking up at her.

Then, she took a deep breath in through her nose.

"So, I was going back over the paperwork you guys gave me when I woke up this morning..."

24

BRIELLE

You know that feeling when you want your eyes to stay closed so badly, but they simply won't? Where you battle your own eyelids for a few more minutes of sleep, only to be pulled awake because they can't stand to be closed any longer?

That was how I felt when I raised myself up from bed.

"Axton?" I asked groggily, swinging my legs over the edge of the bed.

I didn't expect him to be there, especially after everything that had happened. But the lack of his voice and his presence gave me pause. My body ached in so many wondrous ways that it made me shiver. Thoughts of last night raced through my mind, shivering me to my core as if we had never stopped. I raked my hands through my hair, catching my knuckles on knots that made me hiss as I stood to my feet. And after I dragged my ass into the bathroom, I stared at myself in the mirror.

Watching my eyes stare right back at me.

"Jesus," I whispered, turning on the sink.

Splashing some cold water in my face helped my brain to wake up, but I needed coffee. Coffee, and a shower. I needed something substantial if I had any hope of making myself useful.

I couldn't leave things as they were, not when that psycho maniac was still running around out there. For all I knew, my fucking family was in trouble. For all I knew, she had researched me and put my parents in her crosshairs simply for passing her over for adoption.

Why did she get passed over for adoption?

As I gazed at my naked body in the mirror, I thought back to those papers. To that file Dante had given me while I had been in that bath. Jesus, it felt like a fucking lifetime ago. Water dripped off my chin onto my chest, highlighting the fading marks Dante had left behind with his mouth. I grinned as my fingertips danced along their swollen existences. A warmth cascaded through me, like a waterfall spilling over the edge of a hot cliff face. But even as I stood there remembering the carnal desires we indulged the night of the gala, that question kept running circles around my thoughts.

"Why the hell wasn't she adopted?" I murmured to myself.

I yanked the hand towel off its rack and wiped off my face. Then, I pivoted toward the shower and couldn't move quickly enough to turn on the hottest water that I could stand. I was coated in things I didn't even want to look at. I had dirt caked in places that dirt should never touch. The water poured down to the marble shower floor, and as I stripped out of my clothes, I relished the way the steam gathered all around me.

As if it were cloaking me away from the world.

"Oh, hell yeah," I groaned as I stepped into the walk-in.

It felt like I hadn't taken a decent shower in days. Dirt and mud dripped down my body, rolling with the beads of water, carrying the stains of my sins toward the drain. I dipped my head and let the water wash over me like ocean waves battering against a sandy shoreline. I pressed my hands into the tiled wall. Steam filled my nostrils and my lungs, hydrating me from the inside out. The hairs on the nape of my neck stood on end and my muscles involuntarily clenched and released.

Clenched, and released.

Clenched, and released.

"Goddamn it, I love this shower," I whispered to myself.

I took the time to lather myself up right. I took the time to wash my hair and clean myself up. I was tired of smelling like lies and blood. I was tired of walking around, clueless as to when I'd be able to go home. It wasn't that I didn't like it at the clubhouse. Honestly, it was growing on me. It all was. They all were. But I missed my family. I wanted them to know that I was okay. I wanted to make sure they were all right.

Because for all I knew, they were just as much of a target as I was.

And that revelation was enough to pull me out of the shower.

"Shit," I hissed, turning off the water.

I barely got the towel wrapped around me before I dashed out of the bathroom, on a mission for clothing as I threw open drawers and flung open closet doors. I scrounged around until I found a t-shirt that was much too big for me and a pair of sweat-pants that could have drowned me if I gave it the opportunity, and I stopped to draw in their scents. They smelled like my guys. Sandy and wind-torn with just a hint of leather.

I could have crawled into bed and gone right back to sleep in those clothes.

But instead, I threw the clothes on and booked it for the kitchen. Those papers had to be somewhere, and the last place I had seen them were on the table. My gaze fished around the place, and I made a pot of coffee. I threw open cabinets and pulled open drawers, hoping, and praying I'd come across that manilla envelope. If I wanted to help my family and save myself, I had to figure out why the hell my twin sister hadn't been adopted. I had to figure out why in the world she was doing all of this. Maybe it had nothing to do with me, but maybe it had everything to do with me.

And the risk to my family was enough for me to consider all sides of the equation.

"Looking for this?"

Dante's voice popped up behind me and it made me smile. I caught his gaze in the kitchen window and I saw him leaning against the doorframe, looming over the only entrance in and out of the room. I slowly turned toward him, leaning against the countertop as I folded my arms across my chest. And while the coffee percolated in the glass container, he stalked toward me with those hunter green eyes of his, pinning me to my spot.

"Thank you, Dante," I said, fluttering my eyelashes at him.

He chuckled as he settled it silently onto the countertop to my left. "Morning."

I smiled up at him. "Morning."

"Enjoy your evening?"

I blushed beneath his gaze. "Want some coffee?"

He tucked a loose strand of hair behind my ear. "Don't mind if I do, thanks."

He tossed me a playful wink before moving toward the coffee pot. His long, languid movements caught my attention as I mindlessly placed my hand on top of that folder. I knew the answer was in there somewhere. The reason for all of her shit was buried within the contents of the words on the papers Dante had pieced together of his own volition. I watched as he poured himself a mug of black coffee. I watched the way those thin lips of his curled around the edge of the cup, his Adam's apple bobbing with his silent movements.

There wasn't a damn thing about him that I didn't find completely intoxicating.

And he knew it.

"Church calls," he said, turning toward the hallway.

"Will it take long?" I asked after clearing my throat.

"Why?" he asked, making his way to the doorway. "Miss us already?"

I giggled. "Something like that."

He peered over his shoulder. "Don't worry, we won't be long."

Then, he disappeared toward the stairs before floating up them like the fucking ghost he was.

"Wow," I whispered and quickly dropped my attention back to the document.

The coffee was soon forgotten about while I dove into the medical records of our birth. It didn't shock me that they had mine, and I rummaged around for anything to write with as I tried to figure out the medical jargon typed and scribbled about. I finally found a green highlighter, of all things, and found myself perched at the countertop next to the piping hot coffee that sat on the hot burner, just waiting to be chugged.

"Come on," I grumbled as I mindlessly reached up for a mug above my head, "you've gotta be in here somewhere."

But I didn't even get my first sip of coffee in me before my gaze landed on the one word I had been looking for.

And I sure as fuck didn't need Google to tell me what it meant.

"So, I was going back over the paperwork you guys gave me when I woke up this morning," I said, setting my mug of coffee down onto the table in front of me, "and I came across something that I think answers our questions."

"What the fuck is this?"

"Why the hell is she here?"

"Uh, miss, we're having a church meeting. You need to go."

"Do you have information for us?" Axe asked.

I peeked up at him. "I wouldn't be here if I didn't."

"She stays, then," Dante said.

"Since when?"

"Can it, Blaze," Mav said.

The man shot up from his seat. "She's caused us enough shit, don't you think?"

"Shut the fuck up," Axe said flatly.

"He's got a point," a man with disheveled hair and pocked skin on his face said. "She pops up from out of nowhere, and all of a sudden, she's weighing in and running things? It's been disrespectful around here for a while, but this is our crew. Our turf. Our bounty. Our job. She's got no place in it."

"Unless she's got information we can use," Axe said curtly.

The guys fell silent as I dropped my gaze to the manilla folder I still clutched in my hands. I hadn't realized that my presence had stirred things up this way between all of them.

I regretted ever coming upstairs.

"Anytime now," a man with mutton chops murmured. "I'm already getting tired of sitting here."

Dante's face turned to ice, and he stared the man down. "Wolf."

But I simply held out my hand. "Mind if I use your cell phone, Wolf?"

The hairy-faced man looked around before he shuffled in his seat. "Yes, I mind."

"Wolf," Axe barked.

The predator of a man didn't take his eyes off me. "Why my phone?"

I wiggled my fingertips. "Because you're being such a good sport right now. Figured I'd reward you."

"At least she's got spunk," someone muttered.

Wolf scoffed. "If she runs this shit into the ground and gets one of us killed—"

Axe snarled behind me. "Just do it, Wolf."

And with a roll of his eyes, the man lifted his ass, pulled out his burner cell, unlocked it, and then tossed it to me.

"Good thing I got another one to use," he grumbled.

"When I woke up this morning, the first thing that came to mind was that the answers on why my sister is doing this has to be in those documents Dante put together," I said as I pulled up the internet.

"The very first thing?" Axe asked.

I giggled. "You mean, you want me to tell them that the very first thing on my mind this morning when I woke up was the fact that you burped in my ear?"

His face immediately fell. "I fucking did not."

I tossed him a playful wink, though. "It'll be our little secret, no worries."

"I didn't fucking do that, Brielle."

The room came to life with cackles and hands clapping, which only made Axe stare at me harder. I swear, he was the cutest human being with his nose wrinkled up the way it did when he got annoyed.

"You got any other stories to tell us?" Wolf asked with a smirk.

"Quit giving me shit about your phone," I said as I tossed him a playful wink, "and I'll tell you about the time Dante decided—"

"Enough," Mav said, lobbing his gaze in my general direction. "Get on with it, beautiful."

Wolf pointed at me. "You owe me that story later."

"She owes us a fuckton for even being entertained during this meeting," someone grumbled.

"Anyone else would've been killed for barging through those doors," someone else spat.

I knew I was on thin ice standing in front of all of them, and I wanted to make sure I did right by them. But, if embarrassing stories of the guys got them in my good graces, they'd all just have to take one for the team.

Some other time, though.

"Anyway, my point is," I said, pulling up the definition of the condition my sister had been born with on Wolf's cell, "I know why she's doing all of this."

"We're on the edges of our seats," a buff man with a fully-grown beard said.

"And you are?" I asked.

He sat up straight and cracked his back. "Rocker."

I nodded. "Noted. But don't fall off the edge of that seat just yet. It gets a bit convoluted. You can catch up by passing around Wolf's phone and reading those definitions to yourself. That'll make it easier to listen to what I have to say."

A man sitting beside Rocker scoffed. "Really, Axe?"

I peered over my shoulder. "What?"

Dante crossed his arms over his chest and the guys just stared at the phone as if it were a grenade I had pulled the pin on. "Why don't you just give us the bullet points?"

"Or, they could read," I said, fluttering my eyelashes playfully at him.

A man who hadn't yet introduced himself scoffed. "You come into our territory, fuck up our turf, get yourself caught at an undercover sting not all of us were on board for in the first place, and now you expect us to listen to your every whim just because you flounce your tits around and smile pretty?"

"Watch it," Axe growled.

"No," the man said as he stood. "No. We've been through

enough. This crew has lost enough. We've rebuilt stronger than ever after Luca's death. And now, we're casting off all bounties heading our way because we want to chase this very specific bitch down."

"Got a problem with that?" Dante asked.

The man held his head high with pride. "Yeah, I do. We're watching some woman we don't know after only a few days with us touting shit around and bossing us around like she owns the damn place."

Murmurs of approval filtered through the crowd as I took a small step away from my position.

"Not to mention," Wolf said and stood, "these plans. Not all of us have been on board from the beginning. You guys know that. But we trusted you enough to follow."

"Our trust is about to wear thin," Rocker said, standing.

The man beside him stood as well. "And if she's not careful, we're gonna have a dead, innocent woman on our hands while Luca's murderer gets away."

"Again," Wolf said flatly.

"All right, all right," Mav said, holding up his hands, "why don't we all just—."

"You're right," I said.

That froze the room, and all eyes were on me as I tossed the contents of the manilla folder onto the table in front of me.

"You're right," I said again as I gazed around the room, "this is a private conversation meant for a family I'm not part of, and I understand that. But I also understand that I'm now part of this. I was made part of this when I was mistaken for her, held in your basement, starved, beaten, and dehydrated for two solid days."

I looked each of them square in their eyes as I spoke.

"I mean no disrespect, but if we want to talk about who disrespected me first? It's the three men standing behind me. Three men who took me right from out in front of my home on a random Tuesday morning while I was trying to get to work. I was stolen, so if you want to be pissed that I'm part of this? That I have input? That I'm just as much of a target as you guys are? Then be pissed at the three men standing behind me. But I've got information you need to know, and you really need to listen."

"And why the fuck should we do that?" a gruff man asked, tilting his head.

I didn't hesitate. "Because I know why she's doing this, and it makes me more important than even I would have originally thought."

"The hell does that mean?" Axe asked.

"What did you find?" Mav asked.

I felt Dante's gaze on the profile of my face, but he didn't say anything. He simply stood there, leaning up against that wall like he always was, with his hands slid into the tightest pockets I'd ever seen on a pair of pants in my life.

Made for a good view, too.

"Just let me help. Please," I said breathlessly. "Let me make the pain and suffering worth something in my life. Just like you guys are trying to do."

And finally, Wolf dropped back down into his seat. "You still need my phone?"

I shook my head. "Not if I'm going to give bullet points."

"Bullet points are good," someone said as the men sat back down.

"Guess we can listen for a little while."

"Can't hurt to hear what she has to say."

"Worst she can be is wrong."

Mav leaned over into my ear. "Good job, beautiful."

I blushed at his words, but I knew it wasn't over with their crew. I had no respect. I had no place. And if I was going to earn any sort of respect or place among them to watch this all unfold, then I had to play by their rules.

No more crashing church sessions. Got it.

"Okay, so," I said, waving my hand in the air, "it doesn't take a genius to figure out that the reason I was adopted over my sister is because I didn't have the kind of medical problems she had after we were born. I was good to go home after a few days, but she needed a NICU stay for almost a year."

Dante's eyebrows rose. "A year?"

I nodded as I opened the folder onto the table and slid papers in his direction.

"I didn't have any issues other than some oxygenation problems right from the get-go, which is normal for twins. They got me up and running, and I was adopted less than 48 hours after being born. But Rachel? She needed NICU care for blood-related problems."

"Blood-related?" a blond-headed, clean-shaven man asked.

"Name?" I asked.

He nodded. "Locker."

I blinked. "Rocker and Locker. Nice."

Rocker grinned. "We thought so."

"What does your sister have?" Axe asked, getting us back on track.

I cleared my throat. "Anyone know what hemophilia is?"

The guys peeked around at one another, but no one raised their hands.

"Hemophilia is when your blood won't clot," I said plainly.

Wolf's eyes narrowed. "Like that Richard Burton guy?"

Rocker slowly looked over at the man. "Richard Burton?"

Wolf darted his gaze back toward him. "Elizabeth Taylor? Richard Burton? Do either of them ring a bell?"

Dante rolled his lips over his teeth to keep himself from laughing, but the redness of his cheeks alone told me everything that I needed to know. The shade was spectacular on him, and I found myself wanting to find other ways to make his cheeks flush like that.

But I kept myself focused. "Yes, like Richard Burton. Good job, Wolf."

He beamed with pride. "So, her blood doesn't clot. So what?"

"So," I said as I pushed a very specific piece of paper from the files toward him, "the only way hemophilia is treated is via transfusions."

"We're still not following," Mav said, leaning back in his chair and spreading his legs.

I did my best not to drop my gaze right to his cock. "Not only would that make her attached to a medical facility of some sort—"

"If she isn't buying the equipment herself, which we could track down," Axe murmured.

I thumbed over my shoulder. "Bingo. But also, my mother needs regular transfusions."

"Why?" Locker asked.

"Good question," Dante said as he furrowed his brows together.

I smiled at their curiosity toward my life. "That's not important, what's important is that one of the biggest problems with regular transfusions is an iron overload. I've watched my mother battle it a couple of times now over the last few years, and all of those treatments and combative efforts wrapped into one is a seriously expensive venture. Especially if you're paying someone under the table to do them outside of a medical facility."

"She'd have to do it that way," Rocker said as he perked up

and rested his forearms against the wooden table. "The second she walked into a hospital, she'd be arrested."

I pointed at him. "Exactly. But if you add in how expensive doing it outside of a hospital or a facility is, and you add even the possibility of an iron overload? With enough damage, that requires organ transplantation to fix."

Mav shot to his feet when he put it together. "Oh, fuck no. Not happening."

Dante shook his head as his face fell to stone. "Not on my goddamn watch."

I turned to Axe and looked up into his face. "She took you guys for the money, probably for her next round of treatments. But she wanted me for a possible organ transplant. I'm the closest match she's ever going to have a chance of finding."

"And our protocols interrupted her gathering process."

I shrugged. "It's the only thing that makes any relative amount of sense."

Dante's chuckle pierced the conversation. "You're smarter than you look, Brielle."

I wrinkled my nose. "Thanks?"

Axe snickered. "It's the best you'll ever get out of him."

I tossed a playful wink in Dee's direction. "I don't know, I think sometimes he can surprise you."

And God dammit, when I saw Dante's cheek blush again, the guys erupted into bombastic laughter.

"Awww, look at those cute wittle cheekies!" Rocker exclaimed as he walked over and pinched all over Dante's body.

"He's just cute as a wittle, bitty button," Locker said with a massive smile on his face.

Wolf quickly snapped a picture with his cell. "This has to go on a wall somewhere. Or maybe on some wallpaper that we decorate a room with."

"That we decorate the clubhouse with," Mav said, then he shoved a piece of gum into his mouth.

Dante peered over at me, and I swear I watched that shadow of a grin softly crawl across his cheeks. There was something sexy as hell about that man. About the unassuming strength that he had lying beneath his muscles, pulled taut over his body. He licked his lips and his gaze cased me, as if he were envisioning what he'd do next with the body beneath the baggy clothes I had found for myself that morning.

God, I couldn't wait to straddle his face and—

"All right, all right," Axe said, holding up his hands.

I was impressed with how quickly the guys shut up.

"Now that we understand what's really going on," he said, inching his hand back down to his side, "we're going to double down on the security around the clubhouse as well as our back road routes. Leave the main ones clear."

"We also need a detail on Brielle at all times," Rocker said.

Locker nodded. "If her organs are the end game, we have to watch her like a hawk."

"You leave that to us," Mav said as he stood beside me, tall and proud.

"Thank you, guys," I said.

"For what?" Blaze asked.

"For wanting to protect me, even though I've pissed you off."

Wolf came out from around the table and walked over to me. He stalked toward me, really, with his gaze latched to mine and his shoulders hunched. He looked like his name. His eyes sparkled with mischievousness and his hair was wild around his head.

And as he stood in front of me, he dipped down, placing his hands on his knees, and looked me squarely in my face.

"You're with us now," he said plainly, "and you'll be protected as such. Got it?"

Mutters of approval ricocheted across the room, and it took all I had not to burst into tears. "Got it."

He reared back up. "Good. Now, Axe, you were saying something about luring her out?"

"Lure her out?" Dante asked. "You think she wouldn't see through that kind of a plan?"

"It'd give us a chance to snatch her up if we pulled it off," Axe said.

"Is she really that stupid, though?" Locker asked.

Mav shrugged and beat me to the punch. "When your life is on the line, wouldn't you do stupid things to save it?"

"But what if it doesn't lure her out?" Locker asked as he stood to his feet. "We got a backup plan for that kinda shit?"

The man with the scar across his face finally spoke. The one man who had kept his mouth shut while staring me down the entire fucking time.

"Then, it's a good thing I'm always on the hunt," he said gruffly.

"Leave it to Jax, then," Wolf murmured.

I committed the man's name to memory as Axe clapped his hands three times.

"You have your orders. We keep the patrol routes as scheduled, but those who usually patrol the main routes will move their efforts to our back and more secretive routes. That way, if she comes sniffing around, it looks like we're preparing for her worst while leaving our best option open and vulnerable. That should be enough to catch her scent. Church is dismissed."

25

AXTON

"That was a hell of a job you did up there."

I stood with Brielle in the doorway of her bedroom as she tossed the file folder on top of the dresser next to the door. The way she moved beneath that fabric made me lick my lips, but goddamn it those clothes were too big. Those baggy ass pieces of cloth had to go. They covered up her curves way too much, and my eyes didn't like that.

Then again, neither did my fingers, which hadn't yet had a chance to touch her.

Brielle sighed heavily. "Honestly, I don't know how the hell I didn't put it together sooner."

I shook my head. "Don't be so hard on yourself. You were... dealing with a lot."

She walked over to the bed and sank down onto its edge. "She's really coming after me for my organs. My fucking organs, Axe."

I walked over and perched beside her. "She isn't getting anywhere near you. Not again. Not before we catch her."

"It's not that I don't believe you, it's just that—"

I rubbed her back as her shoulders slumped forward. "You did so well up there."

"Mmmmm, thank you."

I slid my hand up and down the length of her spine. "You put things together that none of us would have ever seen coming. How did you know what all of that medical shit meant anyway?"

She shivered as my fingertips danced along her lower back. "Just with my mom and all. You sort of pick up on things."

"Does she have hemophilia, too, or something?"

She pushed herself tighter against my palm as it splayed out over her lower back. "No, she's in kidney failure."

"I'm sorry."

"Me, too."

Silence filled the air between us before I cleared my throat. I wanted to tell her, but the words felt so unnatural. It had been a long time since I'd wanted to talk with someone like that. Since I wanted to reassure someone and protect them from the elements.

The words poured forth naturally, as if the universe itself had already made the decision for me. "I'm proud of you, Brielle."

She swallowed hard before she leaned her head against my shoulder. "I wrote down my address on a piece of paper. It's in one of the bedside table drawers."

"Want us to check in on your parents?" I asked, my fingers migrating to her tangled hair.

She shook her head. "No, but if something happens to me, will you—"

I grabbed her hair, yanked her head back, and forced her gaze up to mine. "Nothing will happen to you, Brielle. Do you hear me?"

She didn't flinch. "But if it does—"

I lowered my face to hers as a growl escaped my lips. "It won't."

She let out a shaky breath. "But if it *does*, Axe—just 'if,' okay?—will you please tell my parents? Will you tell them what happened to me? Will you give me back to them?"

I hated the tears in her eyes. The fear in her voice stilled my heart. The panic in her face made me shake as my hand tightened into the knotted locks of her hair that I wanted to break free from her scalp. That fucking bitch had scared her to death, and as far as I was concerned, that was grounds for termination of life. No one fucked with what was ours. No one left our family shivering in fear the way Brielle shivered against me.

"Please," she whispered desperately, "promise me, Axton."

I nuzzled my nose against hers. "It's the least that I can do. I promise."

"Good."

But my hand didn't move.

"Axe?" she asked.

I swallowed hard. "Yep?"

"You, uh, gonna let me go now?"

I chuckled. "And if I do?"

She shrugged. "And if you don't?"

My cock jumped at her words. "Don't approve something you're not ready for, gorgeous."

"Who says I haven't been ready?"

She clapped her hand behind my head before yanking me down, and I have to admit, the bold move shocked me. I had always been the aggressor. The chaser. The predator that caught its prey. But it seemed as if I had gotten tangled into her woven web first. The instant our lips connected; her sweet taste held me hostage. The warmth of her tongue pulsed my cock, growing it against my jeans. The beast within its cage rattled free, breaking the chained bonds of a promise I had made to myself long ago. I'd never get tangled up with someone again. I'd never allow my heart to slip from my grasp.

Yet, as our lips crashed together, I lost myself.

"Come here," I growled.

It was a sensation I had craved for fucking days, and she went limp against me. I rolled over, towering over her as she placed her hands behind her body to prop herself up. I lowered her down onto the bed. My knee forced her legs open and the smell of that juicy pussy of hers filled my nostrils. A growl dripped from my mouth, rattling against her teeth and she moaned down the back of my throat. Her hands flew to my hair. I placed my own on either side of her head as I hovered over her, feeling the warmth of her curves invite me in for more, and the way her hands tore my leather jacket off sprung my cock to attention.

I had to taste her.

I couldn't wait a second longer.

So, I stood up, grabbed those baggy-ass sweatpants at her thighs, and ripped them down her legs.

"Axe!" she exclaimed breathlessly.

I gazed at her tasty pussy. "Good thing I came hungry."

I grabbed her ankles and pulled them up to me, tossing her legs over my shoulders. I stood there, with her feet wiggling behind my head as my hands splayed out over her calves. I ran them up her legs, watching her pussy folds jump for me while her glistening arousal leaked from her entrance. I'd never seen such a glorious sight. A strong, sensuous woman, bared for me as her excess molded to my muscles.

I wouldn't let her go without a fucking fight, I tell you.

I perched on the edge of the bed on my knees, wrapping my arms around her hips and holding the lower part of her body up to my mouth. Her shoulders sat heavily against the bed as her lower body leaned against mine, seemingly suspending her in midair. I grinned at the way she shoved her cunt into my face. Her soaking wet lower lips unfurled for me, dripping with need as her clit slithered out to greet me. And when I leaned forward, I darted my tongue out for a taste.

She curled her hands into the mangled sheets we had left behind last night.

"Oh, fuck," she groaned.

"Fuck yeah," I grunted.

I held her against me, lapping her pulsing clit as the back of her legs tightened against my chest. My tongue explored her folds, lapping up her offering to me as her moans filled the air. She gasped and groaned. She bowed her back out just to get her clit a bit closer to my lips. And as I watched her contort herself for my viewing pleasure, I had mercy on her body.

"Mine," I growled, folding her legs in half against her chest.

"Axe!" she cried out.

I grabbed her hands and threaded our fingers together before pulling them toward me. I moved between her thick thighs as my morning stubble tickled her sensitive folds. I tugged her arms, bringing that pussy flush with my face before I devoured her, pressing my tongue so deeply into her clit that she froze. She choked on her own sounds as I raked the flat of my tongue against her swollen nub. She struggled to breathe as she choked on my name, over and over again. She drenched my cheeks and bucked ravenously, marking her territory as she climbed the mountaintop to her precipice. And as her thighs clamped around my face, they threatened to smother me as I drank her down.

She tasted incredible, like the salted ocean waves I enjoyed venturing out to on my bad days.

I wanted to drown myself in her.

"Axe! Oh, my God!"

I grunted against her pulsing clit. "Come for me, gorgeous. Come for your king."

"Oh, shit," she whimpered.

I pressed my tongue against her sensitive mound, and she raked herself against me. She used my face for her nefarious purposes, and I pinned her beneath me while she unraveled. The way she hiccuped my name with every pulse that sent her muscles quivering, electricity sizzled through my veins. The way her body quivered for me made my cock jump with pride. She collapsed, going limp beneath me as I stepped back and surveyed my handiwork with her fluids dripping down my neck. Her flushed skin glistened in the morning sunlight streaming through her window and the healthy flush of her body held my gaze hostage. Her shirt, which had damn near worked its way over her head, framed her puckered peaks as her tits jiggled for my viewing pleasure. Goddamn it, she was the sexiest woman I'd ever had the pleasure of pinning beneath me.

I stripped down to nothing, watching her roll over onto her back.

"Axe?" she asked.

I perched my naked body on the edge of the bed and gripped her hips. "Shouldn't tease me like that, gorgeous."

I cracked my hand against the globe of her ass and the yelp she let out intoxicated me.

"Oh fuck, Axe," she groaned.

"That's 'my king to you," I said, wrapping my hand into her hair and shoving her cheek against the bed. "Now, open that pussy wide for me, gorgeous."

Feeling her tight walls collapse around me as I slid into her depths was something I'd never forget. The way she staked herself on my cock, pushing that thick ass of hers into my pelvis damn near brought me to the fucking mattress. Stars burst in my vision as I curled my fingers into her hair. My balls sat against her pussy folds, basting in the heat of her body. Her walls squeezed me. Her ass molded to me. I slid my free hand up and down her back, watching her wiggle for me every time I caressed her lower back. I leaned down and kissed it, fluttering my lips across her delicate skin and she let out a pleasant sigh. Then I pulled out until nothing but my swollen tip filled her, slamming myself back inside.

"Oh, God!" she cried out.

I grunted as I pulled out and swiveled my cock back in. "Theeeere we go."

"Fuck, fuck, fuck. Axe. Jesus Christ."

I yanked her head up. "You like this cock?"

She pushed her ass back against me. "Yes. Oh fuck, yes."

I rolled my hips, swiveling them as my balls beat against her pussy. "You like it when I fill you up?"

"Yes, yes, yes," she moaned.

I grunted as her walls milked me, and I shoved her head back down to the mattress. "Then let me fill you up like the good little fuck toy you are."

Her moans and groans against the sheets filled me with lust as I pounded against her. The sounds of wet skin slapping wet skin filled the spaces between us, and I lost myself in the movements. In the motions. In the sensations holding me hostage. My cock grew thicker than it had ever been before. She pushed me to heights I'd never experienced with any other woman. She pulled something up from deep within my gut. Something that I hadn't entertained in a very long time.

And as my hips stuttered, she choked on my name.

"Ax—ton. Oh—my G—I'm gonna—I'm gonna—oh, fuck. Don't—don't stop. Axe—t—Axe! Oh, shit!"

I yanked her up by her hair and wrapped my arms around her waist. She collapsed against me, her head falling to my shoulder as my cock stuffed her full. Her body vibrated as her walls collapsed around me. I felt her orgasm crash over her body, quivering her muscles blanketing me. I sank my teeth into her neck. I sucked on patches of skin as goosebumps fled across her body. Thread after thread of hot arousal shot from the tip of my cock, filling her to the brim until the pulsing of her pussy finally pushed me out from between her legs. And as we collapsed to the bed in a fit of sweat, I knew my fate had been sealed.

I'd defend Brielle until my very last breath.

"Wow," she whispered.

I scooped her into my arms and pulled her close against me. "You okay?"

She smiled lazily. "King? Really?"

I chuckled and kissed her forehead. "I take it you're feeling just fine."

Her smile was lopsided, and it captured my heart. "Something like that, yeah."

I smoothed a tendril of hair away from her forehead. "Can I get you anything?"

She rolled into me and buried her face in my chest. "Just a few more minutes before you go?"

I wrapped her up and pulled her on top of me, feeling her ear press against my heart. "I'll hold you as long as you'd like."

Heaven. It was the only way to describe how she felt in my embrace. She fit perfectly, her body molding to me as if she had been carved out specifically for my pleasure. I inhaled her scent as I pressed my nose into the crook of her neck. Hearing her soft giggles pouring forth slammed my heart against my sternum. This woman had wrapped us tightly around her finger and wouldn't let us go no matter what we did.

And the guilt overwhelmed me.

"I'm so sorry," I whispered.

"What?" Brielle asked.

I picked my head up as she twisted around, falling to her back so that she could look up at me.

"Axe, talk to me," she said, reaching up and cupping my cheek.

I lowered my lips to hers for a soft kiss. "I'm so sorry for what I did to you."

"Oh, Axe. Are you still on that?"

I grimaced. "How the hell are you not?"

She cupped my face and raised my gaze to hers. "Because I've already forgiven you, that's how."

"I don't deserve your forgiveness."

"Well, you've got it anyway, so shut the fuck up about it."

"I'm so sorry," I murmured as I bent down and kissed just beneath her eye.

"I know you are," she whispered.

"I'm so fucking sorry," I said, moving to kiss her other eye.

"Axe," she whimpered softly.

I picked up her hand and brought her delicate wrist to my lips to kiss. "I'm so sorry, Brielle."

"Axton," she said breathlessly.

I wanted to take her again. As my mouth fell to her neck, I muttered my apologies all across her skin. I lapped at her pulse point, and she spread herself for me. Every form of apology I could think of coated my tongue as I slid it between her breasts. I'd spend my entire life apologizing if she'd let me. I'd spent the rest of my days murmuring them in every language against her curves, if that was what she requested of me. She had me wrapped around her finger so tightly that I had lost all sense of reason, and I never wanted to come up for air. Yet, all too soon, a knock came at her bedroom door.

"No," she whined softly.

I cupped the back of her head so that she didn't move. "Who the fuck is it?"

"Sorry to burst the bubble," Mav said on the other side, "but playtime's over."

"Five more minutes," I called out.

But when Brielle sighed, I knew she was about to give in.

"No," I said before she got a word in.

"Really, go. It's okay."

"I could tell him to fuck off."

"I heard that," Mav said flatly.

She perched herself on my chest and cupped my cheek. "Go, Axe. They need you."

"Do *you* need me?"

She stroked her finger along my cheek. "Would that matter?"

"It matters to me."

Knock, knock, knock, knock. "Come on, Axe, we've got a lot to get going around here."

I groaned as I lifted myself upright, still holding her against me. "You stay put, okay? Doc's orders. Don't go anywhere without someone at your side, even if it's just around the clubhouse, and don't strain yourself in any way. I'll be back as soon as I can."

"You keep yourself safe, too, okay?"

Even though I hated it, even though I wanted to stay there against her for all eternity, I forced myself to lay her back down. I placed a gentle kiss on her forehead and watched that angelic smile creep across her face before I reached down for the sheet and pulled it up over her exposed body. God, what I wouldn't have given for five more minutes with her luxurious playground.

But Mav was right. We had a shit ton of work to get done.

"Promise me," Brielle said as I stood from the bed.

I scooped up my clothes and pulled them back onto my body. "No promises."

"Axton."

I grinned. "That worried, huh?"

"Can you blame me?"

I finished dressing myself before I slipped into my leather jacket. She had a point, and I sure as hell wasn't gonna leave her empty-handed.

Not after everything she had been through with us.

"I promise to do whatever I can to keep you safe," I said, staring her down. "But I can't promise that both you and I will be all right, because if your safety means my—"

Worry flooded her eyes as she held up her hand, stopping my sentence in its tracks. "Just come back, okay?"

I reached for the doorknob. "I'll do my best."

"Wait, before you go," Brielle said quickly.

I spun around. "What's up?"

She held the sheet up, covering her pristine body from me and pointed to the foot of the bed. "If you haven't torn my clothes to shreds, can you hand them to me?"

I smirked. "And if I have?"

"Then, you might want to find some more clothes for me to wear."

I chuckled as I walked to the foot of the bed. I scooped up the oversized clothes, happy that she had found them. There wasn't much for her to wear around here in terms of clothes that fit her, but we were happy to part with some of the things we didn't wear often so that she could have something to cover herself.

I tossed the clothes back to her, watching as she caught them in her hands.

Good, her dexterity hadn't been impacted by her injuries.

"Thanks, my king," she said in a sultry voice that damn near tipped me over.

My cock pulsed at her words. "Of course, my queen."

Then, without another word spoken between us, I headed

for the door and slipped out into the hallway where Mav stood there, looking at me with a goofy grin on his face. His lips moved, but I had no fucking clue what he said, because all I could think about was Brielle. If I stayed in that bedroom long enough for her to ask me again, I'd stay. I'd stay right there with her until this entire saga was wrapped the fuck up.

And my men needed me out there with them instead of curled up with her.

26

DANTE

Axton's heavy footfalls barely touched the steps as he damn near leapt down them. I fell in line at his side, striding with his lumbering footsteps as I gripped a tablet in my hand. Things were moving so quickly that we had to brief him quickly.

And where the hell Mav was, I had no fucking clue.

"What do you want?" Axe asked gruffly.

I whipped in front of him and held out the tablet. "She's already been spotted. She's less than four miles from us."

His face fell blank as he ripped the tablet from my palm. "That was quick."

"Have a look. It's the camera feed from the hospital."

He quirked an eyebrow. "How did you and Mav manage—"

"Just look at it, would you?"

His brow stitched itself together before his stare dropped to the screen, and when it did, he tilted his head. I watched the reflection of the reel in his eyes, clocking his every tick and twitch as the scene unfolded.

"When did this happen?" he asked.

"It's happening now."

He whipped his head up. "She's erratic. Moving a little weird."

"Did you see the thing wrapped around her waist?"

He handed the tablet back to me. "So, that's what I think it is."

I nodded. "She's been shot. And if her blood doesn't clot—"

That grin of his pulled his cheeks taut. "It means that she's going to bleed out. That makes her desperate."

"And I figured we could use that to our advantage."

He searched around the front foyer. "Where the fuck is Mav?"

I thumbed over my shoulder. "Gathering the guys. I figured you'd wanna roll once you saw the footage. You got a plan we can execute?"

CRUNCH! Crunch, crunch, crunch.

CRUNCH! Crunch, crunch, crunch.

CRUUUUNCH!

I didn't even have to turn around to know who the fuck had come up from the damn basement.

"Really?" Axe asked as his voice fell flat. "At a time like this?"

Mav came up to us with a massive apple in his hand. "Gotta keep up my strength."

"Did you find all of the guys?"

He nodded and took another huge bite of that fucking thing. "Yep."

Axe scoffed. "Can't your stomach wait until tonight? I swear, it's like someone's got a bullhorn to your fucking face while you eat."

Mav smirked. "Like I said, gotta keep up my strength."

I placed my hand on his shoulder. "You forgot to brush your teeth this morning, didn't you?"

He shoved my hand off his shoulder as Axe's head fell back in laughter.

"Hey," he said curtly, pointing at me, "it's been fucking chaos around here. Can't fault a man for skipping a brushing or two."

I couldn't help but chuckle. "Just try not to take it with you on the roll-out."

He paused. "We rollin' out? What's happened?"

And still, Axton kept laughing. I swear, I'd never heard him laugh so much in all the years I had known him.

"Guess a good lay does us all some good, yeah?" I asked, nudging him.

He rolled his eyes before clearing his throat. "Dee, did you divert some of our men that are out on patrols toward the hospital?"

I nodded. "I'm still waiting for more footage as the guys tail her, but I'm 90% certain she's headed to the hospital because of her injury."

"Serves her right," Mav murmured before he took another large bite of his apple.

CRUUUUUUNCH!

"Ugh," Axe groaned.

I ignored the chomping for that moment. "This is a very delicate moment, so we have to play it as best as we can. Right now, she's fighting for her life. She's got nothing to lose, and we do. So, we have to be painfully aware of that right now."

"Yep, yep," Mav said with his mouth full.

Axe wrinkled his nose. "Chew and swallow like a good boy before talking, yeah?"

Mav shot him a look, but I simply continued. "We know she's not coming here because she's not en route. The hospital is in the opposite direction, and that's where every single street camera is picking her up. She doesn't have another choice at this point, she needs immediate medical attention, or she dies. And she won't make it far. Judging by the massive stain on that tourniquet around her waist, she's lost at least three pints of blood."

Axe drew in a deep breath through his nose. "Then we make sure we're ready for her, both here and at the hospital. That way, we're covered no matter what happ—"

My tablet dinged out and I pulled it back to my face. "Uh, guys?"

"Yep?" Mav asked, hovering over my shoulder.

"What is it?" Axe asked as he stood at my other side.

"I think... maybe all of us should head to the hospital."

Wolf had sent me another clip, only that time they were sitting in the emergency room parking lot of the only major hospital in town. We all watched as Rachel came into view, clutching her side and stumbling about with a gun waving in her hand. People in the parking lot scattered. She held the gun over her head before two muzzle flashes were seen on screen.

Then, she disappeared through the E.R. doors, pointing her gun at someone in the process.

"Shit," Axe hissed and pulled away from me, "let's go. We have to get out of here. Everyone! It's time to roll!"

His bellow echoed throughout the house as he clapped his hands three times. Men poured from every orifice of the clubhouse, coming up from the basement and rushing their way down the stairs. Mav led the way toward our hidden storage locker at the back of the house, where we stacked ourselves to the brim with weaponry. We strapped pistols to our hips and stuffed grenades in our pockets. All of us grabbed zip ties and knives to hang from our belt loops. Mav cocked his shotgun before stuffing his pockets with ammunition while Dee plucked his scoped rifle off the wooden rack he had carved himself on a whim. I smiled with pride as I reached for Ol' Bessy, my trusty semi-auto rifle with an extended mag and a genuine leather strap tailored specifically to my body.

Then, her voice sounded.

"I'm going with you guys," Brielle said.

"Oh, no you're not," I said before I even turned around good enough to pin her with a look.

However, when I turned around, I found that I was the one being pinned with a look.

"Oh, boy," Mav murmured.

"It's not up for debate," she said as she turned on her heels. "I'm going with you because you guys know I'm the only one she'll stop and listen to."

I shook my head. "I'm not letting you do this. It's too dangerous. She's already on the brink of losing her life."

"And you don't think I deserve to be there should my twin sister bleed out?"

I sighed as Mav walked up to her, abandoning his apple in a trash can as he passed by. He placed his hands on her shoulders, catching her stare when she pulled it away from me. I twirled my finger in the air, signaling to the guys that it was time to mount our bikes.

And as they inched around her, Mav drew in a deep breath. "You can't go with us."

She shrugged off his touch. "I'm what she wants, and if I walk in there, she won't even point a gun at me. You know she won't."

"No," Dee said flatly, "she'll just come into a bathroom, knock you unconscious, strip you of your clothes, and steal you away again."

"But she won't kill me," Brielle said.

I peeked over at Axe and watched his façade crumble.

"You're not actually considering this," I said, turning to face him.

"She's got a point," he murmured.

"See? Listen to your president. I've got a point," she said.

Mav barked with laughter. "God damn it, I like your spunk."

Brielle giggled, and I wondered if that was the last time I'd hear her giggle. If being in her presence at that moment, fighting with her on what she should do, was the last time we'd ever talk. The last time we'd ever have a disagreement. Panic gripped my heart in a way I'd never felt before. Images flashed before my eyes that had no origin. Images of Brielle's face and her bubble-soaked body in that bathtub. I'd never be able to join her for one if things went south and she were with us.

But Axe apparently didn't care about any of that shit.

"Fine," he said, striding past us, "you can ride on the back with me. But what we say goes once we get there, got it?"

Brielle's eyes lit up as she whipped around and fell in stride behind him. "Got it."

"Everyone!" Axe bellowed as Mav came up to my side. "Roll out!"

"She'll come back with us. She'll be all right," he said, trying to reassure me.

I simply turned around and slammed the storage locker door closed, however.

Before making my way toward my bike without another word falling from my fucking mouth.

Not like anyone listens, anyway.

27

BRIELLE

The sheer number of men that poured out of that clubhouse and into the gravel parking lot astounded me. There had to be at least a dozen of them, if not more, and the roar of their bikes as they all struck up at once rattled my ribcage. I studied their bikes as everyone tossed their legs over the leather seats, and I realized something.

Their bikes looked like them.

It was kind of like dog owners who ended up looking like their dogs. With Dee being so lean and taut, with muscles pulled tightly over his tall bones, his camouflaged bike had a very sleek look to it. Every line was perfectly in place, carving out curved patterns around his motorcycle's body that made his legs look even longer than they already were. Mav's bike had splashes of color as loud as his bright white smile, and it didn't shock me one fucking bit when he opened a little compartment hanging off his handlebars and pulled out a sucker.

Was that man ever not eating?

Then, there was Axe's bike. The bike he expected me to straddle. The damn thing had to have been at least twice the size of everyone else's motorcycles if anything to accommodate his mountainous size. Leather didn't stop at the seats, either. Some of the trim on the bike looked like leather, and the sleek, shining black paint job sparkled beneath the sun hanging heavily above our heads. He even had those leather tassels dangling from his own handlebars.

It made me smile as he held out his hand.

"Toss a leg over and I'll stabilize you. It'll take a moment to adjust, but you'll get it soon enough."

"Ah, my hero," I said with a grin as I slid my hand into his palm.

Yes, my entire fucking hand fit into nothing but his palm. And my God, how I loved it. How I loved feeling small and delicate in his embrace. The thought of his body folding mine in half made me shiver as I hiked my leg over his blacked-out bike, and he was right. It took me a few hops before I had to cling to his leather jacket in order to seat myself the rest of the way behind him.

"You good?" he asked.

Every time I shifted, it spread my legs further. It slid me deeper against his body, until my clothed pussy was flush with the small of his back. His body heat pulled my arms around him, and I placed my cheek against his back. The wind kicked up, chasing away the sun's harsh rays as the ground rumbled beneath the tires of the bikes standing ready.

Then, I winced as Axe's voice rose above the cacophony. "All right, everyone! Let's get this show on the road!"

I pulled my head up from his back. "Wait, what should I hang on to when we—oh!"

I squealed, but the sound got eaten up by the bikes that fell in line behind Axe. I clung to his zipped-up leather jacket, gripping it by the handfuls as my legs girded themselves around his body. Wind whipped around us as we soared down the road. My knuckles turned white, and I pressed myself deeply into

Axe's strong, steady body. It felt so weird, rushing down the road like that. Feeling the wind against my face that usually battered my windshield while I drove. I didn't dare open my eyes, though, because I knew I'd be a goner the second I tried rubbernecking at my surroundings. I'd lean right off that fucking bike and slam my cheek into the asphalt at ninety miles an hour.

At least, that was how fast it felt we were going.

Still, there was something comforting about all of it. Freeing in a way. My hair fluttered around my head as my clothes wafted in the breeze that we kicked up, and all of a sudden, my worries faded away. Thoughts of my sister turned to thoughts of sunlight, beaches, and suntans. Thoughts of my capture turned into thoughts of Dee, Mav, and Axe. Their bodies, bared for me. Their cocks, filling my holes. I shuddered at the thought. Three holes and three men. I wondered what it might feel like to be that full. To feel their arousal filling me to the brim before spilling over and collapsing onto whatever surface we had decided to destroy for ourselves. It encapsulated my mind. It puckered my tits as the tires beneath my body roared across the pavement.

But all too soon, the sounds of the wind whipping against my ears turned into sounds of screaming and fear. Pain and punishment.

We had arrived at the hospital, and it was chaos.

I picked my head up and opened my eyes long enough to see security guards lining the emergency room doors. They had their weapons drawn, shooing people away who desperately needed help. There was a young woman with a child in her arms. A man with a woman's bloodied arm slung around his shoulder. Nurses in scrub uniforms ran around like rats in a maze, trying to figure out which way to go and who to tend to first.

I'd never seen such a disaster in all my life.

"What are we going to do!?" I called out to Axe.

He eased into a parking space at the back of the lot, next to a dark corner that was shrouded in trees. His other men followed suit, with Mav coming up to our right and Dee coming up to our left. I lifted myself up a bit, peering over Axe's broad shoulders as cars peeled out of the parking lot and security guards waved their guns like madmen to get people's attention.

And the guys weren't moving.

"What is it?" I asked after they all cut the engines to their bikes. "Why aren't we heading inside?"

"Because we didn't get here before they locked down the hospital," Axe said.

"It means the place is probably already swarming with police," Mav said as he leaned over and murmured in my ear.

I had to admit, the feeling of his warm breath against the shell of my ear gave me pause. But I quickly shook it off. We had other, more important things to tend to that weren't my fucking sex drive.

"So that means you guys can't go in there with me," I said.

Dee whipped his head toward me. "You're not going in alone, so get that out of your head."

I peeked over at him. "How will you do that if there are police here?"

"We can send you in with Jax, our prospect," Axe said as he slid off his bike, leaving me there to fend for myself. "They're not familiar with his face yet, so he can protect you."

"But no," Mav said, offering me his hand. "We can't go in there with you. Not with a police presence already in play."

I took his hand gingerly and slid off the bike, tiptoeing onto the ground in order to swing my leg off. I struggled to unhook it, though. Axe's bike sat high off the ground. Higher than any of the other bikes. And it took him lifting my ankle gingerly before my leg finally let go of that bike.

"Thanks," I said softly.

He nodded. "No problem."

"You rang?" that gruff voice asked as it appeared behind me.

Mav linked my arm with his and turned both of us around. "Jax, you're headed inside with Brielle to talk with Rachel. Keep as low of a profile as you can."

"And leave your leather cut behind," Dee said flatly.

Jax shrugged his coat off, donning a plaid button-up beneath it, and tossed it to Mav. "Got it."

"You armed just in case?" Axe asked.

Jax unbuttoned his shirt and flashed the guns on either side of his body. "We're good."

"Brielle," Dee said.

I felt the warmth of his dexterous fingers wrap around my wrist, and when I turned to face him, worry filled his gaze. It was a look I'd never seen in his confident gaze before. It was a look that unnerved me.

"Dee? Are you okay?" I asked, turning to fully face him.

He walked me out from around Axe's bike before wrapping his free arm around my waist. "Come back to us, okay?"

I cupped his cheek and stroked his smooth skin softly with my thumb. "I'll do my best."

The feeling of his lips pressing against my forehead stoked something within me. Whatever happened, whatever became of our time together after everything was said and done, I knew I'd never be able to leave their side. It didn't matter how things had started. In some ways, I couldn't even blame them for it, because if my twin sister had done to me half of what she had done to these guys, I would've wanted her strapped up in my basement, too.

"See you soon, okay?" Dee whispered.

I reached my lips up and kissed the underside of his jaw. "See you soon, handsome."

Just as I backed away from Dee, however, he reached over Axe's bike and practically snatched Jax up by his fucking shirt collar. He walked the man around the bike, effectively pushing me away with Jax's back, and while his lips moved, I had no idea what the man was saying. Jax kept nodding his head, his face etched with that same serious frown of his. And when the two were done, Dee nodded before releasing the man.

"You're good to go," Dee said, slinging his leg back over his bike.

"Come on," Jax said with a nod of his head, "let's go."

I matched the man, stride for stride, as I felt the stares of all the guys behind us on the back of my head.

"What did Dee say to you? If you don't mind me asking," I said.

But Jax simply shook his head. "Can't tell you. Now, eyes forward. Stay alert."

I snickered. "Fine, then stay out of my way and we won't have any issues."

We crossed the parking lot, and I did my best to ignore the sounds of people crying out for help. Of people cursing out the security guards for turning them away from the hospital. Sirens sounded in the distance, and I peered over my shoulder, wondering if that was the signal for the guys to jump ship. But instead, they simply sat there in the shadows, barely visible from the emergency room doors.

"Holy shit," someone said.

"Is that her? I thought she was inside?"

"You need to let us through," Jax said.

"Not on your life," a hardened voice said.

I didn't like that motherfucker's tone of voice and quite frankly, I was tired and wanted a nap.

"What was that?" I asked as I turned to face the man.

His eyes widened. "You look just like the woman that—"

Jax held up his hand, stopping the man in his tracks. "Let us through. Her sister can talk some sense into her."

The guards looked me up and down as they shook their heads, and at that moment, I hated being related to that bitch. I was nothing like her. Nothing like my sister one fucking bit, and yet there I was, being equivocated to her because we were twins. The hole in my heart suddenly didn't feel as big as it once did. The mystery of who my sister might have been was demolished the second she knocked me out and stole my goddamn clothes. I wanted that woman's head on a pike just like the guys did.

Yet, there was a small, idealistic part of me that felt for Rachel as well.

We all did what she had done. All she did was create a life for herself that she needed in order to survive. It wasn't her fault that she had been born with hemophilia. It wasn't her fault that she had become too much of a burden to adopt. It wasn't her fault that she bounced around between foster homes before being dumped on the street at the ripe young age of eighteen. All of that shit had been done to her, and all she had done was attempt to survive the only way she knew how.

"All right," the security guard said as he stepped off to the side, "but the second your sister becomes volatile, we're putting a bullet in her and ending this. We can't hang up the only hospital in the area for whatever the hell she's demanding."

"It won't take long," I said as I slipped past the man.

"Thanks," Jax murmured, following me inside.

The second the automatic doors closed behind us, it sealed off the chaos. The sounds of people screaming and crying and throwing fits in exchange for services muted itself into nothing but a dull roar, and the silence of the tiled emergency room unnerved me. Jax hovered at my side, his head on a swivel as we searched for any signs of people in distress. But, outside of some drunk slouched in the corner with puke staining the front of his shirt, there was no one else in the E.R.

Except for her, that is.

"Well, well, well," Rachel said in a weakened voice as she came through the metal double doors that separated the waiting room from the rest of the hospital, "if it isn't sister dearest."

She was pale from her blood loss, still dripping down her leg. "You need medical attention, Rachel, but this isn't the way to get it."

My sister leveled a shaking gun at my head. "I knew you'd come. Miss Goodie Two-Shoes. Miss Has to be Perfect in Every Way. Can't miss being the good little girl that you are, can you?"

I took a step toward her, only for Jax to grab my arm. "Brielle?"

I slowly panned my gaze over my shoulder at him. "Does this break whatever promise you made to Dee?"

He shook his head. "No."

I yanked my arm away from his grasp. "Then, don't you dare touch me again."

Rachel let out a breathless chuckle. "Yeah, fuck men, am I right?"

I turned my attention back to her. "I'm going to come closer, all right?"

"If you do, I'll shoot."

"If you wanted to shoot me," I said as I slowly crept closer, "you would have already done so. But you need me alive for my organs, don't you?"

Her eyes widened. "How do you—"

"What do you need?" I asked.

"What?" Jax asked.

Rachel searched my stare. "They should've taken me, too, you know. That's what they always encourage."

I nodded. "I know."

"I heard it my whole fucking life," she said as her lower lip quivered. "I heard all of those motherfuckers encourage people to adopt siblings, not individual kids. And I watched as so many siblings were adopted into amazing homes. But not me. Not with my sibling."

"You should have been with me."

"I should have been with you!" she bellowed, stumbling into the nearest wall.

"Rachel!" I exclaimed, rushing toward her.

I helped her to steady herself before she stared deeply into my soul. "They should have taken me—me, too."

"Tell me what I can do to help you. Tell me what you need. Whatever it is, I can help you negoti—No! Jax! I need help!"

My sister's legs came out from beneath her and she collapsed into my arms. Footsteps sounded quickly behind me before Jax appeared, scooping his arms beneath hers. He hoisted her into the nearest seat in the waiting room where she slumped over, her body hanging over my right shoulder as her blood dripped onto my thighs.

Then, I saw it.

I watched her hand loosen around the gun she held.

"I got her," Jax said.

I slowly raked my gaze up to his and he nodded. So, I went for it.

"No, no, no. No! Stop!" Rachel exclaimed.

But she was too weak to fight me. Too weak to fight any of it, really. Her skin continued to pale as her blood spilled out onto the tile floor, and I knew it wouldn't be long before she bled out, right then and there. I plucked the gun from her weakened fingers and slid it across the floor, watching as it disappeared into the darkness of the hallway in front of us.

"Got anything else we should know about?" Jax asked.

Rachel scoffed. "Fuck you."

I saw a glimmer of something shiny on her hip. "Left hip, you're closer to it."

Jax reached down and pulled a gigantic butcher's knife seemingly from out of nowhere. He studied it before tossing it down that same hallway, and I listened to it clatter before it slammed into the cold metal of the gun that the darkness had swallowed whole.

Then, I gripped my sister's hair and pulled her head up so that her stare locked with mine.

"Anything else we need to pull off you before we get you the medical attention that you need?" I asked.

She snarled. "Over my dead body."

"We can strip search you," Jax said as he stood to his feet, "but something tells me you won't survive it. So, be straight with us. Do you want help, or do you want to die? Because those are your only options."

Rachel rolled her eyes. "On my ankles."

I bent down and plucked the knife off her left ankle and the small handgun off her right.

"And my right pocket," she said flatly.

Jax stuffed his hand inside the pocket of her black bodysuit and pulled out a set of throwing knives.

"Dee would love those," he murmured, tossing them onto the chair beside us.

"Anything else?" I asked as I helped her stand.

She groaned before leaning heavily against me. "Nope, that's it."

"You sure?" Jax asked.

And when Rachel sighed, I rolled my eyes. "Come on, where is it?"

Her legs shook against mine. "Down the back of the suit. See the handle?"

"Jesus," Jax grumbled as he unsheathed...

"Is that a... combat knife?" I asked.

"Yep," Jax said as he set it on the ground at his feet.

"I need a gurney in here! Someone help me, please!" I exclaimed.

"They won't help me," Rachel grunted. shivering violently against me.

"You're in a hospital," I groaned as the metal double doors burst wide open. "They don't have a choice but to treat you."

"Come on, let's get you onto this thing," Jax said, lifting Rachel's limp body into his arms.

I watched as he placed my twin sister down onto that gurney. Nurses were pale in the face and the doctors had obviously been crying, but the second her body touched down onto that rolling hospital bed, they whisked her away. Silence blanketed my ears as I followed them. I followed them through the metal double doors as the disinfectant of the hospital filled my nostrils. Machines beeped wildly. I watched them set I.V.s and place an oxygen mask over my sister's face.

"She's got hemophilia!" I called out after them.

One of the doctors scanned his card before a machine-automated door popped open, and as I tried to follow them inside, someone placed their hand on my chest. I expected Jax to be standing there when I followed the arm, but instead I found a scrub nurse standing there in a bloodied outfit.

"We can take it from here," he said.

So, with a silent nod of my head, I turned to head back toward Jax.

Except, he wasn't where I had left him when I got back out into the waiting room.

"Ma'am, you need to come with us."

Two police officers came from out of nowhere and scooped my arms up. "Has anyone seen a man in a white t-shirt and blue jeans?"

"Just come outside with us. We need your statement."

I craned my head over my shoulder, but Jax was nowhere in sight. "Seriously, his name is Jax. I came in with him. Where is he?"

"It's okay, ma'am, just come with us. We can get you whatever it is that you need."

I yanked away from the police officers just as they led me out of the E.R. "What I need is the man I was with when I came in. Now, where is he? What did you do with him?"

"What man?" one of the officers asked.

His question filled me with dread. My stomach sank to my toes and my heart leapt into my throat as I shoved my way through the growing crowd. People collapsed in tears and clung to those they loved while nurses and doctors alike bounced from crowd to crowd, taking vitals, and checking over wounds. I scanned the parking lot, looking for any sign that Jax had made a break for it. Maybe he wanted to get back to the guys once he knew Rachel was no longer a threat, just to stay beneath the police's radar. But when I stood on my tiptoes and gazed over at the dark corner of shrouded trees they had parked beneath, I found no one sitting there.

No bikes.

No Jax.

No men.

"Brielle?"

Oh, my God. Where did my boys go?

"Brielle."

They wouldn't have just abandoned me like that. Not after what we had all shared. Not after they made me fall in love with them.

Right?

"Brielle! Honey! Over here!"

28

———

BRIELLE

Where are they? Where did they go?

"Brielle, sweetheart. Can you hear me?"

Pressure wrapped around my wrist as my gaze scanned the parking lot. The world around me fell silent, engulfing my head in a swimming feeling and my heart leapt into my mouth. I tried swallowing it back down, chasing the nerves with enough spit to drown a small animal. And yet, as I scanned the ground for any sign of them, I found nothing.

No bikes.

No leather jackets.

No men.

No, they couldn't have. They'd never.

"Princess? Please say something."

That turned my head. Even as the muffled words dawned upon my ears, it wasn't until I turned my body to face the familiar voice that tears leaked down my cheeks. They had left me. Abandoned me. Ran away like cowards.

Had I ever meant anything to them?

"Oh, sweetheart," Mom choked out as she enveloped me in a hug.

Her warm embrace yanked me back to the present. The sounds of people crying and asking a fuck ton of questions battered against the shell of my ears. An involuntary shiver worked its way down my spine. Her arms held me tightly as my soaked cheek descended upon her shoulder. And when those short, plump fingers of my father's hand stroked through my hair, I couldn't help myself.

I sobbed against her shoulder, releasing the demons I'd held at bay for oh so long.

"It's okay," she whispered, kissing my temple, "we're right here. You're safe now, honey. You're safe."

"Here, let's get you home," Dad said. "We need to get your clothes changed. You're covered in blood."

The idea of leaving without my boys yanked my head up from my mother's shoulder. I pulled out of her grasp, studying the ghostly imprint of red I had left behind in my wake. I picked my hands up as the sound of tires squealing caught my ear. I yanked my head toward the sound, hoping and praying to see those bikes rolling into the parking lot, one by one.

But instead, I saw news vans rolling up as people with cameras spilled out of every orifice.

"Shit," I hissed.

"Brielle," Mom whispered, "language."

I curled my nose up at her words. "Says the woman who kept the most important thing about my life from me."

My voice sucked the air out of the spaces between us. Newscasters set up outside the façade of the hospital as Dad wrapped his arms around me. He held me close, stroking his hand up and down my back. I stared mindlessly at all the cameras. Maybe they had left because of those?

It wasn't like they could necessarily be seen on television or anything like that.

Yeah, maybe that's what happened.

"You can't even give your old man a hug?" Dad asked with a nervous chuckle on the tip of his tongue.

I pulled away from his embrace. It felt too confining. It felt unreal, as if I were stuck in some nightmare I'd never shake.

"Why didn't you tell me?" I asked, locking my gaze with his.

Those icy blue eyes that everyone thought I had inherited stared back at me. "How do you tell someone like that, princess?"

"Easy," I said flatly, taking another step backward. "With your mouth."

"Sweetheart, it was so much more complicated than that," Mom said, reaching out for my hand.

I leaned my arm away from her. "How could you leave an innocent baby to suffer in a hospital after adopting me?"

Mom and Dad looked over at each other and I took a moment to draw in a deep breath. As newscasters rattled off what they thought they knew, my hands balled up into fists at my side. I heard them mention my sister's name, Rachel. I heard them mention her arrest record, multiple counts of murder and an outstanding warrant for her arrest. I slowly turned to face them as they talked about hitmen and contracts. Her supposed ties to the seedy underbelly of our country and how she bounced around from foster home to foster home, challenging authority wherever she went.

All because she had been rejected at birth.

Though, they conveniently left that part out of the narrative.

"All right, everyone!" a doctor exclaimed way too close to my ear as he stepped out of the emergency room. "The lock-down has been lifted! Everyone can come inside now!"

The thunderous sound of footsteps stampeded toward me,

and had it not been for my parents yanking me out of the way, I may not have moved. I may have actually allowed them to trample me, because anything was better than the empty ache I felt deep within the pit of my soul. They were nowhere to be found. It was as if they had never existed. The newscasters never mentioned their names. I didn't hear their bikes revving off in the distance. My heart shattered into a million pieces as I finally managed to swallow it back down, and the shards raked against my insides as my soul broke.

They were gone.

And I'd never get the chance to tell them how much I had come to love them.

"Miss!"

I drew in a deep breath as I wiped at the tears leaking down my face.

"Miss!"

"Honey?" Mom asked softly, placing a hand on my shoulder. "I think that doctor is talking to you."

I cleared my throat and turned around. "I know. What can I do for you, Doctor?"

A tired man in a white coat trotted up to me. "You know what I'm about to ask, don't you?"

"We don't," Dad said, stepping in front of me.

I inched out from around him and walked up to the doctor's side. "What does she need?"

"No," Mom said curtly.

"She needs blood," the doctor said, "and as much of it as you can spare. You're the best candidate, and her best chance at pulling through this."

"Absolutely not," Dad said, stepping back in front of me.

"You do not have our permission," Mom said.

The doctor peeked over my father's shoulder at me. "With all due respect to you both, it's her decision."

Both of my parents whipped around on me.

"Don't do this," Dad said.

"She doesn't deserve your help. Did you listen to any of those newscasters over there?" Mom asked.

Dad took my hands within his. "Just come home with us. We can clean you up. Get you some rest. Whatever you need."

"Let's just go home, okay?" Mom asked, tucking a strand of hair behind my ear.

But I simply pulled my hands away from my father. "Yes, Doc. Whatever you need, I can help."

"What?!" Mom exclaimed.

"I will not allow this," Dad said as he pointed to the ground, as if he were making some kind of argument that he figured I'd listen to.

I had changed, though. My men had changed me. The entire situation had changed the scope through which I viewed my entire life, and the words fell effortlessly from my lips as I stood beside the man in the white coat.

"Well, she's my twin," I said, darting my gaze between my parents, "she's the other part of me. So, of course I'm going to help. I'm going to help her the way you should have helped her all those years ago."

"Honey," Mom whispered as tears lined her eyes, "we didn't —we couldn't have possibly—"

I nodded. "I know. But it didn't help. So, I'm going to go in there and be the sister that she deserves, even if this is my only chance to be that to her. And if you love me? If you want me to be okay after all this? You'll let me do it."

Then, without another word from my parents, I pivoted on the balls of my feet toward the E.R. doors.

"Lead the way, Doc."

"Brielle, come on!" Dad called out. "We just weren't equipped to take care of someone like her!"

"You're brave for doing this," the doctor said as he escorted me through the automatic doors.

I heard Mom hot on my heels. "Will she need any tests or anything before she gives blood?"

My head had never moved so fast as I looked over at her. "Really?"

She took my hand and paused both of us in our tracks. "If this is really what you want, you know I'll always support you. I'm just so glad you're all right."

I wrapped my arms around her and hugged her tightly. "I love you, Mom."

She sniffled before drawing in a broken breath as she held me close. "I love you, too, honey."

"No," the doctor said, placing a hand on my shoulder, "but we need to go, she's bleeding out quickly, and she won't last much longer."

I released Mom and dried her tears with my thumbs. "Watch after Dad, will you? He's gonna give himself an aneurysm pacing the way he is."

Mom snickered. "We'll be waiting for you right out here."

"Miss?"

I relinquished my mother and fell in line with the doctor as he walked toward those metal double doors. "Brielle, please."

"Doctor Ingles."

I smiled. "Like the show, right?"

He chuckled. "You have no idea how often I get that question."

"Oh, I'm sure it's enough to make you hate it."

"You have no idea. Follow me, we'll get you set up in here."

He ushered me into a room where a nurse stood, waiting for me to sit in the recliner she had prepared for me.

"Sit there?" I asked, pointing.

Dr. Ingles held out his hand. "Yep. Just make yourself comfortable. I'm gonna go get you some juice and a few crackers to snack on, just in case."

"How much can I give right now?"

"Two," he said without hesitation, "but any more than that is pushing it, so we won't take more than that."

I eased down into the chair, put my feet up, and held out my good arm. "Lay it on me, then."

As I stared up at the ceiling while they prepped me for blood extraction, the guys came flooding back into my memories. They were gone, just like that. Out of my life, for good. The ache in my gut made me sick to my stomach. I had to close my eyes and take in deep breaths just to get through the blood donation. I wanted nothing to do with any food or drinks. I didn't want to get back to work, or go home, or deal with my parents.

It felt like I had lived an entire lifetime with those men.

And I wanted that life back.

"Mom?" I asked.

"We're just out here, honey," she said, sticking her head inside.

I giggled. "I thought you guys were gonna be in the E.R. waiting for me."

"Can you blame us?" Dad asked.

I shook my head softly. "No."

"Do you need something, sweetheart?" Mom asked.

I swallowed hard. "How long was I gone?"

"Seven days," Dad said without hesitation.

I snickered as I shook my head. Seven days. One week. That was all it took to turn my life head over heels. To change every single priority I had ever set out for myself. One week with those men, and I had turned into a completely different person. Those seven days had changed my worldview. Those seven days changed the way I lived, loved, and experienced the world around me. It felt like a lifetime, honestly. And now, I had to live another lifetime without them.

A thought that pulled tears down my cheeks as Dr. Ingles prepared me for the second blood draw.

29

MAVERICK

"She looks misera—"

"SSHH!" Axe hissed.

I took a large chunk out of the roast beef sandwich I had made for myself the second we got back to the clubhouse. Locker had been forward-thinking enough to patrol the outer skirts of the hospital for news crews, something none of us had taken into consideration.

I guess we had all been distracted.

"I hate this," Dee said flatly.

"Shut. Up," Axe growled.

She looked dazed. Confused. Watching her look out over the parking lot shattered my heart in my chest. I took another large bite of my sandwich, trying to keep my jaw distracted, because I knew that if it wasn't moving, I'd grind my teeth from the stress. She looked distraught. She looked as if she were on the verge of tears.

And she was looking for us.

"We can't be seen on camera," Rocker said, walking up beside me. "You know that."

I nodded mindlessly as I shoved the rest of my sandwich into my mouth.

"Someone get him a drink," Axe muttered.

"Already on it," Wolf said, handing me a soda.

I cracked it open and washed it down, but it wasn't enough. Nothing was ever enough, and it would never be enough again. Abandoning her was, by far, the hardest thing I'd ever done in my life. I wanted to wrap her up into my arms and tell her how proud of her I was. I wanted to slam our lips together in a breath-stealing kiss while ripping her clothes off that beautiful body of hers. Yet as I stood there, burning my throat on the carbonation as it slid down my throat, all I saw was her face in my head.

The pain in her eyes.

The searching of her stare.

She was looking for us.

And we weren't there.

"Fuck this, I'm going back," I hissed, crumpling the empty can in my hand.

Axe was on me faster than aftershave on a playboy. "You'll go nowhere. It's too damn risky."

I pointed to the television. "She's looking for us, Axe. You know she is. You really mean to tell me we're just gonna leave her there by herself?"

"She's not by herself," Dee said.

"And she's not even looking at them! She's not even looking at her parents! Look at the television, Axton!"

When he didn't turn around, I grabbed his shoulders and whipped him around, forcing him to look at the screen. Forcing him to see the empty hugs she gave those people as tears slid down her cheeks. Her gaze never wavered. Even one of the cameras caught onto what she was doing and panned over the parking lot, trying to figure out what in the fuck she was staring at.

We knew, though.

We knew what she was staring at.

"We can't," Axe muttered.

I growled. "I need some fucking chips."

"Maybe she's just pissed about her sister. It's understandable. I'm sure she's got a lot of anger toward them right now," Dee said, grasping at straws.

Then, all too soon, she disappeared back into the hospital.

"Where is she going?" I asked as my travels to the kitchen were thwarted.

Axe chuckled. "Of course, our girl wants to help."

Our girl.

The words hung heavily in my head as a grin tugged at Dee's cheeks. "I like the sound of that."

Axe chuckled. "I figured you would."

I swallowed hard. "Why didn't we call her that sooner? It would've made her smile so much."

"Look, I know this sucks," Rocker said as he came out of the kitchen and handed me one of my suckers, "but what the fuck are we going to do about The Heretics? It's not like they're just out there not doing shit."

I took the sucker from him and unwrapped it. "Thanks."

He nodded as he stared at Axe, waiting for an answer. And I had to admit, it was a good fucking question. We had gotten so wrapped up in chasing down that bitch that we had completely forgotten about the puppeteer.

"Well," Dee said, pulling out his phone and dicking around on it, "word on the street is that the bounty on our heads is gone."

"Probably because of the meet-up," I said matter-of-factly. "Can't really say it went their way."

Wolf chuckled. "Serves them fucking right, too."

"The payments clear out, by the way," Locker said, coming up to my side. "Just moved my shit around and everything was smooth sailing."

That made the guys rip their phones out of their pockets. Dealing with the kind of money that we did on a regular basis took patience and time. And sometimes, it didn't always clear, which meant that we had to hit the streets for a nice little warning call. But with the dings and smiles that ricocheted across the room, the mood seemed to lighten.

Despite the fact that Brielle had charged back into that hospital and hadn't yet come back out.

"What do you guys think she's doing?" I asked as I nodded to the newsreel on the television in the living room.

"We could get our regular patrols back out now that Rachel's off the streets," Locker said.

"We may want to go check our stash warehouses, though," Rocker said.

"Good idea," Wolf said, pulling his bike keys out of his back pocket. "Who's riding with me to those warehouses? We can do inventory while we're—"

"There's always gonna be someone," I said abruptly.

The guys turned to face me as I shifted the sucker into my cheek.

"Look," I said, my stare staying connected with the screen. I didn't want to miss a single second of Brielle's presence there. "There will always be someone out there. Someone who wants to get to us. Someone who wants our turf. The point is that we make sure we keep whoever the fuck we don't like underneath our thumb."

Dee smirked. "Blackmail."

I pointed at him. "Exactly. That's what we need. We don't

need firepower or bloodshed. What we need is something to hang over their sorry, fat little heads."

"More shit than we've already got?" Locker asked as he thumbed mindlessly over his shoulder.

I shook my head. "Having records is different than having dirt, and we have surprisingly little dirt on those motherfuckers. Remember why we started chasing that bitch down in the first place?"

Wolf nodded. "It was the only shred of dirt we had on them."

Axe finally chimed in. "Who's on this next patrol route?"

Locker and Rocker raised their hands and spoke in unison. "Me."

Axe turned to face them. "Go back to Plan A patrol routes, but when you're not patrolling? Be digging."

"On it," Wolf said, marching out of the room.

Rocker checked his watch. "We can start our patrol a bit early. You up for a milkshake, Locker?"

The man barked with laughter. "The fuck kinda question is that? Come on, we can start on the opposite end of town and work our way back."

They bumped fists before they headed out of the living room, and I noticed that our silent prospect was nowhere to be found.

"Anyone got eyes on Jax?" I asked as I shifted the sucker into my other cheek.

And that was when a cell phone filled the air around us with its ringing.

"Dee?" Axe asked.

I turned and found Dante holding out his cell phone. Not his personal cell phone, but one of the multitudes of burner phones we utilized for work purposes. The grin on his face was positively devilish, and I peeked over at Axe to see if he had the same look. To see if I had been slow on an uptick, or if I was really supposed to be in the dark.

And he looked just as confused as me.

"Yeah?" Jax asked when he finally answered.

"You got eyes on our girl?" Dee asked.

"What?" I asked flatly.

Axe rushed to his side. "Where is she? What's going on?"

I rushed to Dee's other side and listened intently as Jax spoke. "Sure do. She's home sweet home with her parents."

His phone dinged and Dante's long ass fingers swiped across the screen, revealing the sage green façade of a cookie cutter house out there in suburbia. The pristinely trimmed grass matched the crisp white driveway as the golden numbers of the house twinkled above the double garage door. But, before I got a better look at the place, another picture came rolling through.

"Southview Avenue," I muttered to myself.

"Plan A or B?" Jax asked.

"What?" Axe asked curiously.

But Dee simply chuckled. "You didn't think I'd just let her walk out of our lives, did you?"

My eyes widened as Dee cleared his throat.

"Plan A is a-go. Stay safe, you two."

Then, he hung up the phone, took out the battery, and made his way into the kitchen.

"What did you do?" Axe asked, his tone of voice demanding an answer.

Dee tossed the bits and pieces of his phone into the sink and turned on the hot water. "I did what I do best."

"Which is?" I asked, digging a hammer out of the pantry.

I handed it to Dee, and he firmly smashed the water-soaked phone at the bottom of the sink.

"I made sure we had plans in place to get her back to us," he said.

BOOM, BOOM, BOOM!

And as he shattered the phone into a million little pieces, I slowly looked over at Axe, whose face held a smile I'd never once seen on him.

A smile that matched the happiness swelling in my heart.

30

BRIELLE

"Come here, honey. Why don't you sit down?"

"Want a drink, princess? I've got your favorite in stock."

"Oh! Get her some of those honey and onion mustard whatever things."

"Pretzels?"

"Yeah, those. She loves those. Wanna sit on the couch?"

Mom guided me to the couch while Dad rummaged around in the kitchen, but I couldn't stand it. Even as she eased me onto the worn cushions I had sat on during my youth, I wanted nothing more than to run back out the door. I wanted to rush home, crawl into my own bed, and cry myself to sleep.

I needed to grieve the loss of my men.

"Here you go," Dad said, placing a bowl of my favorite pretzels into my lap. "Where do you want your apple juice?"

I shrugged. "Anywhere is fine, thank you."

"All right," Mom said and picked up the remote, "I think there's a Golden Girls marathon playing somewhere. Wanna snuggle up with your ol' mama dearest and watch some?"

I stared down into my bowl and couldn't help but think

about how much Mav would like the snack she'd brought me. "Yeah, sure. That sounds nice."

"Princess?"

I leaned my head back against the couch cushions. "Yeah, Dad?"

He bent forward and kissed my forehead. "I'm so glad you're home okay."

I'm not. "Thanks, Dad."

He stroked his fingers through my hair. "I'll go get your bedroom set up. We figured you could stay here a few nights. You know, just until you get back on your feet."

It sounded horrible. "Sure, yeah. Sounds like a plan to me."

Mom patted my knee and sat next to me. "I found it, and it's your favorite episode. Wanna watch it?"

I picked up my head and stared blankly at Betty White on the screen. "Yeah, yeah. Sure."

"Princess?"

I resisted the urge to sigh. "Yeah, Dad?"

"Are you sure you're okay?"

"Would anyone be okay after what I went through?"

I couldn't help it. I knew it made them feel bad. I mean, the entire aura of the room changed the second the words fell from my lips. But what the hell did they expect from me? My twin sister tried to kill me, and that didn't count the fact that at one point in time, she had been a killer for money. More than that, though, those men had changed me. I'd never see them again, and they made me feel things I'd never felt with any other human being on the planet. No one I had ever dated made me feel as alive and beautiful as they did. Three different times, I got to feel that way. Three different, wondrous, breathtaking moments with men I knew I'd never forget.

I had become a different person.

How the hell was I supposed to go back to my life after all that?

Mom cackled. "Oh, my God. That Blanche is something else, huh?"

Dad bent forward and kissed the top of Mom's head. "Reminds me of someone that I know."

I wrinkled my nose. "Ew."

Mom giggled as she reached over and took my hand. "One day, sweetheart, you'll understand."

I pulled my hand away. "Yeah, one of these days. Excuse me for a second, I gotta go to the bathroom."

Sitting there and watching some television show felt almost like being strangled. In fact, I would have given anything to go back and be slapped around by Axe than to sit there with my mother like the past couple of weeks hadn't fucking happened. Dad called after me, but I had no clue what he said. I heard my mother's muffled voice, but I didn't care to piece her words together. I needed space. I needed a moment to breathe.

I needed to go home.

"Shower," I said breathlessly as I stripped my clothes off in the hallway, "I need a fucking shower."

"Sweetheart?" Mom called out.

"Just need to get cleaned up!" I exclaimed, slipping into the bathroom.

Finally, some peace.

Knock, knock, knock.

The soft rapping of my father's knuckles made me want to claw my own eardrums out.

"Princess?" he asked.

"What?"

I hated how harsh my voice sounded, but what the hell else was I supposed to do? My life had been turned upside down, and now I missed the three men that I needed the most. They had abandoned me. Left me there, with my psycho twin sister my parents never once told me about, and expected me to... what? Pick up the pieces and move on?

I'd never been so angry in all my life.

"I'm sorry, princess," Dad said softly.

A tear slid down my cheek as my bare back slid down the door. My ass plopped to the cold linoleum floor, and I found myself tucking my knees close to my body.

"We should have told you," he muttered.

"Told her what?" Mom asked.

"About my twin sister," I said flatly.

"Oh," Mom said softly.

Dad cleared his throat. "Why don't you take a shower and—"

"Why didn't you tell me about her?" I asked.

"Oh, sweetheart," Mom whispered.

"Don't change the subject," I spat as tears lined my voice, "I deserve these answers. After everything that's happened, I deserve to know the truth."

"We don't even know what happened, honey," Mom said.

I shot to my feet and ripped a towel from the rack over my left shoulder. I haphazardly threw it around my body, a useless form of protection before I flung the fucking door open.

"You don't know what happened?" I asked.

"Brielle," Dad said, placing his hand on my shoulder, "why don't you take a second and—"

"You don't know what happened!?" I exclaimed as I stepped through the threshold of the bathroom door. "What happened, Mom, is that my twin sister that you abandoned in the hospital for having health issues grew up to become a psychopath, needed my organs for a fucking transplant, and decided she'd seek me out! That's what fucking happened!"

Dad stepped in front of Mom as she gawked at me. "Now,

you watch your tone of voice with her. We've been worried sick about you, trying to figure out what happened after that cryptic phone call a couple of weeks ago."

I stared him down as I ground my teeth together. "All my life, you heard me talk about how I felt empty inside. Throughout the entirety of my teenage years, you wondered why I locked myself away. Why I threw myself so hard into my studies. Why I'd dedicate my time to helping lost little kids when I had, what did you call it, Dad? So much potential?"

"Princess," he whispered as he reached out for me.

I took a step back. "All that time, you watched me cry. Listened to my anger as I tried to describe why it felt like nothing filled the hole I carried around in my heart. You knew I had a twin. You knew I had other family out there. Family that I should've stuck by. And instead, you kept it from me."

Mom's lower lip quivered, and she lowered her head. "We weren't perfect parents."

"And I'm not a perfect daughter," I said flatly, "but I know better than that."

Before they could say anything, I grabbed the bathroom door and inched it closed. I didn't want to talk with them any longer. I didn't want to speak with them. They had done enough. They had contributed enough. And now, it was on me to navigate what the hell had to come next. I couldn't rely on them to give me sustainable information. They'd always advise what they felt was best for them, not for me. Their omission of my second half was proof positive of that.

"Shower," I whispered and dropped the towel, "I need a shower."

Mom sobbed softly out in the hallway, but it only made me turn the water on as hot as I could. The steam seemed to mute the world around me, and as I slowly inhaled, I stepped into the shower. I pulled the curtain and allowed the water to drench my aching body and wash away my tears. Was everyone that I ever loved destined to hurt me? Destined to abandon me at my very moment of need? I let the tears fall. Silently and bravely, I stood there as my body grieved. I grieved the hole in my heart that would never go away. A hole that could have been filled by my beautiful, vibrant sister had she not been left behind. I grieved my guys, and a life I had imagined for myself while in their clutches. I grieved for my sister, and the life she must have lived. The pain she must have endured. The suffering she must have witnessed, to have turned out to be a bringer of that same suffering.

Vengeance was a nasty thing, and I knew I couldn't hold my anger against my parents for long.

But goddamn it, I needed some time to be pissed.

31

———

BRIELLE

I wasn't sure how long I stayed in that shower. All I know is that the water turned lukewarm before I had enough sense to wash the conditioner out of my hair. The steam evaporated, leaving me exposed to the world beyond the shower curtain as I turned off the water and stepped out. I scooped the towel up from the floor and gravitated to the mirror. I wrapped the towel around me, allowing the microfiber to soak up the trails of water that I left behind. And as I reached out to the mirror, wiping the fog off the glass, I saw heavy bags hanging beneath my eyes.

"You look like shit, girl," I said to my reflection.

The house was eerily quiet, and I took my shot. I opened the door and scampered through the frigid air draping the hallway before traipsing into my bedroom. I swung the door shut and sighed. With my hair dripping down my back and the oversized towel double-wrapped around my body, I walked over to the bed waiting for me in the corner and perched on its edge. I glanced around my room, a place that hadn't changed ever since I moved for college. My high school posters were still on the walls. My vision cork board still stared at me with pictures of friends I hadn't talked to since graduation. My desk was still decked out with sparkly hearts I made in art class and doodles in note-taking journals I had crafted in the middle of my math courses.

God, math had been a pain.

"Why did you guys leave me?" I whispered to myself.

"Princess?" Dad asked behind my closed door.

I closed my eyes. "Yeah?"

"May I come in?"

I chewed on the inside of my cheek. "Sure, yeah. Yeah, you can—you can come in. I owe you an apology anyway."

"No, you don't," he said as the door creaked open.

The smell of breakfast wafted through the air. "Mom cooking?"

He brandished a full plate from behind his back, complete with a large glass of orange juice. "She insisted I bring you something to eat."

"I *have* lost weight."

His stare quickly studied my crooked form. "I suppose you have."

I patted the bed next to me. "Just leave it on the nightstand. I'll eat when I'm ready."

"Of course."

He quickly came into the room and shuffled the food onto my nightstand. Then, he perched beside me.

"You're right to be mad at us," he said.

I nodded mindlessly as I stared at my black glitter laced vision board. "I know."

"And, if you're looking for an explanation as to why we did what we did, then I—"

I cleared my throat and clutched my towel tighter. "I already know the reason, right?"

His heavy sigh told me all I needed to know. "Your mother and I were unequipped to deal with the issues your sister had when she was first born. We were just starting out ourselves, and your biological mother? She—"

My gaze fell to the floor. "She what?"

He snickered. "I honestly don't think she knew she was having twins."

I wrinkled my nose. "How the hell do you not know you're having twins?"

"She was young, Brielle. Twenty, if I remember correctly."

"Nineteen," Mom's disembodied voice said from the hallway.

I swallowed hard. "Nineteen? What—what happened to her?"

Mom swiveled into the room and leaned against the doorframe with her arms crossed over her chest. "What happens to most girls that age that have adoptions so young. She was taken advantage of by someone she trusted."

"Jesus," I whispered.

"But," Mom said as she came over and sat on my other side, "it doesn't excuse the fact that we never told you about her."

I peered over at her. "Why didn't you ever tell me, Mom? Why keep something so personal and so monumental from me? Her and I, we could've—"

"Could have what?" she asked plainly.

I shook my head softly and stared out into the hallway. "I don't know, linked up or something."

"Were we not enough family for you?" Mom asked.

"Honey," Dad said sharply.

I jumped to my feet. "Don't make this about you. This has nothing to do with how much family I do or do not have. This is about you withholding information I had a right to know about my life. Don't change the subject because it's uncomfortable for you."

Mom physically gawked. "Well, then."

Dad shoved himself to his feet. "We don't have a good reason as to why we did it."

"I want to hear it from Mom," I said.

She looked up at me. "And why is that?"

I snickered. "Because I honestly believe you think you've done nothing wrong, and you couldn't be further from the truth."

That's when she blinked back tears. "Whatever explanation or reasoning I can give you isn't going to hold up to what you're looking for."

"And yet, you could still try," I said curtly.

Dad walked over to Mom and guided her to the bed. He sat her down, holding her close and wrapping his arms around her as if to protect her.

What the hell had happened?

Dad cleared his throat. "Maybe we should all take some time to—"

"Dad?" I asked.

"Yeah, princess?"

I nodded at Mom. "Stop interjecting and let her get it out. It's clearly been eating away at her for a while. She deserves a chance at peace."

For many people, they never see their father cry. But that wasn't my household. That wasn't the way that I grew up. Dad was the one that taught me about my emotions. He was the one that helped me navigate mood swings during my teenage years. It was Mom that never cried. It was Mom that was the strong, stalwart soldier of the family.

And watching those tears slide down her cheeks broke my heart.

"Mom," I said as I took her hands in mine and sat back down beside her, "just tell me what in the world happened."

She drew in a broken breath. "My health issues had already cropped up by that point."

"And you didn't know if you could afford two children?" I asked.

She shrugged as she gazed over my shoulder. "That, and—"

Dad leaned over and kissed her cheek. "Tell her. I think you need to say it out loud, too."

I squeezed Mom's hands, urging her to talk with me. Urging her to just spit it out. It was clear she was ashamed. Embarrassed of whatever answer she was about to give. But I'd never seen her struggle like that. I'd never seen her work so hard to keep her emotions at bay.

I'd never seen her fail at it, either.

"We were so inundated with medical bills," she said with a tremble in her voice, "and things were bleak. They were—oh God, Brielle, it was probably the hardest time in our marriage."

She sniffled, and I rubbed her back. "Keep going, Mom. You're doing great."

Her watery stare fell toward her lap. "We had signed up to be adoptive parents well before things got bad with my health. We had everything set up, you know? Your room. A savings account for college. A few clothes, some diapers. Things to get us started for when our child finally found us, you know?"

"And then, the downhill started," Dad said.

Mom lifted her gaze and scoffed. "Around the time we got the call that your biological mother was searching for an adoptive family, I was three weeks into being on the transplant list for a new kidney. Dialysis was arduous, and there were a few moments there where I didn't think I was going to make it."

"Oh, Mom," I said softly.

She shook her head. "And I know it's not a good reason to adopt any child, but we decided to go through with things because—"

When she looked over at Dad, I knew. "You didn't want Dad being alone."

"I know it wasn't right," she said as her entire body shivered at her words. "I know it's not right, and it wasn't the right way to make the kind of decision that we did. But I didn't think your father could handle two kids by himself. So, when the doctor told us that your mother had given birth to two girls and not just one, we made the hardest call of our entire lives."

Her explanation didn't do much with my anger. But it certainly didn't add to things. The pain in my mother's eyes was evident. The way Dad wrapped his arms around her and held her close told me everything that I needed to know. She thought she was dying. She thought she was dying, and she didn't want to leave Dad behind to pick up the pieces by himself.

"You wanted to give him something to live for," I murmured, releasing her hands.

"I know it's not—not right," Mom said, her voice hiccupped with her sobs. "I know we've hurt you so—so much. But, I swear, we didn't do it maliciously. We didn't do it intentionally. And when I had that kidney removed and pulled through the cancer, I think your father and I were so desperate to leave all of the stress and worry behind that we just—"

"—didn't talk about it," I said.

"Yeah," Dad said with a nod of his head.

Hurt. Pain. Sorrow. It permeated through my room. It radiated from my parents, and the pain that wafted over their faces as Mom cried on Dad's shoulder, was too much for me. I pushed myself up from the mattress. I walked over to my desk and pulled out the chair. I sat down, watching as my parents held one another. Watching as they cried with one another. Waiting for my reaction. Waiting for me to do something, or say something, or give them something to make things better. We couldn't make things better, though. Not now.

All we could do was... move forward.

"She wanted my organs," I said softly.

Mom picked up her head. "What?"

I picked at a hangnail. "Rachel, my twin sister. I don't know how much you know about what happened to me or whatever, but—"

"Why don't you tell us what you went through?" Dad asked.

Mom stared at me intently. "You're the only one that will be able to tell us how it impacted you from your standpoint. So, if you're willing to talk about it, we're all ears."

I furrowed my brow. "Really?"

"Yes," Dad said as he scooted away from Mom and patted the bed between them, "really."

I dragged my tired body over to the bed and slumped in between them, clinging to my towel for dear life. "You know she was born with a blood clotting disorder, right?"

"Yes," Mom said softly.

"So, you can only imagine the medical costs and tolls that came with it."

"Yes," Dad said just as softly.

"Well," I said, drawing in a deep breath, "her organs are failing, I guess."

"What?" Mom asked.

"Is she all right?" Dad asked.

I shook my head. "No. I'm not sure she'll ever be all right, but it is what it is. I don't think she even realized that I existed until the guys that were protecting me mistook me for her."

"Why were they looking for her?" Mom asked.

I knew better than to tell that particular truth, but that didn't mean I had to lie. "She's a professional assassin, Mom. They were searching for her because she killed someone they loved."

"My God," Dad said.

"She came after you, didn't she?" Mom asked.

I shook my head softly as I turned toward her. "It's hard to say which came first: whether those guys found me first and that brought me to the forefront, or whether Rachel knew about me, and they scooped me up for my protection. Either way, I'm alive because of them. We ended up figuring out that part of the reason why she came after me so hard is because her organs are failing. We all know as well as she does that dialysis and things of that nature are only temporary fixes. It's no way to live a life."

"It takes a toll on everything after a while," Mom said.

"So, imagine doing it pretty much your entire life, just to stay alive. That's what she was doing, and when she figured out that she had a twin out there? Someone who's practically a perfect donor match? She turned her sights on me."

Mom's eyes widened. "She wanted you for your organs?"

I pointed at her playfully. "That was my exact reaction, too."

Dad wrapped his arm around my waist and pulled me tightly to his side. "My God, princess. What in the world have you endured?"

Being wrapped in that man's comforting embrace was all it took for the well to spring forth. He tucked my head against his shoulder and trapped it with his cheek like he always did when I was a little girl, and I collapsed. My chest heaved with heavy sobs that leaked tears of grief down my face. My men had helped save my life, and I'd never see them again. My twin sister would most likely die in that hospital, and she'd never get to be part of my life. I'd never get to know her, or visit her, or have lunch dates with her. All of the would haves and could haves we should have shared would die with her.

And I'd be alone.

Again.

"Oh, sweetheart," Mom said through misty eyes.

"They saved my life, and I'm nev—never—never gonna see —see them again," I choked out.

"We'll get you through this," Dad whispered into my hair.

Mom pulled my legs into her lap and started massaging my feet. "No matter what it takes, sweetheart, we'll get through this. I promise."

And as I sat there in my father's lap, releasing one weeks' worth of anger, shock, and pain, I still couldn't stop thinking about them. I still couldn't snap out of it. I knew that I had to pull myself out of the past, especially since they had made the decision to leave me. They had made the decision to abandon me at the hospital. Hell, for all I knew, that was what Dee had whispered into Jax's ear. *Leave her. Let her go back to her life. We'll sneak out the back before anyone sees us.*

The thought made me nauseous.

I cried so hard that I didn't even feel my parents manipulating my body. All I knew was that dad's shoulder gave way to the comfort of my pillow as tears soaked the fabric beneath my cheek. A warmth blanketed me, fluttering all the way down to my relaxed little toes. And as heat permeated through my tired muscles, my eyes grew heavy with sleep.

"Get some rest," Dad said as he bent down and kissed my forehead.

"We can always reheat your food if you wake up hungry," Mom whispered, kissing my cheek.

"I love you guys," I muttered tiredly.

"We love you, too, princess."

"So much, sweetheart."

Then, as if my best friend were coming to hang out with me, darkness took over my vision. Dragging me under, just like it always had. At least there was one thing I could count on in life.

Even if it was the darkness.

The trilling of a bird outside woke me up. As my eyes peeled open, I watched dust float around in the rays of the sun that filtered through the sheer black curtains of my childhood bedroom. I drew in a deep breath of air as an engine struck up. It revved to life, pulling me upright as I turned myself toward the window. Dad was outside mowing the lawn. Back and forth, back, and forth. The same pattern he had drawn across our front lawn ever since I was a little girl running around with bare feet and dirty sundresses. And as I pulled myself out of bed, I walked over to the window and threw it open. There was nothing as refreshing as birds singing while the scent of freshly cut grass filtered through the screen.

It provided a lovely backdrop while I threw on the first set of clothes that I could find.

"I thought I heard you stomping around in here," Mom said.

I drew in another breath of fresh air, laced with the fresh grass trimmings wafting around outside. "Mmm, morning."

"Here, I figured you could use this."

I looked down at the mug of coffee before I took it from her. "Thanks."

She rubbed my back before guiding me out of my bedroom and toward the kitchen table. "How did you sleep?"

I snickered. "Like the dead."

"That's not funny."

"I didn't realize I had cracked a joke."

I peeked over at Mom, but I found her sharp stare boring a hole in my face.

"I won't say it again," I said.

"We thought you were dead there for a while."

"Honestly? I thought I was, too."

She tucked a loose strand of hair behind my ear. "Who are

these men that you were with? You know, that you keep mentioning."

I peered down into my coffee as steam swirled up from the top. "It doesn't matter."

"It does to us."

"Why?"

"Because we owe them for keeping you safe."

I took a long pull from the mug as the lawn mower engine grew closer to the edges of the house. "It doesn't matter now. They did what they needed to do, found what they needed to find, and now it's back to business as usual."

"And for you?"

"I was talking about me."

"I don't think you were."

I slowly peered over my shoulder at her. "You're doing that thing again."

"The Mom thing?"

"The thing where you act like you don't know anything, but you know everything and you're waiting for me to say it."

She shrugged as a sly grin crossed her face. "Because sometimes I feel like you need to say it out loud."

I snickered as I watched her retrieve a mug of coffee for herself. "Don't pull that trick on me. I just did that with you yesterday."

"And where do you think you learned it from?"

I took another sip of my coffee. "Touché."

She giggled and sat down beside me at the table. "Well, whoever they are, if you ever want to talk about them, just know that we're here. We owe them for keeping you safe."

I listened as Dad continued to move that mower across the yard, kicking up a fresh scent that almost brought tears to my eyes. The rays of sun illuminated my face, warming me from head to toe as caffeine woke up my sore muscles. Mom and I stood there, her arm linked with mine, enjoying coffee the way that we always had over the years.

Sitting at a table, listening to the only non-caffeinated person in our family buzz around outside at nine in the morning without an ounce of coffee in his system.

"He's a freak of nature, you know," Mom muttered as she polished off her coffee.

I grinned. "You and him, both."

"Hey, now."

"Don't tell me you're not a tad bit off for wanting to put barbecue sauce on your scrambled eggs."

"That's good eating right there, Miss Orange Juice in The Cereal."

"That was one time."

"And it was one time too many."

"Says the woman who doesn't like brownies?"

"The gooey middle is a texture issue!"

She threw her head back in laughter and it brought a smile to my face. I clenched my coffee mug as a giggle bubbled up the back of my throat, and when I released it, it took my whole body with it. I leaned forward and chuckled. It turned into a cackle that caused me to howl just to take a breath. And as my stomach started to strain itself from the hilarity of my mother's snorting laughter, it was all we could do to stumble back to my bed just so we wouldn't plummet to the floor.

And I suppose we were laughing so hard that we didn't realize Dad had finished up with his morning chores.

"I hear a good time being had in here," he said, tossing the front door open.

"Oh, my goodness!" Mom exclaimed, trying to catch her breath.

"I still don't know how you do it."

"I swear, we all have the weirdest quirks sometimes," Mom

said breathlessly.

Dad slipped out of his boots. "So, what's got you girls all twisted up with laughter this morning?"

I stood to my feet. "You come sit, Dad. Let me get you some coffee."

He pointed at me. "You, sit and rest. I can get myself a mug."

I snickered. "Dad, it's really not that big of a—"

He brushed past us and pinned me with a look. "Relax."

I held up my free hand in mock surrender. "All right, all right, I know better than to argue."

"We're talking about the kind of quirks we all have," Mom said as she polished off the rest of her coffee.

"Oh, you mean like how you always wear mismatched socks?"

I blinked. "Wait, what?"

Mom tisked as she rolled her eyes. "It's just a little superstition Grandma taught me growing up. What's the harm in that?"

Dad chuckled as he came back toward us with a piping hot mug of coffee clasped in his hands. "Don't make me tell our daughter about the time you wore those mismatched knee-high socks on our fourth date."

Mom smiled so brightly that it almost closed her eyes. "Says the man who carries around a bottle of hot sauce on his keychain."

"I haven't done that in years!"

"Because it gave you food poisoning! Exactly like I said it would."

He leaned down from behind and kissed the top of her head. "Just consider it payback for making me walk you around the grocery store in mismatched knee-high socks."

Rum-rum-rum-rum-rum-rum-rum.

"Dad," I said as I stood from my seat.

I heard him putzing around in the kitchen. "I thought I told you to stay seated."

Rum-rum-rum-rum-rum-rum-rum.

"Dad, did you—"

"Honey, can you grab me an apple?" Mom asked.

"Think fast," Dad said as an apple whizzed past my vision.

I couldn't take my eyes off the front door, though. The still-cracked door that Dad hadn't slung shut yet. Maybe that was the sound that I was hearing. Maybe he simply wasn't done mowing the lawn yet.

"Sweetie?" Mom asked. "What is it?"

I furrowed my brow. "Are you done mowing the lawn, Dad?"

He walked over and stood beside me. "Yeah, why?"

"Then, what is that sound outside?"

The three of us froze, listening to the soft putter of an engine whirring outside. Dad moved toward the door, his shoulders rolled back and his posture tight as he clutched his coffee mug in his palms. Mom took my hand, yanking me back down into my chair before she placed her hand on top of mine. Weighing me down, as if that would stop me from leaping out of my seat.

Could it be?

Was it possible?

Rum, rum-rum-rum-rum-rum-rum.

Dad peered through the crack he left in the door. "There's someone outside on a motorcycle, I think."

"What?" I asked as I shot back to my feet.

Rum, rum-rum-rum-rum-rum-rum.

"A motorcycle?" Mom asked. "Does anyone we know own a motorcycle?"

"Let me see," I said, abandoning my coffee on the kitchen

table.

I rushed toward my father, scooting off to the side as I ripped the front window curtains away from the paned glass. My hands pressed flush with the cool surface with that sound dancing against my eardrums. My eyes searched. My toes curled into the ground to keep me rooted. Every ounce of me wanted to believe it was them. One of them, or all of them, or maybe even Jax.

But there was nothing outside but that fucking sound.

"Where is the motorcycle?" I asked.

I felt Mom standing behind me before she placed her hands on my shoulders. "I don't know, I think that's just what it sounds like."

"Could be nothing," Dad muttered.

"I need another angle," I said as I pushed away from the window.

"Princess, what's going on?" Dad asked.

I rushed over to the other front window that framed the door. "The guys that saved me rode motorcycles, you guys. So, just give me a second."

My parents were hot on my heels as I abandoned my post and slipped out onto the front porch. Their footsteps damn near matched mine as the sound ricocheted around inside of my head. I knew I wasn't dreaming of it. I knew that I wasn't just hearing things. They heard it, which meant that it was real.

And as I walked out into the driveway, I turned in every direction, searching for the source of the sound.

Then, finally, out of the corner of my eye, there was movement.

"Who is that?" I whispered to myself, whipping toward the moving shadow.

HONK HOOOOONK!

All I saw was the outline of the bike. I knew someone had to be sitting on it, but for all I knew it was someone from that bull-shit crew that tried to take us all out. My heart stopped in my chest. The hairs on the nape of my neck stood on end. I heard the front door close, but I couldn't yell at my parents to get back inside and get down.

Would they start shooting at the house?

Was that my sister?

Had she escaped?

Were we about to die?

"Do you know who that is?" Dad asked as his voice sat close to my shoulder.

I jumped at his presence and my heart plummeted to my toes. "Jesus, Dad."

He placed his hand on my shoulder. "Do you know who that is across the street?"

"So, you see him, too?" I asked.

He nodded. "I do."

And as a set of feet moved that motorcycle out of the shadows, I got a good look at a remarkably familiar face.

"Jax?" I asked.

I wasn't sure when the hell he had arrived, or how in the world he knew where to find me, but there he sat, with his jeaned-up legs straddling his motorcycle while the engine idled aimlessly. He perched himself across the street with his tight white t-shirt clinging to his chest, and I saw the bulge of his cigarette packet rolled up into his sleeve.

He raised his hand over his head and wiggled his fingers, and I smiled as I wiggled mine back.

"Mom?" I asked as I turned to face her.

She stepped off the porch and came toward me. "Yeah, princess?"

"Did you mean it when you asked me if there was anything you could do to repay those men for keeping me safe?"

She smiled softly. "Of course."

"Who is that man out there?" Dad asked.

I turned my stare toward him and reached out my hand. "Come here."

He stepped toward me and took my hand. "Who is that? What's going on?"

"Mom asked me if there was anything you guys could do that would repay those men for taking care of me during all of this."

"Is there?" he asked, threading our fingers together.

I nodded. "Mom said that you two owe those men for keeping me safe."

He cupped my cheek. "She's right, we do."

I looked over at Mom. "And you mean that?"

"Yes," she said, "now, what's going on?"

I drew in a deep breath through my nose. "Let me go with him."

Dad didn't hesitate. "Absolutely not."

Mom didn't speak, though.

"Dad, you have no idea what—"

"You're right," he said, his voice growing curt, "we've got no idea what you've been through this week. But you also have no idea what we've been through. We just got you back. We *just* got you safe. I'm not letting you walk away from this house with someone we don't know."

I released his grasp and pointed toward him "That's Jax."

"Jax?" he asked.

"He's the one who escorted me into the hospital and stayed by my side while I did my best to help Rachel. He's the one that watched my back to make sure no harm came to me while we were there. That's who's sitting on that bike across the street."

Dad swallowed hard. "I don't want to let you go. Can't you just... stay one more night? Please?"

HONK HONK HOOOOOONK!

He blared his bike horn like a last call at a bar, and it took every ounce of strength I had saved up for myself to keep standing there with my parents.

"Dad," I said as I reached up and cupped both of his cheeks, "you have to let me go."

His gaze watered over. "I can't. I-I-I—"

But it was Mom that pressed a kiss to the side of my head. "You want to go with him, don't you?"

Dad's stare begged me to say no, but I couldn't. "We're still on for Sunday lunch, right?"

He swallowed hard before shaking his head. "How can I ever let you go back outside after all this, princess?"

I wiped his tears with my fingertips. "If you want to help me, Dad, if you want to repay those men for keeping me safe, then you'll let me go live my life."

The tears that threatened to soak his face broke my heart. "I'm so sorry."

"I know."

"I'm so sorry that we ever hid things from you."

"I know you are."

Mom wrapped her arms around my waist and hugged me close. "I'm so sorry that we ever let you down."

I released Dad long enough to turn around in her grasp and wrap her up tightly. "Then, don't keep doing it. Let me do what I know is best for me."

Dad stroked the back of my head. "I'm so proud of you, Brielle."

I smiled as I pulled away from Mom and turned back to Dad. "You want to know why everyone thinks I inherited your eyes?"

Dad snickered. "Because we have the same-colored eyes?"

I smiled up at him. "No. Because we always have the same

look in our eyes once we understand something. That same accepting, kind, perceptive look. You taught me that."

Tears lined his stare. "Do you feel safe with them? Can you honestly tell me that?"

I threw my arms around his neck and hugged him close. "I'd be dead if it weren't for them."

"But do you feel safe with them?"

It was the most honest answer I had ever given in my life. "Yes."

He sniffled hard before placing his hands on my shoulders and pushing me softly out of our hug. "Then, go. Live your life."

Mom pointed at me. "But if you don't show up for Sunday lunch—"

I wrapped my hand around her finger, pulled her toward me, and kissed her cheek. "I'll bring them to Sunday lunch so you can meet them. How does that sound?"

Mom smiled brightly. "I'll make sure to make extras."

"I love you, princess."

I pulled Dad into a hug as well. "I love you, too, Daddy."

Mom brushed my hair away from my forehead before tucking a loose strand behind my ear. "Go, before I change my mind and chain you to the kitchen table for dinner."

"Wise words," Dad murmured as he gave my cheek one last kiss.

I giggled softly as he relinquished me. "Sunday lunch, okay? Just like usual? 12:30?"

She did her best not to start crying again. "Just like usual. 12:30. Promise?"

I held up my pinky finger and she wrapped hers around it. "Promise."

HOOOOOOOOONK!   **_HOOOOONK!_** **_HOOOOOOOOONK!_**

I whipped around and smiled at Jax. "Love you guys."

"Love you, too," they said in unison.

And that's when I took off.

Everything moved in slow motion after that. I tore across the street, even as tears streaked my neck. I threw myself into the shadows and didn't bother looking back as I ran toward Jax and his bike. Even he had a grin on his face, a smirk that overtook his usually stone-cold features. And as he slid his sunglasses down onto his face, I threw my leg over the back of his bike.

I looked over at my parents and found them waving at me.

"Love you guys!" I exclaimed, waving back.

"Stay safe, honey!" Mom called out as she cupped her hands over her mouth.

"See you Sunday!" Dad bellowed, waving his hand at me over his head.

"And don't forget to bring your friends!" Mom yelped.

"Your momma a good cook?" Jax asked.

I wrapped my arms around his waist. "One of the best."

He chuckled as he revved his motorcycle engine. "Count me in for Sunday, then."

Feeling the wind whipping around my body as he kicked off and soared down the road lifted my heart out of its dark cavern. The closer we grew to the clubhouse, the more my soul took flight. I thought they had forgotten about me. I thought they had left me behind, discarded me like my sister had been the day we were born. And for the smallest of moments, I felt for her. For the smallest of moments, I felt what it had been like to realize you had been left behind. To realize you hadn't been loved enough to have been considered in decisions.

If she pulled through things, I'd make sure she knew someone cared.

Even if the guys didn't agree with my efforts.

The world zipped by us like lightning as I focused on the desert unfolding in front of us. Jax took a sharp left, pulling off the asphalt and soaring through the cracked, cactus-laden desert. Dust kicked up around us and I had to bury my face against his back to keep from breathing it in. How he kept his head high while he drove was beyond me. The dust damn near suffocated me as is.

But when his rumbling motorcycle came to a stop in front of the place I had called home for the last week, I couldn't throw myself off that bike quickly enough.

"Axton!" I roared.

I scrambled up the steps and slammed my way through the front door.

"Maverick! Dante! Where are you guys!?"

"There's our girl," Axe said as he turned the corner and came out of the kitchen.

"We were wondering how long it would take Jax to pick you up," Dee said with a grin, coming down the stairs.

I heard the crunching of food before I ever saw his face, and yet I knew exactly who it was. "I don't know what you're eating, Mav, but I'd like a piece of it."

And when I turned around, he held out the sandwich he had been chomping on. "Hope you like ham and turkey."

I leaned forward and took a gigantic bite as my gaze locked with his. "Mm, mm, mm. This is good."

He chuckled, gripped my chin, and swiped something off my lower lip. "So are you, beautiful."

"Come here," Axe said gruffly.

Feeling him scoop me against his body brought tears to my eyes. He hugged me from behind, my back flush with his bulging muscles as Dante scooted around Mav just in time to wrap his long, taut arms around us both. He squeezed tightly as his lips brushed the shell of my ear, and the heat of his breath made my knees quiver.

"I thought you guys had left me," I whispered, throwing my

arms around Dee's neck.

"You didn't think we'd let you go that easily, did you?" he murmured before kissing my forehead.

Mav sneaked his way in between me and Dee, and his arms disconnected Axe from my back as he pulled me close. He enveloped me, drowning out the rest of the world as it threatened to creep back in. His hand tucked my head into the crook of his neck. His body heat alone comforted me, relaxing me so much that my legs gave way. Tears of happiness flooded his shoulder, and he held me close to him, refusing to let me drop. Then, my body levitated through the air, rising up a set of steps my feet never once touched.

And when my back touched down against that mattress, I looked up to find all three of them staring down at me with smiles on their faces.

"Welcome home, my queen," Axe said.

Dee perched at the foot of the bed and pulled my feet into his lap. "Let's get these off. I'm sure you feel stifled."

Mav clambered onto the bed and lifted my head, placing it softly in his lap. "You hungry?"

I shook my head. "No."

Axe stood at my side and reached down for my hand. "Thirsty?"

"Mm-mm."

Dee eased my shoes off my feet. "Tired?"

I drew in a deep breath. "No, actually."

"Can we get you anything, then?" Mav asked.

And as I tilted my head back, looking at his handsome upside-down face, only one thought crossed my mind.

"The three of you," I said as I reached up and cupped the back of his head. "I want the three of you. Now."

I pulled his lips down to mine, crashing them together in an earth-shattering kiss.

I knew nothing else except his tongue as it brushed against the roof of my mouth. Maverick intoxicated me, sliding his hand down between my breasts before he gripped the fabric of my shirt. He yanked it up and I felt someone dip their hands into the cups of my bra. Those long fingers, sliding their way along my puckered peaks as he freed them from their confines made me gasp against Mav's lips.

But it was Axe's voice that made me smile.

"Everyone!" he bellowed down the hallway. "Clear the clubhouse! Go have a fucking life for once! See you for church tomorrow morning at noon! Spread the word!"

"Perfect," Dante whispered as something warm touched down against my nipple.

"Fuck," I groaned as Mav sucked on my lower lip.

"So tasty," Mav whispered.

I heard the door close as a stampede of footsteps rumbled around downstairs. Mav grabbed my shirt and lifted it over my head, disconnecting our kiss long enough to remove it from my body. He leaned me up and popped the hooks of my bra apart, and as it tumbled down my body, Dee linked the strap of my bra around his finger. The bulging veins of his forearms came into view when he lifted my tattered, broken-in bra up to the light that streamed through the window. It swung there, in midair, and the bed creaked and groaned with Axe's weight as he sat down next to me.

And as Mav's lips connected to my bare collarbone, I chanced a whimper as Dee tossed my bra off to the side.

"We can get you better shit than that," he said, turning back toward me.

The halo of light around his languid body wet my pussy. He grinned and pulled his shirt over his head, and for the first time, the full force of his body came into view. My jaw slowly unhinged from my face as he dropped his shirt to the floor. His muscles pulled taut over his bones, and the pelvic lines he had that disappeared beneath the hem of his jeans made me lick my lips.

"Christ, Dee," I said as Mav sucked a hickey against my shoulder, "where the hell have you been hiding all of that?"

He chuckled and stepped out of his pants. I couldn't help but to stare at his bulge. Jesus Christ, that cock was thick, and the chiseled expanse of his legs made my mouth water. He was nothing but sheer strength wrapped up in a tight casing that formed mountains of muscle against his body. His eyes, twinkling with their hunter green beauty, darkened as he discarded the last of his clothes and stood there in all his lean, powerful glory.

With his cock leaking from its tip.

"You know you're welcome in this room anytime," Dee said, kneeling against the edge of the bed.

"He's right," Mav murmured as his lips found the shell of my ear. "We'll keep this room open for you."

My heart took flight as Mav sucked on my earlobe. My head fell back against his shoulder when he reached around and cupped my tits. I watched their excess spill through the slats of his fingers. I watched him pinch my nipple, sending electricity rocketing straight to my clit. My legs spread for them. My body fell weak against their assault. Dee planted himself onto all fours, crawling up the bed toward me as if he were a tiger ready to feast on his dinner.

It was Axe who slid his hand behind my head and picked it up for him, though.

"There's a good girl," Dee whispered before he leaned his lips into mine.

"Mmmm," I whimpered.

I felt Mav shift beneath me before my body plummeted to the bed. I squealed against Dee's mouth, but it only opened my lips further for his intrusion. His tongue filled me, raking against the roof of my mouth as someone grabbed my ankles. They pried my legs open, and I felt Dee's cock slide between my soaking wet thighs.

Before Mav's voice was heard. "Why don't you move so I can flip her over?"

Dee chuckled down the back of my throat before he released my lips. "Sounds like a plan to me."

"Hold on," Axe said with a grunt as the bed shifted with his movements, "just let me get in here really quickly."

"Ready?" Mav asked.

I tried to peer over my shoulder, but it was no use. "Guys, what are you—"

"Ready," Axe said.

"Aaaaand, there we go!" Mav chirped as he crossed my ankles and flipped me over without a second thought.

Before I face-planted right into Axe's massive cock.

"Perfect," Dee muttered as his knees perched in between my legs, "now, raise those hips for me like a good little girl."

I stared at Axe's pure strength, completely uncovered for my viewing pleasure. I had no clue when the hell he had stripped down or where he had tossed his clothes, but I didn't fucking care, either. Dante lifted my hips into the air as an offering as my gaze lingered upon Axe's pulsing muscles that wrapped around his substantial body. He grabbed the base of his thick cock and touched it to my lips. He bounced it around, coating my skin in his precum. Dee stroked his cock in between my pussy folds.

"Open wide," Mav said, threading his fingers into my hair.

And as my stare locked with Axe's, I opened my mouth and stuck out my tongue.

Before Mav staked my throat on Axton's cock.

"Holy fuck," Axe growled.

Dee plunged into my depths. "There it is. So tight for me."

"Oh, fuck," I moaned around Axe's cock.

"Shit," Axe hissed and shoved my head further down his shaft, "that's the stuff right there."

Dee pounded against me as Mav removed his hand, and all too soon, Dee's replaced his. He kept my head shoved down Axe's cock, and my throat closed around the intrusion as my pussy clamped around Dee's cock. I laid there, allowing them to use me as I raked my fingernails up and down Axe's legs. His muscles jumped for me as his skin flushed from head to toe, and the way his head rolled back as those growls left his lips was something I'd forever commit to memory.

That behemoth, in a pool of growls and grunts and at my mercy.

It was intoxicating.

And I knew then and there, that I loved him.

I loved all of them.

"Oh, God," I whimpered.

"So close, sweet girl. So good for me," Dee said with a grunt.

His hips stuttered as he yanked my head up from Axe's

cock. Axe growled in anger, and for a split second, I thought he'd grab me off Dee's cock and put me back in my place. He didn't, though. He simply sat there with his legs spread and his cock seated against his pelvis as he watched Dee take me from behind. The man wrapped his arm around my neck, holding me hostage as his free hand gravitated toward my core.

It was then that Mav, in all his nakedness, stepped up to the plate.

"I got this one," he said as he perched on the edge of the bed.

I peered down at him as Dee pounded into me from behind, sinking his cock into me, over and over. Mav simply smiled up at me with his toned muscles and his sparkling white smile when his fingers pierced my pussy folds, searching for my aching clit.

"Shit," I hissed the second he graced over it.

"There she is," Mav said, his voice darkened.

His fingers swirled around the edges, shooting me into the heavens as my eyes rolled into the back of my head. I gave myself over to him. I gave myself over to the sensations and they rolled over me like thunder across a landscape. Fireworks burst behind the darkness of my eyelids. Mav's fingers and Dee's cock pushed me to the edge, threatening to spill over as I climbed to the top.

But it was Axe's voice against my ear that sent me over the edge.

"Come for me, my queen. Let me watch you unravel."

"Oh—fu—ck," I choked out.

"Yes," Dee grunted as he slid into me one last time, "there it is. You want me to fill you up."

"Yes," I said breathlessly.

Mav kept up his smooth, subtle movements as my orgasm crashed over my body.

Then, Dee cupped my chin and pulled my head back so

that I stared up at him from upside down before those glorious words fell from his lips.

Words I never thought I'd hear from any of them, but less from Dante.

"I love you, sweet girl," he murmured as his cock filled me to the brim.

Mav slowed his movements and my body collapsed against Dee. "I love you, too. I love you so much, Dante."

His kiss was so unlike his movements. His cock was forceful. It took what it wanted without a second thought. And yet, his lips pressed to mine in such a kind fashion that I couldn't help but to cry. Tears slid down my cheeks, coating my skin in a happy little twinkle as a smile crossed my face. Dee chuckled down the back of my throat and my pussy pushed his cock out from between my thighs. I felt the evidence of our love for each other dripping down to the bed. He leaned forward, easing my stomach back down onto the bed before I rolled over, allowing my arm to flop into Mav's naked lap.

Axe's shadow came into view.

"Well, well, well," he said, his spit-soaked cock casting a shadow over my stomach, "what do we have here?"

Mav dipped his fingers in between my legs before he scooped up the mixture between them. "Open wide."

I parted my lips and sucked it off his fingers, lapping and twirling my tongue around his digits. I hummed at the taste. At the way Dee's arousal tasted when intermingled with mine. My body started moving again, despite the fact that I didn't move it. Someone pulled me to the edge of the bed, and I let them. Someone sat me up, and I let them. But when Axe perched on the cushion in the bay window and beckoned for me, I rose without a second thought.

I straddled his gargantuan pelvis and felt his cock teasing my entrance.

"Good girl," he purred against my ear.

"I love you, my king."

The words flowed forth so effortlessly that I damn near shocked myself. But it wasn't as if they weren't true. I loved them. All of them. And as Axe gazed deeply into my eyes with those brooding brown orbs of his, he thrusted his hips forward.

Staking me on his long, thick cock.

"Fuuuuuuck," I groaned as my forehead fell to his shoulder.

"I love you, too, my queen," he murmured, stroking my hair. "But I sure as hell am not gonna fuck you like I do."

My body shuddered at his words before he stood to his feet. With his cock still filling me up, he cupped the globes of my ass and pinned me to the first wall that he found. He raised my hands above my head, threading our fingers together as my tits dangled helplessly against my chest. His hungry gaze locked with mine and he dipped down, raking his tongue against my puckered peaks.

And when my pussy jumped for him, he pulled back out.

Only to slam right back into me.

"Axton!" I cried out.

"Such a good little slut for us," he growled.

I gasped at his words. "Fucking hell, you feel so—so good."

He pounded back into me and watched my body jump. "You have no idea how beautiful you are staked on my cock, do you?"

Dee and Mav answered in unison. "We do."

I couldn't help but giggle, however the sound was silenced by his lips. He kissed me with such a passion that it robbed me of my very breath, and the timing of his thrusts matched the beating of my heart. He overwhelmed me. He cloaked me away from the world. As I wrapped my legs around him, hanging on for dear life, his cock pulsed heavily against my walls. I sucked on his lower lip. He dipped his face down to my tits and buried himself in them. And the entire time, he kept me helplessly pinned.

Until his stuttering hips began swiveling.

"That's it, my king," I whispered, "come for me. Fill me up. Please."

He bit into my neck and his growl ricocheted through my bones.

"Oh, fuck! Axe!" I cried out.

His growl was the only thing that I knew. The only thing that rattled around in my head as my body locked out yet again. My juices dripped down to his balls as they smacked against my ass, coating my cheeks in the smell of our sex. My jaw shivered. My pussy quivered. It milked his cock for all he had when he stuffed himself into me one last time.

He sank to his knees, carrying me with him as his cock unloaded into my body.

"Goddamn it, my queen," he murmured before he kissed my bare shoulder, "what have you done to me?"

My head fell against the wall behind me. "I could ask you the same question."

"My turn!" Mav chirped, grabbing my arm.

Axe's growl as he ripped me off his cock made me giggle, but the sound didn't last very long. Mav crashed his mouth to mine, drinking down my sounds as arousal continued to drip down my thighs. He backed me up to the bed. I fell with a bounce, his body covering mine as he continued to heave me up the bed. He wrapped his arm around the small of my back and hoisted me upward until my head sat against one of the softest, fluffiest pillows imaginable.

He hovered over me with that boyish smile on his face, and I couldn't help but smile back.

"Hey there, pretty girl," he said with a wink.

I giggled. "Hey there, handsome."

"How you feelin'?"

I shook my head softly. "Like I've died and gone to heaven."

"No dying," Axe said curtly. "That was the promise."

I nodded. "No dying, got it."

Mav's nose nuzzled mine. "Do you love me?"

The softness of his words broke my heart. Almost as if he thought I'd leave him out. So, I cupped his face, gazed deeply into his eyes, and smiled.

"You were the first one that I loved, Mav."

His smile beamed from ear to ear. "You hear that, guys? Suck it."

Axe perched at my right shoulder. "That's her job."

Dee perched at my left. "If she wants it, that is."

I leaned up and captured Mav's lips softly. "I love you, handsome. So, let me show you how you should be treated when someone loves you."

He cupped the back of my head, suspending it in midair. "I love you so much, Brielle."

I reached my lips out and kissed him softly. "Whenever you're ready, so am I."

I could only imagine how hard it was for him. I mean, after what his brother had done to him? After his family ignored what had happened? I could only imagine how hard physical intimacy was for him. After all, he was the only one that hadn't fully taken me yet. The only one that had resisted the urge to fill me up the second he got me beneath his thumb.

I didn't want him to feel pressured if he wasn't ready.

"Mav?" I asked softly. "You don't have to do—oooooooh, shit."

He plunged into my depths. "Goddamn it, beautiful, why the hell did I ever deny myself this?"

I raked my nails up his arms. "Don't stop. Please, Mav."

Hands descended upon my body, and I didn't know who

was who. Someone stroked my hair while someone else stroked my thighs, and as their hands migrated, so did my love for them. Mav kept to a slow and deep pattern, filling me so completely that it brought tears to my eyes. He pinned my wrists above my head, exposing my tits to the room, and all at once, I watched Dee and Axe dip their heads down. Mav perched above me with a decadent grin on his face. He watched my every movement, as if committing the entire thing to memory. And when Dee and Axe flicked their tongues over my sensitive peaks, I bucked my hips hungrily against Mav.

"Shit, shit, shit, shit, shit," I hissed.

"Such a dirty mouth you have, beautiful," Mav grunted.

Dee crooked his finger beneath my chin and tilted my head off to the side. "Maybe someone should stuff her mouth full if she's gonna be such a bad girl."

Axe chuckled. "Highly recommended, by the way."

"Oh, fuck," I whimpered as Mav's cock grew thicker against my walls.

"Fucking hell," Mav growled, and Axe wrapped his hand around my throat.

"Why don't you open wide for Dee like a good little girl?" Axe asked.

I parted my lips and stuck my tongue out as Dee shuffled himself toward me. He perched on his knees and dropped his hand into my hair and Mav slowed his movements. I felt overwhelmed as Dee dropped the tip of his girth to my tongue, inching his way into my mouth. I gagged around his intrusion, a sensation that pulsed my pussy walls and pulled a groan from deep within Mav's body.

And as Dee sank down the back of my throat, he caught his falling body against the headboard. "Jesus, Axe, you weren't kidding."

Axe chuckled as his hand slid down my body. "Now, where is that fun little toy of mine?"

I whimpered against Dee's cock and Mav pulled back. He tossed my legs over his shoulders and pulled my hips closer to him. Axe played with the stubble growing against my folds. Dee shifted with the movements, his cock never once wavering from down my throat, and as Axe's fingers traced the outline of my oversensitive mound, my hands curled up into the sheets of the bed.

Before Mav took off.

"Oh, fuck!" I cried out as my body jostled with his thrusts.

"That's it," Dee hissed, sliding his deft fingers into my hair, "just like that, sweet girl. Hooooly fuck."

"Oh, God," Mav choked out.

Axe flicked his fingers wildly against the tip of my clit. "Come for us, my queen. Show me what your kings can do to you whenever we want."

"Mhm, mhm, mhm, mhm, mmmmmmmmmmmmm-mmmmmmmm."

The orgasm was forceful, and heated. I growled around Dee's cock as his entire body shivered, and I swear to hell on high, I'd never seen anything so beautiful in all my days. Mav's sounds overwhelmed me as he staked me on his cock one last time. And as his throbbing cock emptied itself into me, tears of happiness lined my eyes. I'd never felt so full in all my life. As Axe's movements around my clit slowed with the relaxing of my body, Dee managed to fish his cock out from the tight confines of my throat. I swallowed hard and gasped for air. Axe patted my pussy softly before Mav slid out, unleashing a torrential downpour of arousal toward the bed beneath my ass.

And as the room around me tilted on its own axis, there was only one thing to say.

"I love you guys so much," I said breathlessly.

Dee leaned down and pressed a kiss to my forehead. "I love you, too, sweet girl."

Mav leaned forward and kissed my belly button. "I love you, too, beautiful."

But it was Axe who dropped his lips to mine and captured my mouth in a searing kiss. "I love you, too, my queen."

Tears of happiness streaked down the sides of my face as a smile overtook my lips. "If you guys aren't careful with this shit, I may end up moving in."

Axe settled beside me, and Dee helped to turn my body toward the behemoth. He grabbed my leg and hiked it up over his, and I felt his cock still standing at attention.

God, I loved that we weren't done.

"Don't have an issue with that," he said as his cock slid between my swollen pussy lips.

Dee settled behind me, and I felt his fingertips breach my ass cheeks. "You may be sore after a while, though. Might need a break."

I reached my hand back and threaded it into his auburn hair. "Bring it on."

Then Mav perched just above Axe's head, gripped my chin, and tilted my face toward him. "You're a wild ride, beautiful."

I smiled up at him. "I guess wild is just in my blood, handsome."

"Now," Axe said, easing his thickened girth back into my pussy, "relax for us."

Mav's thumb traced itself along my lower lip. "The more you relax, the better this will be."

I darted my tongue out toward his thumb as Dee pierced a finger into my puckered hole. I groaned at the sensation as my asshole tightened up, but it was Axe that reached around and stroked my clit softly.

"There we go," Dee murmured against the shell of my ear. "Just relax for us, sweet girl."

I felt something wet dripping against my asshole before Dee pumped his finger in, and out. In, and out. In, and out. I'd never felt anything like that before. I'd never felt so full in all my life. Axe, with his cock stroking my walls, and Dee, with his finger stroking my asshole.

But nothing could have prepared me for the carnal lust that took over the second Mav filled my mouth with his cock.

"Oh, it feels like coming home," he grunted when my throat welcomed him.

"Oooooh, that's pretty relaxed," Dee said as he bent down and kissed my skin, "such a good girl for us."

Axe's cock held firm and he continued softly stroking my clit with the pad of his thumb. "You're doing so well, taking us all like this."

My jaw shivered with anticipation. "Only the best for my kings."

Axe growled. "And don't you forget it."

"We'll take this as slow as you need, all right?" Dee asked.

The tip of his cock seated itself against my asshole and my eyes widened. How the hell would he ever get inside that small little hole? My body clenched. Mav growled as my throat closed around him. Axe even grunted as my pussy pulsed around his aching length. However, as he swirled his thumb around my clit even faster, my body continued to relax.

Until Dee's cock took my asshole's virginity with a pop.

"God fucking damn it," he growled.

"Oh, my God," I whimpered as my eyes squeezed shut.

"Now?" Mav asked breathlessly.

Axe removed his hand from my clit and traced my juices along my lips. "Ready, my queen?"

I barely got my eyes opened before I darted my tongue out along the trail he had left behind.

"Ready when you guys are," I whispered.

Ecstasy. It was the only word I had for what happened next. They synchronized their movements, pumping into me at the same time as they filled my holes. I laid there as my moans and groans became stifled with the growing of Mav's cock. Someone fisted my hair, but I didn't know who. All I knew were their cocks. Their warmth. Their bodies, hovering over mine and filling me to the brim as my heart took flight for them. Electricity robbed me of my ability to see. Fireworks burst in the dark expanse of my head. And as I laid there, allowing them to take whatever the hell they wanted from me, I knew I'd never be able to live without them.

I wanted them.

I needed them.

I fucking *craved* them.

"Oh, shit," Axe grunted.

"This asshole is mine; do you hear me?" Dee growled.

I nodded and I hollowed out my cheeks around Mav's cock. "Mhm, mhm, mhm, mhm."

And he was the first to pop.

"Fuuuuuuuuuuuck, beautiful," he groaned, tilting his head toward the ceiling.

"Sweet girl," Dee said breathlessly as his hips stuttered, "you're gonna need a bath after this."

Mav's cock still sat deep against my throat, and he leaned down toward the headboard to keep himself upright. Dee's movements ceased as Axe continued pounding into me, and as his cock filled up my asshole, I smiled. Hearing their sounds and feeling their sweat dripping against me was something I'd never expect to enjoy, and yet there I was, begging them to drench me.

To fill me. To mark me, over and over until I passed out from the sheer joy of it all.

"Fucking hell, my queen," Axe growled as his hand linked with mine, "you're never going to get rid of me."

"Or me," Dee said, flopping down to the mattress.

"Or me," Mav said, picking up my head and placing it into his lap.

And as Axe exploded inside of me, my pussy pulsed so hard that it pushed him out.

"Oh," was all I could muster as the whimper fell from my lips. "Oh, my king."

Axe kissed my forehead. "I love it when you call me that."

My lopsided smile grew. "Will you guys just stay here with me for a bit?"

Dee chuckled and threaded his arm around my waist from behind. "You have us all day."

"And tomorrow," Mav said, stroking his fingers through my hair, "until church at noon."

Axe slipped my leg between his and stroked his calloused fingers along any inch of skin that he could find. I'd never been so relaxed and so content in all my life. I felt safe. I felt beautiful. I felt like I could conquer the world.

But I couldn't help the question that fell from my lips. "What'll happen to Rachel?"

I peeked open my tired eyes and found Axe staring back at me. "We don't have all of the answers there. But she's lucky to have you on her side."

"So, she's still in the hospital?" I asked.

"Mhm," Mav said, massaging the nape of my neck with his fingertips, "but just know that however you choose to proceed with her, we'll stand by you."

It was Dee who provided the warning, though, even as he

held me closely against him. "But if she fucks with you, sweet girl? She's dead."

"Here, here," Axe muttered.

"I can get behind that," Mav said.

I giggled softly before I drew in a deep breath through my nose. "One more question."

"Hit us with it," Axe said.

"What's the rule on eating takeout in bed?"

Axe leaned up without a second thought. "How does Chinese sound?"

"Oooooh, yeah. I haven't had sesame chicken in forever," Mav said as he wiggled out from beneath me.

My head bounced against the mattress as Dee turned me to face him. "What would you like to eat?"

"Other than you?" I asked cheekily.

"Hey, now," Mav said, pointing at me in all his naked glory, "that's for dessert."

"Did we... not just have dessert?" I asked.

Axe peeked over at me, and he kept his head bent toward his cell phone. "No, we didn't."

I blinked. "Then, what was that?"

Mav smirked. "A preview."

I moaned at the thought and rolled over onto my back. "Dee?"

"Yes, sweet girl?"

"Will you stay in bed with me while they get the food ordered?"

And as he tucked himself against me, he rolled me back toward him before enveloping me in his long, strong embrace.

"I'd love nothing more," he whispered.

"Ah, yes," Axe said as he turned his back to us, "I'd like to place an order for takeout."

"What's your poison?" Mav mouthed in my direction.

I kept my voice low and hushed. "Vegetable lo mein and crab rangoons."

Mav gave me a thumbs up before he leaned over and whispered into Axe's ear, and I laid there, relishing the feel of Dee's protective warmth wrapped around me. Had anyone told me even a couple of weeks ago that my captors would have turned into the loves of my life, I would have asked them what in the fuck they were talking about. I would have laughed in their face, waved my hand in the air, and changed the subject. Yet, as I laid there, listening to Axe place the order while Mav continued to smile at me and Dee continued to hold me close, I knew there was no other life that I wanted to lead.

There was no other place I'd rather be than at their sides.

And I'd spend the rest of my life making sure they knew it.

Turn the page for a sneak peak at Twisted Hearts!

They think I'm afraid of them. But I'm only scared of how much I want them…

I've drifted through my life wanting more but never knowing what was missing—until three members of the Shadow Boys MC walked into my bar and changed everything.

Lance. Pike. Blaze. They're all I can think about.

The attraction is electric, and not even seeing firsthand how dangerous they are can stifle the sparks that flare in me when I'm around them.

They don't think there's a place for me in their brutal world, but I refuse to back down until they see that I'm not too fragile to handle them and everything they stand for.

I don't need to be protected, and I'm determined to prove it —but my need makes me reckless. I've set in motion something I can't undo.

And it just might get us all killed.

Twisted Hearts is a complete stand-alone why choose motorcycle club romance. It is a part of the Twisted Intentions series, which features a new harem in each book. These books are not connected and can be read in any order.

"Goddamn it, Dalia, you make a hell of a blue motorcycle, you know that?"

I peered over my shoulder and tossed one of my many loyal customers a playful wink. "Only for you, handsome."

He tipped the rest of his glass up. "Two more for the booth over there?"

I spun around and scooped up his drink. "You got a good tip in it for me?"

He grinned. "Don't I always?"

I dumped the ice out of his cup into the sink. "Give me five minutes and they'll be up."

He rapped his knuckles against the bar top. "You're the best, babe. Thanks."

I blew him a kiss as he walked away. "I only get this way through you guys!"

"I love it when you say shit like that!"

I barked with laughter and set out piecing together two more drinks for the tipsy duo toward the stage. Every Friday night, we had live music in the bar, and I made sure to work because it wasn't as if I could sleep through the damned thing.

Living above my place of work had its perks. Especially when my boss loved staring at the spread of my hips. I knew what I looked like, a big girl with thick tits and thighs that rubbed together. I knew what kinds of thoughts raced through their minds after a couple of drinks at my bar.

And I most certainly used it to my advantage.

"Hey, luscious!"

I snickered, slapping my rag over my shoulder. "Anyone ever tell you that I hate that nickname, Bryce?"

I sent out the two blue motorcycles with my runner for the evening before yet another loyal customer came belly-upping to my bar.

"You know what I like," he said.

"Ah, a margarita with a beer tipped up into it?"

"And float me an extra shot of tequila."

I winked at him and pulled a glass down from the rack above my head. "Sounds like a rough day on the job."

Bryce snickered. "If only my wife were as intuitive as you are."

"Maybe she should know your drink order. That might help."

He barked with laughter, but it almost sounded cynical in its origin. "She can't even figure out how to put on her lingerie half the time. I don't think she'll stand a chance with my drink order."

"Well, you can always come here."

He slapped a twenty onto the counter. "That's why I do. Two drinks, and a tip. Thanks, Dalia."

I threw the contents of his drink into a blender then blew him a kiss. "Always, Bryce."

I mean, what the hell was a high school drop-out like myself supposed to do, anyway? Work in a grocery store my entire life? It wasn't as if anyone would take a chance on my intelligence without at least a G.E.D. And a girl had to pay the bills some-how. I wouldn't have it any other way, however. The Mule was my home, especially since I lived in the studio apartment just overhead.

I loved this place, and it had accepted all of me from the very beginning.

Which was more than I could say for any physical person in my life.

Including my own mother.

"There you go," I said, handing Bryce his drink. I slammed the top of the beer bottle against the counter, using my hand to shield the crack as the bottle cap flew off. My customer clapped his hands and whooped, as if he were at a circus or some shit. Then I tipped the bottle up quickly enough to slam it down into the blended mango margarita.

I took one of my stirring spoons, turned it over, and poured a shot of tequila right over the top of the drink.

"Enjoy," I said with a smile, "and plug your ears."

He put his hands over his ears and I drew in a deep breath.

"LAAAAAAST CAH-AAAAAALL!"

Deep down inside, I was ready for the night to dwindle down. While I didn't mind closing, I hated the way my mind raced as the bar dwindled from packed to nothingness. It made me wonder things I didn't like pondering, like whether or not life had more for me than slinging drinks six times a week just to pay bills. I mean, sure, I had a good thing going with reduced rent upstairs, but it wasn't as if I didn't know why. My landlord, who just so happened to own the bar as well, loved staring at the sway of my hips whenever I came or went. I wasn't an idiot. I knew the way he looked at me. And while my mother always taught me to "use what God gave ya," I didn't want to follow in her footsteps.

I didn't want to prostitute myself for money and luxuries.

Not much for high school dropouts in this world, though.

I don't know. I did my best to try and not compare myself to my mother. But with her dropping out of high school around the same time I did, it was hard not to. I watched men come and go from our house, leaving scores of money she used to treat us to nicer wardrobes and fancy dinners. I couldn't blame her, either. She had a kid to take care of and no man in the house. No one to love or care for her. No one to give her a break or come babysit so she could go out and enjoy what it felt like to be someone other than Mom. I loved her despite her flaws and the struggles we had as I grew up, and I'd never fault her for what she had to do to keep a roof over our heads.

I simply wanted something *more.*

That was all.

"Two glass bottle beers and a whiskey neat."

The shiver that ricocheted down my spine stiffened my tits against my bra. As I stood there, cleaning the blender I had used to make Bryce's margarita, the deep, resonant voice held me hostage. I put on my best smile before I placed the blender onto the drying rack. I raised my arms and got them around the crooks of my breasts, pressing them together as I brought my arms back to a normal position. I turned around, slapping my rag once again over my shoulder and came face to face with the man who possessed a voice that could stop God Himself in his tracks.

And as my gaze landed on the man in the leather jacket, it took all I had just to remember to breathe.

"Got a preference for beer?" I asked, nodding toward our beer cooler full of glass bottles.

The jet black hair that contrasted the playful amber eyes of the man standing in front of me had absolutely nothing on the way his shoulders and arms tugged at the leather bindings of his jacket. The damned thing looked like it was crying out for mercy, and when he slid his stare down my body , I took the opportunity to do the same to him, finding the muscles of his chest damn near ripping his black t-shirt off his torso.

"Surprise us," the man purred.

I tossed him a playful wink. "Coming right up."

I stepped up to the bar as the man turned his back, and I mindlessly made a whiskey neat, watching him backtrack to a booth. He sat down with two other men who donned the same kind of leather jacket, and I wondered if they were in a club together or some shit. It reminded me of my childhood, honestly. The bike crews rumbling down the street, revving their engines and forgoing their helmets because they didn't like the way they sat against their necks.

Those men were old as fucking dirt, sure. But Mom never ceased to try and throw herself at them.

After all, a man with toys was a man with money, right?

Ah, life lessons from Mom.

I barely made it through the whiskey neat before I walked over to the beer cooler. I dropped the glass onto a runner's tray before pulling out two of our finest glass bottle beers: a couple of stouts made locally up the road. I popped their tops and placed them on the tray, and Lisa came up, ready to take the tray from me.

But I waved my hand and picked up the tray myself.

"I got this one. You start cleaning up the tables that aren't taken any longer."

She pointed at me. "On it. I'm ready to get out of here, too."

With the tray balanced in the palm of my hand, I sauntered toward the men. I swayed my hips a bit deeper and jiggled my tits a bit more as my hair swayed along my shoulders. I arrived at their booth, tossing them playful winks while I divvied out their drinks.

And the entire time, I wondered why the fuck they hadn't come in earlier.

I could have gotten them to buy drinks from me all night.

"All right, who's got the whiskey neat?" I asked.

The guy stuffed into the corner flashed me a set of sea foam green eyes that stole my breath away. "Thanks."

I put the drink down and slid it toward him. "Then, you two must be the beer guys."

The man who originally came up to the bar chuckled. "Thanks, doll."

"Mm, mm, mm," I hummed as I looked over at the other man. "I hope you enjoy."

Blond hair and blue eyes were always a classic combination, but the other man's gaze seemed to sparkle like stars in an endless night sky.

"Thanks, beautiful," he said with a wink.

I smiled brightly. "Anytime, guys."

While Ocean Green and Rumble Voice stared at me from over their drinks, the guy tucked in the corner stared way too hard into the top of his whiskey neat. Huh, a bit of a challenge I see. Nothing wrong with that.

"If you need anything else before we close in an hour," I said, tucking the tray beneath my arm, "you know where to find me."

"We certainly do," the man in the corner said, throwing back his entire drink and sliding the glass toward me.

"I'm good for another," he murmured.

I quirked an eyebrow. "Were you guys not in here when I yelled last call?"

Mr. Luscious Voice crooked an eyebrow. "Is it really last call, though?"

I winked at him. "Depends on how much you want to tip."

"Would... this be enough?" sea foam asked.

And when I watched him pull a wad of cash out from the breast pocket of his leather jacket, I did my best to keep a lid on it.

Men who carried around money like that were always trouble.

But who didn't love a spot of trouble every now and again?

"Two beers and another whiskey neat, coming right up," I said.

Want more? Twisted Hearts is out now!!

ABOUT THE AUTHOR

Savannah Rylan is a romance writer that spends most of her time writing and reading. When not writing about sexy bikers and the women that love them, you can find her chasing around her toddler and two fur babies with her husband. She used to live in warm sunny California but has since moved to the East Coast where she has to deal with snow now, which she isn't too pleased about.

You can join her mailing list here!
Check out her website!

Box Sets

The Bad Disciples MC Box Set
The Road Rebels MC Box Set
Marked Skulls MC Box Set
Dead Souls MC Complete Collection
Black Hornets MC Box Set
The Lost Boys MC: The Complete Collection
The Callaghan Mafia Box Set
The Black Cobras MC
Dragon Riders MC
Dirty Misfits MC
Steel Scorpions MC

Series

Twisted Metal
Twisted Glass
Twisted Hearts
Twisted Flames

Bender (Steel Scorpions MC #1)
Angel (Steel Scorpions MC #2)
Goose (Steel Scorpions MC #3)
Viper (Steel Scorpions MC #4)
Reaper (Steel Scorpions MC #5)
Fangs (Steel Scorpions MC #6)

Brooks (Dirty Misfits MC #1)
Porter (Dirty Misfits MC #2)
Asher (Dirty Misfits MC #3)
Cole (Dirty Misfits MC #4)
Tanner (Dirty Misfits MC #5)
Finn (Dirty Misfits MC #6)

Link (Dragon Riders MC #1)
Bowser (Dragon Riders MC #2)
Ash (Dragon Riders MC #3)
Knuckles (Dragon Riders MC #4)
Sly (Dragon Riders MC #5)

Declan (The Callaghan Mafia #1)
Brody (The Callaghan Mafia #2)
Gael (The Callaghan Mafia #3)
Flynn (The Callaghan Mafia #4)

Cage (Dead Souls MC: Prospects #1)
Bear (Dead Souls MC: Prospects #2)
Saint (Dead Souls MC: Prospects #3)
Ryker (Dead Souls MC: Prospects #4)
Toxin (Dead Souls MC: Prospects #5)

Texas (The Lost Boys MC #1)
Stone (The Lost Boys MC #2)

Bronx (The Lost Boys MC #3)
Notch (The Lost Boys MC #4)
Diego (The Lost Boys MC #5)
Puck (The Lost Boys MC #6)
Frost (The Lost Boys MC #7)
West (The Lost Boys MC #8)

Jace (The Black Hornets MC #1)
Maverick (The Black Hornets MC #2)
Duke (The Black Hornets MC #3)
Colt (The Black Hornets MC #4)
Thor (The Black Hornets MC #5)
Jagger (The Black Hornets MC #6)

Knox (Dead Souls MC #1)
Grave (Dead Souls MC #2)
Brewer (Dead Souls MC #3)
Rock (Dead Souls MC #4)
Diesel (Deal Souls MC #5)

Girth (Marked Skulls MC #1)
Rodeo (Marked Skulls MC #2)
Abe (Marked Skulls MC #3)
Oz (Marked Skulls MC #4)
Dash (Marked Skulls MC #5)

Hawk (The Road Rebels MC #1)
Talon (The Road Rebels MC #2)
Snake (The Road Rebels MC #3)
Fox (The Road Rebels MC #4)

Gunner (The Bad Disciples MC #1)